WHEN HE WAS A ROGUE

The Duke's Legacy
Book 2

Tess Thompson

ARE YOU SIGNED UP FOR DRAGONBLADE'S BLOG?

You'll get the latest news and information on exclusive giveaways, exclusive excerpts, coming releases, sales, free books, cover reveals and more.

Check out our complete list of authors, too!

No spam, no junk. That's a promise!

Sign Up Here

www.dragonbladepublishing.com

Dearest Reader;

Thank you for your support of a small press. At Dragonblade Publishing, we strive to bring you the highest quality Historical Romance from some of the best authors in the business. Without your support, there is no 'us', so we sincerely hope you adore these stories and find some new favorite authors along the way.

Happy Reading!

CEO, Dragonblade Publishing

Additional Dragonblade books by Author Tess Thompson

The Duke's Legacy Series
When He Was a Duke (Book 1)
When He Was a Rogue (Book 2)

CHAPTER ONE

James

J AMES ASHFORD'S BOOT crashed through the rotted floorboard with a splintering crack that echoed through the empty halls of Ashford Manor like a gunshot. He cursed under his breath, extracting his leg from the jagged hole while rainwater dripped steadily from the ceiling above, pooling around the faded Turkish carpet that had once been his mother's pride.

Twelve years. Twelve years since he'd last walked these corridors, since the night they'd dragged his father away in chains on charges that still burned like acid in James's throat. Twelve years of watching from afar as his family's ancestral home crumbled under the Crown's indifferent oversight, windows boarded, gardens choked with weeds, servants scattered to the wind.

Now, with his father's name finally cleared and the estate restored to Ashford hands, James faced a different kind of reckoning. The manor seemed determined to punish him for every season of abandonment. First the loose banister that nearly sent him tumbling down the main staircase, now this treacherous floor that threatened to swallow him whole.

ABOVE HIM, HIS father's portrait watched from its gilded frame. His brother Sebastian looked so much like their dear Papa, with his dark hair and eyes. However, James and Sophia favored their fair-skinned, blonde mother, who had died giving birth to his baby sister. James had sworn on his father's grave to restore the Ashford name along with these walls.

He only prayed the house was salvageable. Thus far, he had his doubts.

The more he explored, the more he realized what a momentous task it would be to bring Ashford Manor back to its previous glory. At the moment, it seemed rather hopeless. However, he'd hired an architect to help him. A George Fairfax from Brighton. From what he could gather, the gentleman had a stellar reputation for restoration.

He pulled the crumpled letter from his waistcoat pocket, reading George Fairfax's bold script once more. *I shall arrive Tuesday next to assess the restoration requirements.* The architect came highly recommended for transforming other fallen estates, but James wondered if Fairfax had ever tackled a house that had died of shame as much as neglect.

James had signed the contract just last week, sending the paperwork back with a messenger to Brighton. He expected Mr. Fairfax to arrive at any moment.

Anxious, James paced around the once-grand entry hall, dim and echoing, its marble floor veined with cracks and grit. The great chandelier overhead, once a glittering constellation of cut glass, now hung askew, several arms snapped, the crystals dulled by soot and cobwebs.

To the left, the drawing room yawned open, its double doors permanently crooked. Inside, the wallpaper had peeled back in long, curling strips like shed skin. Mice had long since made a nest in the gutted settee, and what had once been rose-colored velvet was now the color of old bone. Water-stained ceilings sagged ominously in places, and mold traced dark veins across the cornices like ink bleeding through parchment.

He moved down the hall, each footfall sending puffs of dust into the stale air. A cold fireplace sat empty, its grate warped and blackened. The portraits of long-dead Ashford family members, spared from looters only by their size and weight, still lined the walls—watching him with grim disapproval from beneath thick layers of grime. One had fallen and lay cracked across the floor, the painted eyes of some forgotten viscount staring blindly at the rafters.

In the library, the shelves still stood, though many had buckled under time and damp. A layer of mildew clung to the spines of the books like a second skin. His father's desk remained, though warped and slumped at one corner, drawer handles missing or rusted through. He hadn't touched it. Not yet.

The smell was the worst part—old soot, damp wood, decay. A scent of rot and time, thick as fog and clinging to everything.

When their titles and finances had been restored after twelve years, James and his brother Sebastian had agreed that they must restore their old home to its former glory. Sebastian, although the elder of the two, had married a woman with a thriving estate of her own and was needed there. That left James to take care of Ashford Estate. It was his pleasure to do so.

He'd recently sold his tavern and the apartment above so that he could return to the place that had been snatched away from him when he was only ten years old.

He hadn't expected the title but Sebastian had insisted.

Lord Ashford. Once a name whispered with disdain in drawing rooms and taverns alike, now spoken again with a careful kind of deference. The dukedom restored, the Ashford name reinstated, and with it a courtesy title granted by his elder brother who had discovered a small barony long buried in the family line, revived to mark James's part in reclaiming their father's honor.

It was a kindness, really. A public gesture from Sebastian, the newly restored Duke of Ashford, meant to signal that the family's disgrace was over for them all.

"The family name needs more than a duke," he'd said. "It

needs visible unity. Restoration in full. And you've earned it—many times over."

James had been a soldier. A tavern owner. A man with dirt beneath his nails. Being called "my lord" still made something in his chest go tight. As if the ton might all realize the truth and take it back again.

He hadn't asked for a title. Wouldn't have, even if it had been offered by the Crown itself. But Sebastian, ever the strategist and diplomat, had insisted.

The barony had once belonged to a distant Ashford uncle, a minor title folded into the estate's legacy generations ago. Forgotten, mostly. But Sebastian had petitioned to revive it as a courtesy title. A symbol. A shield.

And so James became Lord Ashford. Not by inheritance. Not by entitlement. But by redemption. He must always remember his brother's kindness and do good with what had been restored and gifted to him. He would set it all right again. Bring back his family's manor and the village and farms associated with the Ashford name. His family was not the only one who had suffered when they'd wrongly sentenced his father to death.

He paused at the bottom of the staircase, hand on the balustrade. The wood was dry and splintering beneath his palm. Upstairs, the bedchambers waited like tombs. Rooms that had once held laughter, firelight, his father's voice. Now they were only shadows and sagging beams.

He inhaled sharply, letting the air burn his lungs. This was his now. His to rebuild. His to rise from the ashes.

A knock on the door startled him. Had the architect come on foot? Surely not? He rushed to the door, expecting George Fairfax. Instead, a gray haired woman clutching a bag to her bosom stood before him. For a moment, he couldn't place her. Then, it came back to him. Mrs. Ellsworth. Their former housekeeper. She'd been good to them after they'd hanged their father. While the rest of the staff had scattered like dandelions in the wind, she'd stayed with them until they'd been sent to live with the Langstons. In fact, if he remembered correctly, Mrs. Ellsworth had wanted to keep James and his sister and brother, but she was unable to, given her financial limitations.

Yet, here she was. Still rosy-cheeked, with kind hazel eyes. A small woman, who moved with birdlike swiftness and had run their household with graceful efficiency.

"Mrs. Ellsworth?" James asked. "Is it really you?"

"You know me?"

"Yes, of course I do. What are you doing here?"

"I heard in the village that you'd returned and I had to see it for myself." Her gaze swept the length of him. "You're quite large."

James chuckled. "I'm no longer the scrawny boy you remember?"

"You were always sturdy. Constantly outside, running about and getting your clothes muddy." She smiled, shaking her head. "Goodness me, you look fine though. Handsome. Just as I knew you'd be."

"I'd invite you in for tea but I'm afraid there's no staff. The architect I've hired will be here shortly. I'm afraid to say, the estate is in a terrible state."

"Then the rumors are true? You've come back and plan to live here?"

"Indeed. I plan to return Ashford Manor to its original beauty."

"I've come to greet you, of course, but also to offer my services. If you need a housekeeper, you need look no further."

"You're not currently employed?"

"I have been. Until recently. The woman I worked for in the village passed away. God rest her soul. I've been staying with my sister and brother-in-law the last few weeks. When I learned of your return, it seemed divine intervention. I've missed working here all these many years. And your family too. I'd been employed by the Ashfords since I was a young woman. It was all I knew and then suddenly it was no more. It broke my heart to send you children away but there was nothing I could do."

"Mrs. Ellsworth, it would be an honor to welcome you back. However, I'll need a few weeks to repair the kitchen and staff quarters to make them habitable once more. I don't know if it's safe to reside here, to be perfectly honest."

"Are you living here?"

"Yes, I brought a cot with me to sleep on and managed to clean the chimney in the main bedchambers to help with the chill. I must say, it's not making much difference. The rooms are frigid and damp. I'm used to rough dwellings. But it wouldn't do for you."

"I'm available to start right away," Mrs. Ellsworth said. "I can stay with my sister until we have the staff quarters restored. If you need me, I can help to put the kitchen back into working order. I know several women in the village here who would be happy to help. Work is hard to come by these days."

"Yes, that would be most welcome. My cook will be arriving next week. If we can have the kitchen in working order by then, I won't have to eat at the pub every night. Mrs. Honeycutt cooked for me at the tavern I owned in Brighton and she's agreed to come to the manor."

Mrs. Ellsworth was shaking her head. "I heard rumors you won that tavern in a card game. Is it true?"

"Indeed, I won the tavern in a bet." He grinned, tickled by her horrified expression.

"Well, I'm glad that life is behind you now."

"Yes, now here we are. The Ashford name's been restored and I plan to do the same with the manor."

"It will take some time to do so," Mrs. Ellsworth said, peering over his shoulder at the manor.

What must she think, seeing it like this? Did it break her heart as it did his own to see how the wind caught the broken shutters? Or how weeds had overtaken what was once a sweeping, manicured lawn? Ivy crept like rot up the facade of the great house, choking the windows and curling over the cornices.

He crossed his arms against the chill and stared up at the cracked windows of the east wing, where water damage had turned the plaster walls to flaking parchment. The old ash tree near the gate leaned like a drunkard over the crumbling boundary wall, its limbs bare despite the spring thaw. Beyond it, the stables sagged under the weight of disuse.

Before he could offer to take Mrs. Ellsworth inside, the sound of a carriage drew their attention. "This is the architect," James said to Mrs. Ellsworth. "I've not met him yet."

"I'll let you alone then," Mrs. Ellsworth said. "But if it's all right, I'll call on you tomorrow. I'll be ready to do whatever needs doing."

"Wonderful. I'll look forward to it." He resisted the urge to take her hands. Instead, he gave her a sincere smile and thanked her again for calling on him.

The carriage was almost to them by then. Mrs. Ellsworth gave a wave and then set back down the road toward the village on foot, pulling her coat tighter around her small frame.

The carriage halted and the driver stepped down to open the doors.

He really hoped the architect wasn't a pretentious dandy type in garish clothing.

He needn't have worried. It was not a dandy.

Worse. It was a woman.

She was tall and slender, her movements brisk and unflustered despite the wind tugging at her hem. A fitted gray-blue walking dress hugged her frame with quiet precision, practical but well-cut, and a dark Spencer jacket nipped in smartly at her waist. Posture so straight it looked like she had practiced carrying a book on her head from the moment she could walk. She wore her bonnet low, tied neatly at the chin, a single charcoal feather curling from the side. In one gloved hand, she held a sketch case; the other adjusted her bonnet against the breeze but not before he caught a glimpse of white blonde hair.

James blinked, then looked past her, expecting a man to follow. No one did. Instead, a slight woman with flaming red hair stepped from the carriage.

The blonde turned to face him fully, her expression cool and composed.

"Lord Ashford, I presume?"

James scowled. "That's right. Who are you?"

Her mouth curved, just barely, and her gaze faltered. "I'm Georgiana Fairfax. Your architect."

"Surely there's been a mistake? I was expecting a man. Perhaps your husband?"

"My husband, Robert Fairfax, has passed away. But I can assure you, he taught me everything he knew."

This woman was an architect? Surely not. For one thing, she was extremely pretty and delicate. Light blue eyes that took up half her face. Pointy chin that paired perfectly with her full mouth. She was young, too. No more than his two and twenty years. How could she be a widow already? "No, I'm afraid this won't do. I need a real architect. A man."

She lifted her chin, eyes flashing. "You of all people should know better than to judge someone merely because of their gender or station in life. Seeing as you were a tavern owner instead of a gentleman not so long ago."

"How did you know that?

"Your family's been the talk at many social events since the news came from the King." Georgiana turned toward the other woman, who stood a good foot behind. "This is my younger sister, Cecily. She acts as my secretary."

James inspected the redhead more closely. Now that he knew they were sisters, the resemblance was obvious. They shared a similar facial structure and fair skin. However, Cecily possessed a pair of hazel eyes and she lacked the fierceness of the woman claiming to be an architect.

Speaking of which: Women were not permitted to study architecture formally at universities or architectural academies. Institutions like the Royal Academy or the Society of Civil

Engineers were closed to women, and the field of architecture was considered strictly masculine and professional. In fact, James had often heard it referred to as a gentleman's art, often passed down through apprenticeships. "Isn't school required for the title of architect? Which you wouldn't have been able to attend. Am I right?"

The sooner he sent her back down the driveway, the better.

Georgiana's fingers tightened around the strap of her sketch case. "I wasn't formally educated, Lord Ashford. As you mentioned, women aren't permitted in the architectural academies. Sadly." Her voice remained steady, though a hint of steel threaded beneath it. "I studied in my father's library from the time I could read. As an adolescent, a tutor taught me drawing, geometry and technical sketching. I had a natural ability that blossomed through hard work. I then married a respected architect at age eighteen. After we married, I worked at Robert's side—drafting plans, managing site visits, consulting with clients. He encouraged me, saying I had an instinct for proportion and a mind for structure. The firm you hired bears his name, yes. But much of its work bears my hand. All of it, actually, now that Robert's dead."

"They can't just send you out here and expect me to trust you with the restoration of my family's legacy!" James kept his voice even but inside anger flared. How dare they send this chit of a woman out here?

"*They* is me, Lord Ashford. I am the sole owner of the firm you hired. The contract bears my name."

"The contract does not bear your name. It says George, not Georgiana."

She flushed and gazed down at her boots peeking out from under the hem of her dress. "I am known as George or Georgie in my professional circles and friends."

"Well, George, that may well be—but the truth is—I have no intention of hiring you. I apologize for your trouble but I must ask you to leave."

Cecily retreated backward several inches but Georgiana did the opposite. She stepped closer. "Our contract is legally binding. I'm afraid you're stuck with me. Or out the large retainer you already paid me."

Despite the cool temperatures, perspiration had broken out on his forehead and the back of his neck. He'd paid a sizable sum to hire Fairfax Architecture. If he'd known it was a woman, he would not have done so. However, he was a practical man. Losing that much money was not something he could do and sleep at night. He narrowed his eyes, studying her further. Was it possible this wide-eyed beauty could take on this kind of project? He guessed he was about to find out.

"Shall we go inside?" Georgiana asked. "It looks as if it might rain."

The triumph in her eyes irritated him. But what choice did he have?

HE SHOWED THE ladies inside, rather reluctantly. James led them through the wide front hall with its checkerboard floor of cracked marble, the sound of their footsteps echoing off the vaulted ceiling.

"To the right here is the drawing room." James pushed open the heavy double doors and held them open for the ladies before following them. Seeing this room in such disrepair stole his breath for a moment, just as it had the first day he arrived. It was as if their former life had frozen in time, leaving behind ghosts of the past. Every inch of the room held memories that made his chest feel heavy and sore.

Furniture sat draped in old linen sheets, now grayed with age and scattered with mouse droppings. One sheet had slipped off a rosewood settee, revealing torn upholstery and stuffing peeking through like old wool. A grand mirror over the fireplace, gilded, but cracked across one corner, reflected the room in slanted, distorted lines. The gold leaf had blackened in places, curling like burnt parchment.

The wallpaper, once patterned in soft florals, now peeled back in curling strips, revealing the cracked plaster beneath. Water stains traced down from a place in the ceiling where a leak had spread. On the mantel, a faded ceramic vase still held the long-dead skeletons of dried roses—more dust than flower now. Who had placed them there? After all this time, he had no idea.

The fireplace was choked with ash and debris, an iron grate tipped sideways, half-buried beneath old soot. A tarnished hearth brush leaned forgotten in the corner. Framed silhouettes hung askew on the walls, some with their glass smashed, others missing entirely, their outlines marked by faded wallpaper shadows. A pianoforte sat in the far corner, keys yellowed and warped, one leg splintered. A single music sheet still rested on the stand. Sophia was learning to play in the months before their father's arrest. He'd forgotten that until now.

On a small escritoire, a drawer hung half-open. The once-luxurious Axminster carpet, now threadbare and water-stained, was stiff with time and grit underfoot. In the corner, near the window seat, a child's forgotten wooden horse leaned on its side, one wheel missing, the paint flaking from its saddle.

"It was once my favorite room in the house," James said. "We spent many happy times here as a family."

"Then we shall bring it back to what it was," Georgiana said stoutly.

He had to admit, there was something very reassuring about the woman. Hopefully, she would be as competent as she seemed to think she was.

Georgiana stepped lightly across the worn rug, seeming to take in the ruined moldings. "We will fix it, Lord Ashford. You will have happy times here again. When my husband was alive, he allowed me to decorate the interiors as well as the structural elements of our projects. I like nothing more than making a room beautiful again."

"I see." Was it true? He really hoped so.

James took them to the ballroom next. "The floor's warped from water damage. There's a leak above the ceiling, which will have to be repaired before we do anything in here."

"Will you host a ball, Lord Ashford?" Cecily asked.

"I suppose I will. I hadn't thought much about it," James said. "The house needs so much work that I'm afraid to get too far ahead of myself."

"Very wise," Georgiana said.

Across the corridor, he paused outside a tall set of double oak doors. "This is our library. All of the books are still in there. But mold has gotten into a lot of them."

"Oh dear," Cecily murmured. "How sad."

"I'll have to sort through them and decide what to keep and what to toss," James said.

"We can save some of them, if you wish. They'll need to be dried out before we dust any mold spores from their pages." Georgiana turned to her sister. "Please note that we'll need to make some drying racks."

Cecily nodded and scribbled the directive into her notebook.

Down a narrow passage, they reached the dining room. A long mahogany table bowed in the center. A single candelabrum still stood, tilted at a mournful angle.

"What a beautiful room it once was." Georgiana ran a gloved hand along the table. "We'll have this table restored somehow."

"Servants' stairs are here." He lifted a tarnished latch and gestured for them to follow. They descended into the dim, cool underbelly of the house. The smell of damp stone and ash met them at the base.

"The kitchen's over this way. It used to feed twenty on staff and whatever guests came calling." He pushed open a door to reveal the cavernous space—blackened hearths, rows of rusted pots, a butcher's block scarred with decades of use. The scullery beyond was filled with overturned basins and a cracked pump handle. "We'll have staff again soon. But not until it's habitable again. Right now, it seems unsafe."

"Yes, agreed," Georgiana said. "But none of this is impossible. In fact, the structure of the manor seems intact, although we'll have much to repair. Inside, will be mostly cosmetic changes."

"Staff quarters are down that corridor," James said. "There's mold on the walls and furniture, which will have to be cleaned up before I can think about hiring anyone."

They returned to the main staircase, its carved balustrade worn smooth beneath his palm. He took them upstairs to show them the bedrooms, all of which were in similar states to the other rooms.

"This is the main bedchamber, where I've set up a temporary living space," James said.

James slept on a narrow cot with a wool blanket he'd brought with him and relied on the fire for warmth.

Georgiana looked around the room, nodding to herself. "Soon enough, these will be quarters fitting a gentleman."

He paused at the room that had once been the nursery. He'd not had the courage to open this door but it must be done. Georgiana should see everything if she was to help him.

"This was our nursery," James said. "I've not looked at it yet. I couldn't face it."

The door stuck slightly as James forced it open, the wood swollen from years of damp. The air inside was colder than the rest of the house and heavy with the scent of mildew, old wool, and something sweeter underneath, like lavender sachets long gone stale. Wallpaper, once pale blue and patterned with tiny stars or flowers, peeled in wide, curling strips. Mold traced the corners of the ceiling. A child-sized rocking chair sat overturned near the hearth, one of its rockers splintered clean through. A faded rag doll, its stitching unraveling at the mouth, lay nearby, half-covered by a crumbling quilt.

"My sister was only eight when we were sent away," James said. "It's as we left it."

In the corner stood a narrow iron bed, the mattress sagging, sheets grayed with time and stained by mice. The pillow still bore the faint indent of a small head, though whether that was memory or imagination, James couldn't say. A once-bright toy chest, its lid warped and open, revealed a scatter of wooden blocks, a tin whistle rusted to silence, and the shredded remains of a storybook nibbled at the corners.

Near the window, a child's chalkboard easel stood crooked. A stick of white chalk still lay in the tray, and on the slate Sophia had once drawn a crooked sun with rays and a smiling face. The smile had faded, washed half away by time. Rain had seeped in through the roof, staining the far wall with a long brown streak and warping the floorboards. In the worst corner, a puddle had formed beneath a hole in the ceiling, fed by every storm since the house was abandoned. Tucked beneath a windowsill, a small book of fairy tales sat open, its pages fused together, the ink bled into clouds.

He sighed, memories flooding him of the happy afternoons they'd spent in the room with their governess. Sebastian and Sophia had been good, obedient students, but James had been fidgety, wishing he could be outside instead of stuck inside learning his lessons. Looking back, he could see how good he'd had it. If only things had been different. They should have had more time together. They should have been allowed to grow up and leave this room when it was the right time, not pushed out as they had been.

"This will be a wonderful place for your children someday, Lord Ashford," Georgiana said.

"I don't plan on having any," James said. "But perhaps my nieces and nephews will enjoy it."

"May I ask why?"

He shrugged. "I don't imagine I'd be a good father. In addition, it seems cruel to bring another life into the world. Not after everything I've seen."

HE LED THEM back downstairs to show them his father's abandoned study. Knowing it would take an emotional toll, he drew in a deep breath. This was where his father had spent many hours, running the estate with a benevolent hand.

James paused with his hand on the door, the worn brass handle cool beneath his fingers. "This was my father's study." He pushed the door open.

Dust swirled in the shaft of light from the tall, narrow window. Old smoke, paper, and time had worked its way into the oak-paneled walls. The great desk dominated the room, its surface littered with scattered papers, a cracked ink pot, and a stack of ledgers long gone stiff at the edges. One drawer sagged open slightly.

A cracked brandy decanter sat on a silver tray, alongside two dusty glasses, one of which bore a long fracture spidering through the rim. He didn't touch it. The fireplace was cold, the iron grate bent at one corner. In the ash, he could just make out the blackened scrap of a letter, words burned to illegibility.

Above the hearth, the map of Ashford lands hung askew, the parchment yellowed and curling at the edges. His father had traced those lines with pride, explaining acre by acre to a boy who didn't understand any of it yet.

His mother's portrait still hung on the far wall. In it, his beautiful mother sat in a simple chair, with her hands folded in her lap and a gentle smile splayed on her rosebud mouth. James felt the old pressure behind his ribs and looked away. He'd been only two when she died, leaving him with no memories of her whatsoever. Instead, Papa had been his and his siblings' whole world. Regardless, he wished then and now that he could have known her. It gave him some comfort to think of his father and mother somewhere together in an eternal love match.

"You look like her," Georgiana said.

"Yes, I do," James said. "My sister as well. Our mother died in childbirth." He wasn't sure why he'd felt compelled to tell her that detail but it was out of his mouth before he could think too much about it.

"I no longer have my parents either," Georgiana said. "No matter what age we are when we lose them, grief remains."

For a second, he and Georgiana locked gazes and a mutual understanding passed between them. She, too, had had troubles. He felt certain of it. What were they exactly? Who was this woman? And why was he so intrigued by her?

She walked toward the hearth, running her gloved hand gently along the mantel. "This is lovely. We can make it so again."

Cecily followed in silence. She knelt near a small table tucked under the window and lifted a faded book from the dust. A dried flower slipped from its middle. "Someone pressed flowers in this." She knelt to fetch the dropped flower but the petals were paper thin and disintegrated between her fingers. "I'm sorry. I should have left it alone."

James looked away again, a painful knot in the back of his throat. "My sister used to press flowers often in a few of our books." Did Sophia remember that?

No one spoke for a moment.

He cleared his throat. "We'll likely turn this into a receiving room, eventually. Or a second library."

Georgie turned to face him then, eyes steady. "Or you could restore it as it was. And use it while you run the estate as it should be run."

He held her gaze. "Maybe."

"It's strange how rooms can bring emotion and memory to us in an instant," Georgiana said. "That's one of the reasons I love architecture. The spaces in which we dwell become a part of us. Losing them is painful."

"Restoring them will be less so," James said. "Or at least I hope so."

CHAPTER TWO

Georgiana

GEORGIANA'S HAND TREMBLED as she set down her teacup, the delicate porcelain clicking against the saucer with more force than intended. The cramped inn room felt smaller with each passing hour, made more so by the weight of what lay ahead. Beside her, Cecily bent over a sheaf of notes, her pen scratching industriously across the paper.

"There," Georgiana murmured, forcing steadiness into her voice as she reviewed the proposal one final time. The figures swam before her tired eyes—labor costs, materials, timeframes. Everything hinged on Lord Ashford's approval. Everything hinged on her ability to convince a man who had every reason to distrust her that she could restore his family's legacy.

The scent of tallow candles and old wood permeated their small chamber, mixing with the faint aroma of the beef stew drifting up from the taproom below. Georgiana's stomach growled from hunger.

"You've done excellent work today," she said, glancing at her sister. Cecily's cheeks were flushed with purpose, her eyes bright despite the late hour. "Shall we venture downstairs? I find I'm rather famished."

They had spoken little of the morning's events, other than Lord Ashford's thunderous expression when he discovered George Fairfax was, in fact, Georgiana. She had anticipated his fury, had even planned for it. The deception sat uneasily in her chest, but what choice did a woman have in this world?

Robert would have understood, she thought, gathering her shawl about her shoulders. Her late husband had been a master of necessary compromises.

The taproom below buzzed with conversation and the clink of pewter mugs. Georgiana selected a table near the hearth, grateful for the warmth that seeped through her wool dress. The fire cast dancing shadows across the rough-hewn walls, and she found herself studying the flames as she waited for their ale.

"What manner of man do you suppose his lordship to be?" Cecily asked, her voice pitched low beneath the tavern's din.

Georgiana considered the question, turning her pewter mug between her palms. The metal was warm from the ale within, and she savored the simple comfort of it. "A complicated one. He carries his wounds like armor—necessary protection, but a heavy burden."

She had seen it in the rigid set of his shoulders as he'd toured them through the manor, the way his jaw tightened when he spoke of his father. Ten years old when he witnessed that horrible injustice. The very thought made her stomach turn.

"The gossips say Sebastian, the eldest, disguised himself as a gardener to infiltrate the Wentworth estate," Georgiana continued. "He sought proof of their father's innocence."

"And found love instead," Cecily said softly. "How romantic."

"Romance is a luxury we can ill-afford," Georgiana replied, though the words tasted bitter. She had learned that lesson well enough in her marriage to Robert—a union of convenience that had bloomed into deep friendship, if not passion.

The memory of their wedding night still had the power to steal her breath. Robert's halting confession of his preference for men, her own tears of disappointment, the long conversation that had followed. *I cannot love you as a husband should, he had said, but I can offer you partnership. Knowledge. Freedom of a sort.*

And he had kept that promise. Every evening spent hunched

over architectural drawings, every lesson in structural engineering, every patient explanation of load-bearing calculations had given her a trade, a means of independence. She would not squander that gift.

The taproom door swung open, bringing with it a gust of January air and the tall figure of James Ashford. Georgiana's breath caught as he surveyed the room, his gaze landing upon them. Snowflakes clung to the shoulders of his greatcoat, and his hair—that fascinating shade between gold and brown—curled damply at his collar.

"Oh dear," Cecily whispered. "Do we bid him join us?"

The question became moot as James approached their table, hat in hand. Up close, Georgiana could see the way the cold had heightened the color in his cheeks, could catch the faint scent of winter air and a note of sandalwood, perhaps, or cedar.

"Mrs. Fairfax. Miss Cecily." His voice carried that same measured courtesy from the morning, though his eyes seemed less guarded now. "I trust you've found comfortable lodgings?"

"Indeed, my lord. Pray, will you not join us?" Georgiana gestured to an empty chair, acutely aware of how her pulse quickened at his proximity. *Foolish woman. You've no time for such nonsense.*

"If I shall not intrude upon your evening."

"Not at all."

He settled into the chair with fluid grace, and Georgiana found herself studying the long lines of his fingers as he signaled for the serving girl. Those hands had once pulled pints and wiped down tables. A gentleman reduced to common labor by circumstances beyond his control. She understood that particular desperation all too well.

The serving girl fairly fluttered as she took his order, her cheeks pink with more than the tavern's warmth. Georgiana felt an unexpected stab of something that might have been jealousy, which was ridiculous. She had no claim on Lord Ashford's attentions.

"A warming meal for such a bitter evening," James observed once their bowls of stew had arrived. Steam rose from the rich broth, carrying the scent of herbs and tender beef.

"Do you find yourself missing the tavern life?" Cecily asked, her voice carrying that particular sweetness that made men lean closer.

James dabbed at his mouth with his napkin, considering. "Aye, more than I anticipated. The work itself, and the rhythm of daily tasks gave me a sense of satisfaction."

"And the people?" Georgiana asked. "You spoke of your cook with such fondness."

A genuine smile transformed his features. "Mrs. Honeycutt is formidable. My sister Sophia calls her 'a force of nature,' which is a charitable way of saying she brooks no nonsense from anyone. She'll have the manor's kitchen running like a military operation within a fortnight."

"Will she adapt well to country house management?" Georgiana asked. "The scale seems quite different from tavern cooking."

"Mrs. Honeycutt could organize a siege if required. I've no doubt she'll master whatever challenges Ashford Manor presents." James's eyes crinkled with humor. "Though I pity any servant who thinks to slack under her watch."

As the evening progressed, Georgiana found herself relaxing despite her better judgment. The ale had warmed her from within, and James proved to be unexpectedly easy company. When he turned his attention to Cecily, asking about her plans for the Season, Georgiana studied his profile in the firelight—the strong line of his jaw, the way his eyes gentled when he spoke to her younger sister.

"The Season depends rather heavily upon our current circumstances," Cecily admitted, her cheeks coloring. "I've a modest dowry, but whether it shall prove sufficient..."

"You undertook your husband's profession to secure your sister's future?" James's gaze returned to Georgiana. There was no judgment in his tone, only understanding.

"Among other reasons," Cecily said. "Georgiana possesses remarkable talent. She's not merely maintaining Robert's business. She's improving upon it."

"No easy feat for a woman in such a field," James said. "I begin to understand the necessity of your creative correspondence."

Heat crept up Georgiana's neck. "Would you have engaged my services otherwise?"

"In all honesty? No." His directness was refreshing, even if the answer stung. "But I've learned that desperation teaches one to value results over conventions. And I confess myself curious to see what you'll make of the old place."

"I pray I shall not disappoint you."

"I suspect disappointment is the least of my concerns." Something in his tone made her pulse quicken. "Tell me of your plans. How shall we tackle such an undertaking?"

They spoke at length of practical matters—labor requirements, material sourcing, the coordination of various tradesmen. James listened intently, occasionally asking pointed questions that revealed his own keen understanding of such projects.

"I noticed you've been residing in the master's chambers." Georgiana immediately regretted the observation. It seemed too intimate, too suggestive of her having noted his sleeping arrangements.

"The cot serves well enough for now." James shrugged, as if it was of no consequence. "Though I confess I look forward to proper furnishings."

"We shall begin there, then. And the kitchen quarters—they'll require immediate attention if Mrs. Honeycutt is to work her magic."

"Agreed. Mrs. Ellsworth, our former housekeeper, returns tomorrow. She'll prove invaluable in organizing both staff and local laborers."

"Former?" Cecily asked.

"She worked for us when we were children. When she heard of our change in circumstances, she came calling. It was quite something to see her again after all these years. We were very fond of her. It is a dream come true to welcome her back to the manor."

Georgiana could not help but feel moved by his sentimental streak. As they discussed timelines and priorities, she found herself stealing glances at James's hands as he gestured, noting the way his voice deepened when he spoke of restoring the village's prosperity. This was a man who had learned to care for others, who understood responsibility born of hardship.

Dangerous thoughts, she warned herself. *You've worked too hard for independence to surrender it now.*

But when he insisted on settling their account and walked them to the foot of the narrow stairs leading to their chambers, she could not ignore the flutter in her chest as he bid them goodnight.

"Until tomorrow, then." His eyes lingered on her face. "The beginning of our grand endeavor."

"Indeed," Georgiana said, her voice steadier than she felt. "Good evening, my lord."

She climbed the stairs with measured steps, acutely aware of his presence below until the taproom door closed behind him. Only then did she allow herself to exhale fully, one hand pressed to her rapidly beating heart.

"He's rather magnificent, isn't he?" Cecily whispered as they prepared for bed.

"He's our employer," Georgiana said. "Nothing more."

A few minutes later, as she lay in the narrow bed, listening to Cecily's soft breathing and the wind rattling the windows, sleep remained elusive. Her mind churned, not with worry over the project itself, but with thoughts of the man who'd commissioned it.

James Ashford was a contradiction that unsettled her. She'd heard tales of his reputation as a rough tavern keeper who'd never backed down from a fight, yet tonight he'd been nothing but courteous. The raw emotion she'd witnessed in his father's study lingered in her memory, as did the way his voice had gentled when speaking to Cecily.

With a soft sigh, she slipped from bed and padded to the small table beneath the window. When restless thoughts plagued her, drawing had always provided solace. It offered a way to focus her mind on form and shadow rather than fruitless worry.

She opened her sketchbook, her pencil moving almost of its own accord. The precise recall that had always seemed natural to her—though she'd learned it was quite rare—allowed her to capture James as he'd stood in his father's study. The slope of his shoulders beside the cracked hearth, the rigid line of his jaw as he'd struggled with old grief.

Her father had possessed artistic talent as well, though he'd used it only to occupy his restless nature during the long decline that preceded his final, devastating choice. The gambling debts. The scandal. The gunshot that had stolen not only his life but their future. In one terrible night, her promised Season had vanished along with their home and security.

She shaded the drawing carefully, adding depth to James's profile. Perhaps that shared experience of loss was what drew her to him. She recognized in him someone who understood what it meant to have everything stripped away by forces beyond one's control.

Setting the sketch aside, she gazed out at the frost-covered window. Tomorrow would bring early rising and whatever challenges James Ashford might present. But tonight, she allowed herself this moment of quiet fascination with a man who'd surprised her in ways she hadn't expected.

One thing remained certain—he wanted his home restored, and she intended to give him exactly that.

CHAPTER THREE

James

J AMES ROSE BEFORE dawn, unable to sleep for the second night running. The cot in his father's chamber was too small for his large frame, but it wasn't discomfort that kept him wakeful. It was the weight of what lay ahead.

Mrs. Fairfax and her sister would arrive in a few hours, ready to begin the monumental task of restoration. Ample time to take a ride around the countryside and into the village. He'd not had much time to explore the community he'd been forced to leave behind and it felt important that he do so.

He saddled his stallion in the pre-dawn darkness and set out toward the village as the first pale light crept across the horizon. The gravel drive gave way to a rutted country lane bordered by hedgerows heavy with winter's grip. The horse's hooves fell into a steady rhythm against the packed earth.

To his right, fields that should have been prepared for spring planting lay neglected, the soil hard and unworked. The Barton farm had always produced the finest grain in Sussex, but now the farmhouse windows stared blindly at the morning, no smoke rising from the chimney to signal the early stirrings of a working household.

The abandoned mill came into view, its great wheel motionless and green with moss where water once flowed. Before his father's hanging, it had churned day and night, the heartbeat of their little community. Now silence ruled where industry had once thrived.

James slowed his mount as they approached the Widow Collins's cottage. The garden, once famous throughout the county for its herbs and vegetables, had grown wild with neglect. A thin trail of smoke rose from the chimney. At least someone still lived there. But the cottage looked smaller somehow, as if poverty had compressed it.

The lane widened as it curved down toward the village, revealing more signs of decline with each passing furlong. Fences sagged where once they stood straight. A cart with a broken wheel lay abandoned beside a field where two old men labored to do the work of ten. Without the Ashford estate's employment and custom, everything was slowly coming undone.

James's grip tightened on the reins. The false accusation that had sent his father to the gallows had torn more than one family apart—it had unraveled an entire community. The weight of that responsibility settled heavier on his shoulders with each passing yard.

The road widened as James guided his horse into Ashford-on-Wey proper. The village green, once immaculately maintained by estate groundskeepers, now sprouted weeds between the cobblestones. An ancient oak stood at its center, the wooden benches beneath it weathered and empty where once they had hosted gossiping housewives and resting laborers.

The inn and tavern where he'd dined the previous evening looked different in the harsh morning light. What had seemed atmospheric by candlelight now revealed itself as simply worn. The sign hung askew, paint peeling from the once-fierce beast. Beside it, Perkins's Bakery stood with shuttered windows. A faded notice hung on the door. *Closed until further circumstances allow.* He remembered Mrs. Perkins's currant buns from childhood visits, how they'd filled the morning air with their sweet fragrance. Now only emptiness remained behind those dark windows.

The butcher's shop displayed a meager selection behind cloudy glass. Through the window, he could see Mullins arranging what little stock he had. The man had served his family for decades, but now operated on scraps where once he'd sold the finest cuts in the county.

The chandler's shop remained open, though the display looked thin. Next door, the seamstress had converted half her establishment to mending. A practical pivot when few could afford new garments. A hand-lettered sign advertised darning and patches at fair prices.

Where Cooper's workshop had stood, crafting barrels for the estate's ale and preserves, only a vacant building remained, its windows boarded against weather and vandals alike. The blacksmith's forge still operated. Horses needed shoeing regardless of fortune, yet the rhythmic ping of hammer on anvil sounded sporadic, hesitant.

James dismounted near the village well, his boots crunching on the frost-covered cobblestones. A woman drawing water straightened warily as he approached, but it was the thin man emerging from the tailor's shop who caught his attention.

"Mr. Drayton?" The name came to him suddenly. The man had been young when James was a boy, apprenticed to his father who had measured the Ashford children for their Sunday clothes.

The tailor paused in sweeping his threshold, recognition flickering across his gaunt features. His clothes, James noticed with a pang, were impeccably mended but showed the telltale signs of a craftsman who could no longer afford new fabric for himself.

"Master James." Drayton straightened, setting aside his broom. "We heard you'd returned to us."

"How do you fare?" James kept his voice gentle, remembering how the young man had always taken such pride in his work, even as an apprentice.

Drayton's laugh held no humor. "I manage, my lord. Mending and patching mostly now. Not much call for new garments when folks can barely afford to keep their old ones whole." He gestured toward his shop window, where James could see the sparse display of thread and simple notions. "My eldest is apprenticed to a tailor in Brighton now. More opportunity there, you understand."

That hurt him to hear. The Drayton family had served the estate faithfully, and now the next generation had been forced to seek fortune elsewhere.

"Your father made fine clothes for us when we were children," James said. "I remember how carefully he measured my first proper jacket."

"Aye, he'd be pleased to know it. Though I doubt he'd recognize what his shop's become." Drayton's voice carried the weight of a man watching his legacy crumble. "Still, we endure. As we must."

"That will change," James said quietly. "There will be work again—proper work. The manor will need furnishing, and I mean to employ local craftsmen wherever possible."

Drayton studied his face for a long moment, as if assessing whether he spoke the truth. "There's been talk around here. Hopeful talk. First time in a long time."

"There's reason for hope," James said. "You mark my words."

"I certainly will," Drayton said.

"I'll need a whole new wardrobe, so we'll get started on that soon, if it suits you?"

Drayton's face lit up. "It surely does. Just let me know when and I'll be ready for you."

James urged his horse toward the eastern edge of the village, where St. Michael's church maintained its dignity despite the surrounding decline. The Saxon tower stood as a reminder of permanence amid change, though even the vicarage garden had grown wild without proper tending.

A handful of children played listlessly near the village pump, their clothes more patched than whole. They paused to stare as he passed, their thin faces curious but wary. They all knew who he was. For whatever reason, it hadn't occurred to him that he would be the talk of the village.

He was lost in thought as he guided his horse back through the village, Drayton's words echoing in his mind. The morning mist was beginning to lift, revealing clearer details of the decay around him. He was so absorbed in his observations that he nearly missed the solitary figure walking purposefully along the lane ahead.

A woman in a dark blue cloak, her step brisk despite the early hour. Something about her bearing made him look twice, and recognition dawned with a start of surprise.

"Mrs. Fairfax?"

She turned at his call, and he saw her face brighten with what looked like relief. "Lord Ashford. I wondered if I might encounter you."

He dismounted, leading his horse as he fell into step beside her. "You're abroad early. I trust you slept better than I did?"

A faint smile played at her lips. "I'm afraid sleep proved rather elusive. I found myself too restless to remain abed, so I thought a walk might soothe my nerves."

"Have you found anything of interest?" He found himself genuinely curious about her perspective on the village. Would she see what he did?

She was quiet for a moment, her gaze moving thoughtfully over the landscape. "I feel our work extends far beyond the manor walls. This community is like a body that's been weakened by illness—every part of it suffers when the heart fails to beat properly."

Her insight struck him immediately. "You see it too, then. The connection between the estate and everything else."

"How could I not? Architecture isn't merely about buildings, my lord. It's about the lives that shelter within them, the communities that surround them. A house without purpose is merely stone and timber. Your father's legacy will be restored in more ways than one."

"It was my thought exactly."

They walked in comfortable silence for a few moments, and James stole glances at her profile in the growing light. She seemed less guarded this morning, more relaxed in his presence. The early hour and chance encounter had stripped away some of the formality that had marked their previous interactions.

"I spoke with Mr. Drayton just now," James said. "The tailor. His eldest son has gone to Brighton seeking work. A family that served mine for generations, now scattered to the winds."

Georgiana's step faltered slightly. "How many such stories are there, do you suppose?"

"Too many." The admission felt good to say out loud to someone who clearly understood. "Every empty shop, every abandoned cottage represents a family suffering because of the injustice done to my father. All these years, I didn't think much about what effect it would have on the people who live and work here. I feel ashamed to admit it, but it's true enough."

She looked at him then, and he caught something in her expression that made his pulse quicken. "One must look out for themselves before they can look out after others."

They had reached the turnoff to the manor, and James realized he was reluctant to end this unexpected intimacy. There was something about encountering her here, in the quiet morning light, that felt more honest than their formal discussions of contracts and timelines.

"Are you returning to the inn this morning?" James asked.

"No, I left a note for Cecily to come out after she's had her breakfast. Since I'm up, I might as well get started."

"I wish I had breakfast to offer you but without a cook, I have only a loaf of bread and a chunk of cheese."

"I had something easier, so please don't trouble yourself," Georgiana said.

The manor house came into view as they crested the hill together, its damaged walls glowing pale gold in the strengthening light. He wished they could keep walking. The realization caught him off guard—he wanted to remain by the side of this woman who saw that rebuilding was as much about mending souls as restoring structures. Well, they would spend the day together, regardless. He looked forward to it.

How strange.

The restoration of Ashford Manor wasn't merely about reclaiming his family's legacy. It was about breathing life back into an entire community that had withered in their absence. Every stone they repaired, every room they restored, every servant they employed would send ripples of prosperity through those empty shops and struggling farms.

Mrs. Fairfax had asked about finding laborers for their project. Now he understood that the question wasn't whether they could find willing workers, but whether they could hire enough of them to make a real difference to the local economy. The village was full of strong backs and willing hands. They simply needed honest work at fair wages.

The weight of that responsibility should have daunted him. Instead, his vow to bring prosperity back to the good, hard-working people of the farms and shops was a fire in his belly. He would bring it all back. No matter how long it took.

And perhaps, he thought, glancing at the woman walking beside him, he wouldn't have to shoulder that burden alone.

CHAPTER FOUR

Georgiana

IN THE WEEKS since she'd first arrived at the manor, Georgiana had one thing to say about James Ashford. He didn't waste any time. Clearly, he was a man of action. He knew what he wanted and was determined to make it all happen, sooner rather than later. Although he made her nervous, what with the intense way he looked at her and his clear desire for speed and efficiency, she could see already that they made a good team. She, too, was decisive by nature. If she was correct in assuming so, she thought James had come to respect her after seeing her extensive project plan and all the components laid out in a precise manner. She'd been surprised to see him working physically as hard as any of the men and boys they hired.

Today, when she and Cecily had arrived, he was dressed in a rough cotton work shirt and a pair of wool trousers. He had the shirtsleeves rolled up to his elbow and his neck was bare of a cravat. The sight of his muscular arms and strong neck had made her stomach feel strange and her legs wobbly.

This was most certainly not good.

She'd not allowed herself to be attracted to any man while she was married. It was silly, given that her husband hadn't felt the need to keep his desires at bay. Still, there was a part of her that respected her marriage vows, even if they were never to be man and wife in the usual ways. After his death, she'd been too busy trying to figure out how they were going to stay off the streets to worry much about womanly yearnings. Thus, she had been quite unprepared for the storm of desire that raged within her at the mere glimpse of James Ashford.

Despite all that, it was only late January and already the project was underway. Ben Thatcher had come straightaway after she'd written asking if he was available to help her with such a large project.

Georgiana had worked with Ben on many of Robert's jobs. She knew him to be competent and trustworthy, although slightly intimidating. He was a large man, broad through the chest and shoulders, with a thatch of dark blond hair that never quite laid flat and low, booming voice that had scared more than one of his workers over the years.

James had offered his father's former study for their temporary office space. When they arrived that morning, they found that James had cleared and scrubbed the desk and had a chimney sweep out to clear debris out of the fireplace so they could have heat while they worked.

She and Cecily were leaning over her blueprint of the manor when Ben arrived. He and his men had spent most of the day in what would be James's bedchambers.

"Mrs. Fairfax, I have good news and bad news. Which would you like first?" Ben grinned, stopping in front of the desk.

"Bad please," Georgiana said.

"I found a family of mice living in the old wardrobe. They have been relocated."

"By relocated, do you mean you've killed them?" Cecily asked, lower lip trembling.

Her sister never met an animal she didn't love.

"No, Miss Cecily. I managed to get them into a crate and took them out to the stables where they will be safe and dry," Ben said.

Georgiana wasn't sure he was telling the truth but Cecily seemed placated.

"And the good news?" Georgiana asked.

"We are ready for his lordship to pick new wallpaper and paint. My woodworker has sanded down some of the furniture and will begin staining tomorrow. If we keep going at this rate, Lord Ashford will have a bedchamber in less than a week's time."

"I'll meet with him straightaway," Georgiana said. "We have samples and ideas for him."

"Excellent. The boys and I are going to call it a day. Looks like it's going to rain and I want to get back into the village before it grows dark."

"That's fine."

"We'll be back bright and early tomorrow," Ben said.

He and his workers headed out just as a bolt of lightning lit up the sky. Georgiana hoped the rain would hold long enough for her to meet with James about his bedchamber choices before she and Cecily headed back to the inn but at this rate it seemed unlikely. James had provided them the use of his horses and carriage, hiring a young man from the village to drive them back and forth, but carriages were no match for muddy roads this time of year.

"I'm going down to speak with Lord Ashford before we head back to the inn," Georgiana said to Cecily. "I'd like him to choose paint and wallpaper tonight so that I can order them in the morning."

Cecily glanced up from their master ledger, nodding distractedly. Her little sister loved numbers and accounting. Thank goodness, because Georgiana didn't care for that type of task. Nor was she good at it.

Georgiana ventured down the worn stone steps to the manor's kitchen, portfolio clutched against her chest and a nervous flutter in her stomach. She hoped Lord Ashford would like at least one of the choices she planned to propose for his bedchambers. His quarters must be just right for the lord of the manor and she didn't feel as if she had his aesthetic fully figured out as of yet.

What she found at the bottom of the stairs stopped her momentarily. They'd drastically improved the kitchen since this morning. In fact, she believed it would be ready for the cook when she arrived tomorrow.

Stone-flagged floors had been scrubbed to a honey color. The massive hearth dominated the far wall, its blackened stones now revealed as warm russet where the village boys had scraped away years of accumulated soot. A small fire crackled there now, warming the air and scenting it with woodsmoke.

Copper pots hung from the overhead beam, most showing fresh polish though some still bore tarnish too stubborn for a single day's attention. The deep sink beneath one window remained stained by a hundred years of use, but the brass tap gleamed with unexpected warmth. A stack of wooden spoons and paddles dripped onto a cloth nearby, their grain raised by recent washing.

The enormous oak worktable anchoring the center of the room showed the honorable scars of a century of chopping, kneading, and rolling. Its surface had been scrubbed to a clean paleness that spoke of lemon and sand and considerable muscle.

In the midst of this transformation stood James, sleeves rolled to his elbows, forearms glistening with perspiration as he worked at a stubborn hinge from one of the pantry doors. He looked up at her footsteps, a streak of grime across one cheekbone, making him look more like a blacksmith than a lord. Regardless, he was beautiful.

"Mrs. Fairfax, is everything all right?" He straightened, though not apologizing for his disheveled state.

"Yes, why wouldn't it be?"

He smiled, his expression soft. "You have a worried look in your eyes."

"Ah, yes. I mean, no, nothing's wrong. I'm amazed by how much you've accomplished. I'd not expected you to do any of the work yourself."

"For now, I remain more of a tavern owner than lord, Mrs. Fairfax. Until the manor is restored, I fear I will be unable to show much improvement."

"None is necessary, my lord."

The corners of his eyes crinkled. "You're too kind. But I fear society would not agree.'

"I have some proposals for your bedchambers, my lord," she said, stepping fully into the kitchen. "If you've a moment."

He gave the hinge a final twist before setting it aside. "I can hardly wait."

"Do you mean that?"

"I do. Very much so. I care deeply about every inch of this house. It's a way to honor my father."

Her eyes pricked with sudden emotion. "This is a home. One that will hold happy times again."

He nodded and for a second their gazes locked and an understanding passed between them. She'd felt it with him several times since they'd met. A kinship of sensibilities, perhaps?

"Shall we gather at the table?"

"Yes, please." He set aside his tool and joined her at the table that surely had fed countless staff over the decades. Not the last one, sadly. But the one to come, surely.

A faint scent of lye and soap lingered in the air, almost but not quite masking the deeper notes of old woodsmoke and herbs that had permeated the walls over decades. The kitchen range nearby, a massive iron affair with multiple ovens and hotplates, had been blackened with stove polish, though rust still peeked through in places where the neglect had bitten too deeply to remedy in a single day's work.

"I find myself unsure if you'll like any of them now that I'm here to show you what I've gathered."

"What's the worst that could happen?" James asked. "If I don't like them, then we'll try again."

"My husband used to tell me something similar when I was fretting about this or that."

"He sounds like a wise man."

"He was. And he certainly didn't suffer from any feelings of insecurity when it came to his work."

"You must borrow some of his confidence. Just as I will have to learn to be a gentleman."

From somewhere in the depths of the kitchen came the scrape of a boot on stone as one of the village boys continued his work in the scullery or cellars below. Three doors led off from the main kitchen. The first revealed what must be the pantry, its wooden shelves visible through the partially open door and mostly barren save for a few lonely jars and sacks. The second door presumably connected to the scullery, where faint sounds of clattering dishes and running water could be heard. The third and narrowest door, with its weathered handle and ancient hinges, likely concealed a steep staircase winding down to the damp cellars beneath the house.

Georgiana set her portfolio on one end of the table. "All right, then. Here's what I have." She opened the portfolio to reveal her selections. "These are the options I believe would suit the east-facing master chambers."

James leaned in, bracing his hands on the table's edge. Those hands. How strong and capable they were.

She arranged five squares of wallpaper across the scarred oak surface. "This first is a damask in Prussian blue from Ackermann's Repository. Very fashionable in London this season." Her fingers moved to the next sample. "This is a more traditional striped pattern in forest green with gold accents, which would complement the existing woodwork."

"Hmm." He reached for the third sample. His touch was surprisingly delicate for such work-hardened fingers. "And this one?"

"A subtle tartan-inspired design in burgundy and navy. Less ornate than what's currently favored in Town but elegantly masculine." She glanced up to find him watching her rather than the paper. "It would pair well with mahogany furnishings." *And you.*

The fourth sample was simpler—a textured paper in a warm cognac shade. "This would create a particularly inviting atmos-

phere for evening. The texture absorbs candlelight beautifully."
She presented the final sample, a rich crimson-flocked damask.
"What do you think?

James leaned over them, studying each one. His finger absently traced a deep knife scar on the table, one of many that told
stories of countless meals prepared for generations of the Ashford
family.

Georgiana slid three paint samples from the portfolio. "If
none of these appeal, we might consider a painted finish instead.
A deep green-blue for elegance, this warm gold for brightness, or
this terracotta for warmth."

James straightened suddenly, running a hand through his
disheveled hair, leaving it standing at odd angles. "You favor the
burgundy."

Georgiana blinked. "I… yes. How did you know?"

"Your voice softened when describing it." His eyes met hers,
unexpectedly perceptive. "Why that one?"

She hadn't expected him to notice, much less care about her
opinion. "It suits the manor's character, in that it's traditional but
not outdated. And it would complement the eastern exposure
without darkening the room." She hesitated. "It also seems to suit
you."

His eyebrow rose. "Does it?"

"Dignified without ostentation." The words escaped before
she could reconsider them. "Masculine but elegant. Like you, my
lord."

"High praise." Chuckling, he glanced down at his soiled shirt.
"Though perhaps misplaced at the moment."

"Clothes do not make the man. Your character remains, no
matter what you're wearing on the outside."

He simply gazed at her for a moment, his eyes soft. "You're
kinder than I thought you'd be."

She laughed. "What do you mean? And should I be insulted?"

"I don't know. When we first met, you came in so fierce and
determined, I was afraid we might be at odds. I've been known to

be stubborn and fierce myself."

"It was only that I was nervous. About the lie about my gender, mostly. I over-compensated, I suppose."

"Well, the world's not dealt us fair hands, but here we are just the same. Scrappers."

She returned his smile, feeling shy but also understood. "Scrappers. Yes."

James returned his attention to the samples, his fingertips resting on the burgundy paper. "What else? The bed, for example?" He glanced back at her, his eyes twinkling. Was he flirting with her?

A shiver went down the back of her spine.

She told herself to stay composed. Acting like a lovesick schoolgirl would not help her cause. "Dark walnut four-poster with navy wool for winter, something lighter for summer. White linens with this subtle pattern at the edges." She pulled out a small fabric swatch.

"Yes, these are lovely. You've captured my taste very well. I'm not sure how." Something unexpectedly gentle had entered his voice, at odds with his rough appearance. He tapped the blue sample once, leaving a faint smudge on its edge. "This one is right. As are the rest of your suggestions."

"Very well." Georgiana began gathering the samples, conscious of his gaze. "I'll put the orders in tomorrow before I come out."

"Mrs. Honeycutt will arrive tomorrow. Do you think she'll approve of our work here in the kitchen?" James asked.

"You've done very well, my lord. I'm impressed."

"Good. Because Mrs. Honeycutt's not the type to suffer fools. She's been known to make grown men cry."

"Surely not?"

"You'll see," James said, grinning. "She's marvelous."

A boom of thunder rattled the pans hanging overhead.

"Goodness me," Georgiana said, shivering. "I hate thunder and lightning."

James nodded. "I am not fond of it either. The thunder reminds me of the war. Let's go upstairs. I fear it may be difficult to get you back to the village if this keeps up."

"Yes, my lord. Good idea." She really hoped it wasn't as bad as it sounded from down here.

BY THE TIME they reached the main floor, sheets of rain crashed against the windows, turning the drive to soup and the garden paths to rivers. Cecily stood in the front hall, looking worried and pale.

"How will we get back to the village in this?" Cecily asked. "And the lightning's terrifying."

Georgiana's stomach clenched. Since Robert's death, Cecily had been frightened of storms. It was no mystery as to why. If the storm had not come that day, Robert would not have fallen from the scaffolding. That day had changed everything for Georgiana and Cecily. They'd thought they were safe but Robert's death had been just another sad twist of fate in their lives. Now, it was up to Georgiana to make sure her baby sister was well taken care of. Doing well on this project was important in so many ways. Creating a reputation as being one of the best in her field was the only way she could continue working. There were only so many times she could trick a client into thinking he was signing with a male architect.

James stepped back from the window. "I don't want you out in this. It won't be safe. You'll have to stay the night. I'll find cots and set them up for you in the study. I have bread and cheese from the shops in town and ale. We'll make it a party."

"I don't know," Georgiana said. "We hate to put you out."

"It would put me out worse to have you perish in a carriage accident," James said.

A sudden, sharp knock echoed through the manor.

Then a louder one.

"Who could that be?" James crossed the hall to the front door, brow furrowed. "No carriage could make it up that road in this mess." His voice was tight, wary. "It may be trouble. Stand aside until I assess the situation."

Another knock thumped—this time with a string of muttered curses audible behind it, colorful enough to make a sailor blush. But if she weren't mistaken, the voice belonged to a woman.

James opened the door, one hand resting near the small of his back where Georgiana suspected a pistol might be concealed. "Mrs. Honeycutt? What in God's name are you doing out in this weather?"

"Took you long enough to open the door, young man. I could catch my death out there." In stepped a woman shaped like a pot-bellied stove, round in the middle with twiggy limbs. Her soaked cloak clung to her like seaweed, unruly copper-red curls escaping from a dozen metal pins, cheeks bright red from the wind. Water pooled instantly around her mismatched, mud-caked boots, creating a small lake on the once-fine marble floor.

"I've come to save you from starvation and by the looks of you, I've come too late. You look awful." The woman's voice was like a market bell, booming yet musical, as if she were always halfway through a story worth hearing. She sniffed the air. "This place is a wreck. I hope the architect you've hired knows what he's doing."

James tugged at the collar of his shirt, making him look momentarily boyish. "Mrs. Honeycutt, this is Mrs. Fairfax, my architect, and her assistant, Miss Cecily."

Mrs. Honeycutt turned her attention toward them, her sharp blue eyes taking in every detail as laugh lines crinkled at their corners. She seemed not to have realized they were in the room until just that moment. "She's a she?"

"Correct." James's tone left little room for further questioning. "You're not supposed to arrive until tomorrow."

Mrs. Honeycutt scowled for a second, her broad shoulders

squaring beneath her patterned gown—at least two decades out of fashion and looking suspiciously like repurposed tavern drapery. Then she grinned, transforming her round, ruddy face. "Well, I'll be. A woman architect. I never knew such a thing was possible."

"It's a pleasure to meet you," Georgiana said, catching the distinct scent of rosemary, roasted garlic, and rain that seemed to emanate from the woman's very being.

Cecily stepped forward to greet the robust woman. "Good afternoon, Mrs. Honeycutt."

"Mrs. Fairfax. Miss Cecily. The pleasure's mine," Mrs. Honeycutt said.

"Why are you here a day early?" James asked, holding out his hands for her drenched cloak.

Mrs. Honeycutt dropped her basket with a dramatic thump. "I had a little trouble back home that made the need for my departure somewhat hasty." Her sharp eyes turned to Georgiana, then Cecily, assessing them with the practiced gaze of someone who had spent decades determining who needed feeding and how much.

"You're both as skinny as one of those whippet dogs. You need some meat on your bones. Thank goodness I'm here. I may not look fancy but I know how to cook." She smirked and crossed her arms over her ample chest. "I'll say it's a real step up in the world to be cooking for a Lord. I won't miss kicking drunks out of the tavern, now will I?"

"Why are you on foot?" James asked, his tone a mixture of disbelief and admiration.

"Well, let me tell you, I'm lucky to be alive." Mrs. Honeycutt shook out her skirts, sending droplets flying across the entryway like a dog after a swim. "Carriage went sideways on our way here and I told the useless driver I would find my own way on foot." She paused to catch her breath, wild wisps of silver and copper hair dancing around her face. "I'm not afraid of much, but the man was reckless and incompetent. Not a good combination, if you know what I mean? I could've been killed."

Cecily coughed behind her hand, clearly trying to contain her laughter.

"I'm glad no such tragedy has occurred," James said, his eyes sparkling with humor. "As luck would have it, some boys from the village and I have just finished cleaning the kitchen. In preparation for your arrival, Mrs. Honeycutt."

"I must see it at once." Without waiting for permission, Mrs. Honeycutt swept past them, water dripping from the hem of her dress.

"Shall we all go?" James asked. "It's nearly time for supper. We can eat downstairs, if that suits you ladies?"

"Absolutely fine," Georgiana said, stifling a laugh.

What an evening this had turned into.

CHAPTER FIVE

James

JAMES LEANED AGAINST the doorframe, watching as Mrs. Honeycutt circled the kitchen like a queen bee in her hive. She'd rolled up her sleeves, revealing freckled forearms corded with muscle he knew so well. He'd inherited Mrs. Honeycutt when he bought the tavern and he'd often thought she was the most valuable of any of his other staff put together. She might be bawdy, foul-mouthed and opinionated but she was also smart, loyal and hilarious.

"This is a fine kitchen indeed." Mrs. Honeycutt ran her hand along the freshly scrubbed workbench. "If only my mother could see me now, in such a place as this. She'd be proud."

"I'm glad you're here," James said. "I've missed you."

Mrs. Honeycutt snorted. "'Course you have. There's only one Tilda Honeycutt in the world." She set the pot down with a clang that echoed through the cavernous space. "Right then. Let's see what you've managed for provisions."

Without waiting for direction, she marched to the pantry, throwing open the door as if expecting an ambush. "Lord have mercy," she muttered. "A half-wheel of cheese, a loaf of bread and some butter? What exactly were you planning to eat tonight, my lord? The furniture?"

"The storm upended our idea to eat at the pub in the village," James said. "The ladies are staying at the inn and planned to return but I didn't want to send them out in this weather. I've been eating supper with them at the inn most nights."

"I see." Mrs. Honeycutt crossed her arms. "Speaking of which, where will any of us sleep?"

"I hired some boys from the village to clean several of the staff rooms," James said. "Our housekeeper is to arrive tomorrow as well."

He didn't mention that he'd assumed Cecily and Georgiana would take those rooms tonight. Now, he was short a room.

"This housekeeper—who is she and will I like her?" Mrs. Honeycutt asked.

James chuckled. "She's the housekeeper who worked for us when I was a boy. She's perhaps the sweetest lady in England. You'll like her."

"We'll see about that. I won't have anyone telling me what to do in my own kitchen."

"I doubt she'll be heavy-handed," James said. "But she'll be invaluable when it comes to teaching us both about proper etiquette when it comes to entertaining and staff. My sister-in-law has promised to advise us as well. She's a proper lady. And I'm not exactly a proper lord."

"There's no finer man than you, James Ashford, and don't let anyone tell you otherwise."

Mrs. Fairfax caught his eye across the room, her lips pressed together in what might have been an attempt to suppress a smile. Cecily made no such effort, grinning openly as she perched on a stool by the hearth.

"I had planned to visit the village tomorrow," James said, straightening. "To arrange deliveries."

"This won't be the first time I've fed a household from a nearly bare kitchen," Mrs. Honeycutt said. "My mother, God rest her soul, fed a family of six on mostly nothing at all."

"Thank you," James said. "I can't speak for the ladies, but my stomach's rumbling."

"Good thing I've arrived early then." Mrs. Honeycutt went

back into the pantry and emerged with the bread and cheese in hand. "Let's get a fire started. And I'll need a skillet." She disappeared into the scullery, emerging moments later with a cast-iron pan.

James offered to make the fire in the stove. He knew at some point he would have to start acting like a gentleman but for now he could still be himself. A man who knew how to build his own fire.

Georgiana and Cecily sat at the table, watching Mrs. Honeycutt with amused expressions.

Soon enough, James had a fire going and had poured them all glasses of ale. He knew Mrs. Honeycutt enjoyed an ale most nights after she'd finished feeding his patrons at the tavern.

Mrs. Honeycutt set about slicing the bread with efficient strokes of a knife she'd produced from seemingly nowhere. "Mrs. Fairfax, how does a woman come to be an architect? I always thought that was men's work, all that measuring and mathematics."

James tensed, worried his outspoken cook would upset Georgiana, but she merely smiled. "My late husband was an architect. I'd always dreamt of being one myself. He agreed to teach me everything he knew."

"Unusual, ain't it? A man willing to teach a woman something valuable?" Mrs. Honeycutt slapped butter onto the bread slices with the enthusiasm of someone beating a rug. "Most men want to keep knowledge to themselves. Otherwise, women have too much power."

"My husband was an unusual man. He understood my ambitions." Mrs. Fairfax's voice remained steady, though James noticed her hands clasped together tightly in her lap. "He was rather progressive in his thinking."

"Was he now? Rare breed, that." Mrs. Honeycutt paused in her preparations, pointing her knife at Mrs. Fairfax. "How long's he been gone, then?"

"A little over a year."

"I'm sorry to hear. I lost my husband young too." Mrs. Honeycutt returned to her work, placing thick slices of cheese between the buttered bread. "Tavern brawl. Knife to the ribs over a game of cards. I was spitting mad at the time. Such a waste."

"How awful," Cecily murmured.

Mrs. Honeycutt placed the assembled sandwiches in the skillet with a satisfying sizzle. "Well, he wasn't much of a husband anyway. Drank and gambled away all our money and couldn't keep his hands to himself where the serving girls were concerned."

Miss Cecily's eyes widened to saucers. "Our father was a gambler too," Cecily said. "That's how we got into so much trouble. He gambled away our fortune, then took his own life."

"Oh, dear me, that's horrible," Mrs. Honeycutt said.

James's chest ached, thinking about what it must have done to his daughters. He'd seen it himself back at the tavern. Men who gambled away homes or businesses, always thinking one more bet would restore whatever they'd lost previously. In fact, that was the very scenario in which he'd won the tavern. Although, that man had had no family. If he had, James wasn't sure he could have taken it from him, even though he had won it fairly. James liked cards, but he never cheated. Now that his fate had changed for the better, he'd lost the taste for cards. He'd played out of necessity. Once he'd discovered his talent for winning any game he played, he'd used gambling for financial gain. Having nothing forces a man to do things he otherwise might not. He would have no need for gambling now.

For some odd reason, a thought popped into his head. Would Mrs. Fairfax think less of him if she knew he had often gambled? Now that he knew about her father, he worried she might see him in a different light. An unflattering one.

"Did you ever consider remarrying?" Georgiana asked Mrs. Honeycutt.

"Good heavens, why would I? Once was quite sufficient." Mrs. Honeycutt flipped the sandwiches with expert precision. "I found it easier to make my own way. You?"

"I wouldn't be opposed," Georgiana said. "But it's unlikely. We're hoping Cecily can have a Season. I married a working man but our father was a nobleman. Unfortunately, as Cecily said, we had nothing after our father's death. I had to find a husband quickly but I had no dowry. Fortunately for me, Robert took a shine to me. If not for him, I'm not sure what would have happened to my mother and sister. Or me, for that matter. As you can imagine, it's important for me that this job goes well. I'm hoping to provide a dowry for Cecily so that she can marry well."

Mrs. Honeycutt looked at Georgiana and then back to Cecily. "You look alike, except for the hair."

"We've heard that all our lives," Georgiana said. "Cecily takes after our mother. She is a ginger too."

"This hair is a curse, ain't I right?" Mrs. Honeycutt asked Cecily. "I blame it for my temper."

"Cecily doesn't have much of a temper," Georgiana said, her eyes softening as she glanced at her sister. "Isn't that merely a stereotype?"

"I suppose so." Mrs. Honeycutt said, grinning. "But it's been a good excuse for my wild nature."

"I'd like to be wild," Cecily said, perched on the edge of her chair.

"I don't recommend it," Mrs. Honeycutt said. "It's gotten me into some trouble."

He wondered what she'd done to necessitate an early departure from Brighton. He'd have to ask her later. The ladies were not ready for one of Mrs. Honeycutt's stories.

Mrs. Honeycutt lifted the skillet from the fire and slid the sandwiches onto plates. "Not my finest work but it'll keep body and soul together until I can get to the village tomorrow. I've a list long as your arm, my lord, and I'll need coin for it."

"Of course." He brought two of the four plates to the table, placing them before the ladies. The aroma of toasted bread and melted cheese made his stomach growl embarrassingly.

Mrs. Honeycutt brought the other two plates and James waited for her to settle her substantial frame on a chair that creaked in protest. Once James was seated, Mrs. Honeycutt said, "Go on then. It won't improve with waiting."

James took a bite, the buttery crunch giving way to molten cheese. It was ridiculously simple, yet somehow perfect.

"Tomorrow," Mrs. Honeycutt announced between bites, "I'll set things properly to rights. Need herbs from the kitchen garden—if there's anything left of it—and proper meat. Can't have His Lordship and two beautiful ladies living on cheese and bread like mice."

"I'm afraid the kitchen garden is quite overgrown," Mrs. Fairfax said. "Lord Ashford has plans to have it cleared and planted this spring."

"We have a lot to do," James said. "But Mrs. Fairfax is doing splendidly so far."

"I'll do what I can with what I can find in the village. By this time next year, the pantry will be stocked full of summer's bounty." Mrs. Honeycutt fixed her gaze on Georgiana. "So, Mrs. Fairfax. Accident or illness?"

"I beg your pardon?" Georgiana dabbed at her mouth with a napkin.

"Your husband. Was it accident or illness that took him?"

"He fell from scaffolding on one of his job sites. Hit his head in the fall. It was a sudden storm like today and it made for slippery conditions. He died instantly, though. That gives me peace."

"What a shame." Mrs. Honeycutt shook her head. "Mine lingered for three days after the stabbing. Cursing and raving the whole time, as expected." She snorted. "Still, I gave him a decent burial. More than he deserved, truth be told."

Cecily made a small choking sound.

Mrs. Honeycutt turned back to Georgina. "Now then, how long have you been working on great houses? Must have taken some doing, convincing the gentry to trust a woman."

Georgiana glanced at James. "This is my first project without my husband. We shared the workload when he was alive, but our clients didn't necessarily know that."

"And my James hired a woman? Never thought I'd see the day," Mrs. Honeycutt said, nodding toward James.

"She used a man's name on the contract." James spoke without malice. If anything, he sounded amused. "So what was a man to do? Anyway, she's more than capable. From what I've seen so far, I'd have to say she's extremely talented."

"Thank you, Lord Ashford," Georgiana said, her chest warming with gratitude. "I am appreciative of your openness to working together."

Together.

He liked the sound of that.

"And what exactly needs fixing in this grand old place?" Mrs. Honeycutt asked, turning to Mrs. Fairfax. "Everything?"

"The roof will need to be repaired in some places and there's water damage to the floors in some of the upstairs bedrooms and the ballroom," Georgie said. "But it's mostly cosmetic. The structure is solid."

"We chose furnishings and wallpaper today," James said. "For my bedchamber."

Mrs. Honeycutt's blue eyes twinkled. "I do hope you're considering finding yourself a lady of the mansion." She leaned forward conspiratorially. "You're not getting any younger."

A startled laugh escaped Miss Cecily, who quickly covered her mouth.

"I've no need for a wife," James said. "I'm simply happy to return to my family's home. That will be enough for a good life."

"Ridiculous. Of course you need a wife," Mrs. Honeycutt said.

"I'm not sure anyone would want me, given the scandal of my family." It was the truth. Although their family's estate and titles were returned, there was still stigma attached to the Ashford name. What woman would want to be his wife, given all it entailed?

"Any woman would be blessed to have you." Mrs. Honeycutt stood, collecting the empty dishes with efficient movements. "And you might be surprised. The right woman could appear at any moment and she wouldn't care one bit about the past. Not if she's truly in love with you."

He flushed, feeling the gazes of all three women upon him. "Shall I show you to your room? I imagine you're tired."

"Yes, I suppose I am tuckered out." Mrs. Honeycutt gestured toward Georgiana and Cecily. "Where will these two sleep?"

"We can share the other room," Georgiana said quickly. "Sisters are accustomed to sleeping together when necessary."

"That's very accommodating of you, Mrs. Fairfax," Mrs. Honeycutt said. "Looking at you, I would have thought you'd be a right prig but you're all right."

"I'm not sure I've ever had a better compliment," Georgiana said.

The women exchanged smiles.

Georgiana Fairfax was nothing if not surprising. She'd managed to win over Mrs. Honeycutt in the span of thirty minutes.

He wasn't the only one charmed by the lovely architect.

CECILY AND MRS. Honeycutt were yawning by the end of their meal and left for bed, leaving James and Georgiana alone. She mentioned that she had more samples to show him, this time for the drawing room. Before he could stifle the impulse, he asked if she'd like to join him upstairs for a brandy while they looked through her suggestions.

"We can get the fire going in the study to keep out the chill."

"Yes, why not? I'm not feeling tired enough to sleep," Georgiana said. "I'm a night owl."

"I am as well. All the years running the tavern ruined me for mornings."

They went up the stairs and into the study. While he lit the fire, Georgiana poured them each a brandy. He brought two chairs and a coffee table close to the hearth. They smelled of dust but it was better than sitting on the floor. She took her portfolio from her desk and brought it over to the table.

She opened the swatch book. Beneath the flap of linen were layers of fabric samples, paper sketches, and watercolor renderings of color pairings. She brushed her hand over a pale duck-egg blue silk damask. "For the drawing room, you'd mentioned you'd like it to reflect the past. From what you've shared and what I've uncovered, I think I have a good idea of what to do."

He nodded. When they'd talked about the drawing room, he'd shared with her his memories of what it had once looked like and asked that she bring it back.

"This was the original tone of the wall panels. It faded, of course, but I had one section removed from behind the hearth where it was better preserved. Do you like it? Or would you rather have some other color?"

"No, it's exactly as I remembered it."

"I thought we might restore the palette with this." She held out the fabric for him to inspect. "The blue and gold complement each other, don't you think?"

She showed him two coordinating trims. One was a braided silk, the other a masculine linen binding. He stared at them longer than she expected.

"Which do you like?" James asked.

"The linen binding suits you, I think."

"How strange this all is. I'm flooded with memories."

She hesitated, unsure what to say. "I can imagine being back here after all these years brings forth a myriad emotions."

"Indeed it does. My mother chose every furnishing and decor herself when they first married," James said. "After she died, my father kept everything the same."

"How old were you when she passed?"

"She died giving birth to Sophia. I was only two. Sadly, I have no memories of her."

"I'm sorry."

"Sophia looks exactly like her," James said, gesturing toward the oil painting of his mother hanging on the wall.

"She was beautiful."

"My sister is too," James said. "My brother and I are hoping to convince her to have a Season next year, like Cecily. Perhaps they will become friends."

"That would be most welcome."

"What did you hear about my family before you arrived here?" James asked.

"Only what was reported in the newspaper and gossip, of course. It was Cecily's idea to approach you about the restoration. She'd heard that the younger of the Ashford brothers wanted to bring the family home back from ruin."

"It was resourceful of you both."

"No one knows what happened to you and your siblings after you left here and before your return. I have to confess to being curious."

"Yes, well, it's a sad tale. Are you sure you want to know?" James asked.

"I do."

"Fine. But then you have to tell me more about your own sad tale."

She smiled. "Whatever you wish to ask, I shall answer."

"When Papa was hanged and our home and assets taken by the government, we were sent up north to live with a distant cousin. She was our only living relative on either side of the family. Baron Langston and his wife, Eugenia, were not exactly thrilled to have three children to take care of. They already had two of their own. We were not taken into the fold. Instead, we were treated as free labor. Sebastian was assigned to the gardening staff. I to the stables. Sophia, at age eight, became a scullery maid."

"That's awful. There's a place in hell for the Langstons, I

suspect."

"Yes, I believe so. It would have been bad enough to be treated as servants but it was worse than that. My brother and I were often whipped for minor infractions or ones made up by their children. They hated us from the moment we arrived and made an art form out of finding ways to get us into trouble. Sophia was denied food and sent to bed hungry more nights than any child should have to endure."

"How did you get away?"

"Sebastian and I joined the military, hoping to provide a way out for our sister. We lied about our ages and enlisted when we were still in our teens. Sadly, we had to leave Sophia behind. She was only twelve."

Georgiana's mouth dropped open. "So that means you joined up when you were fourteen? Lord Ashford, it's unspeakable what they did to you."

"Sebastian and I are tough and lucky. We managed to stay alive through the Peninsular campaigns. When we returned to England after the Battle of Waterloo, we weren't sure how we were going to survive. As luck would have it, I'm a good poker player. I won the tavern in a game."

She flinched, as if he'd smacked her. "You won the tavern in a poker game?"

"Yes. Your gossip sources didn't mention that part?"

"No." Her jaw set and she suddenly seemed very interested in the contents of her glass.

"Does that make you think less of me?" James asked. Was it as he'd feared?

She lifted her gaze to his. "My family lost everything because of my father's gambling. I cannot help but think of that when you tell me such a thing."

"This may make no difference to you, but I would like to mention that a man in my situation had little going for him, other than his skill at card games. Like you, I found success in a less than morally ideal way. Just as you have."

"You mean pretending to be a man?"

"That's right. I mean no offense or even judgment but no matter how you look at it—you lied to me. Tricked me into signing a contract."

She nodded, before taking a sip of her drink. "As you say, those of us without many choices are often forced into doing something they never thought they would, just to survive."

"I have to admit, however, hearing you speak about your father and what his gambling did to your family, gives me pause. The man who I won the tavern from didn't have a family. I suppose that's how I convinced myself it was my right to take it, as I won it fairly. Anyway, my gambling days are behind me. I left the tavern and the cards in Brighton. I no longer need them. You, on the other hand, are still fighting to make a life for you and your sister. Perhaps we can agree that sometimes the morally messy choice is the only one we have."

"I want only to give Cecily a chance."

"I understand. I feel the same way about my own sister." He glanced toward the fire, thinking he should throw another log into the flames, but didn't. "Where's your mother now?"

"She's staying with a friend in London."

He could tell by her tone that there was more to the story. "What is she like?" James asked.

Georgiana sighed, looking down at her glass. "There's no way to say the truth and remain kind. Simply put, Mother's selfish and helpless, but doesn't know it. Cecily and I find her challenging in every way. She has not adapted well to her change in circumstance since my father's death. She's staying with a friend in London now, but I fear it won't last. She has a way of alienating those who are doing their best to help her."

"She sounds difficult."

"Since I was young, I've taken care of her, emotionally, and now financially. If I'd not found Robert, I don't know what would have become of us. He was the perfect husband for me."

"You loved him very much?"

"I did."

The idea that she'd loved her husband bothered him. Which was ridiculous. Firstly, the poor man was dead. Secondly, why should he care about Mrs. Fairfax's love life? It was none of his concern.

None whatsoever.

Then why did it make his stomach feel so odd?

CHAPTER SIX
Georgiana

GEORGIANA WOKE THE next day to the smell of bacon. Mrs. Honeycutt must have gone into the village already and returned with supplies. She might be a bit bawdy, but the woman knew how to get things done. No wonder James loved her so dearly.

As she lay in the narrow bed, fragments of the previous evening drifted through her mind. The warmth of the brandy, the flicker of firelight across James's face as he spoke of his past, the way his voice had gentled when he'd made her feel safe. She touched her fingers to her lips, remembering the way he'd looked at her when he'd called her beautiful.

Cecily had already risen and dressed. Georgiana could hear her talking to Mrs. Honeycutt in the kitchen, their voices mingling with the sounds of breakfast preparation.

Her sister had left her a basin of warm water, which she used to give herself a thorough washing before putting on her dress from the day before. After pinning her hair with extra care—though she told herself it had nothing to do with a certain lord—she headed toward the wonderful smells.

Morning sunlight spilled across the long worktable, catching in the rim of chipped crockery bowls and a basket of golden scones. Mrs. Honeycutt bustled between the hearth and the table in her apron and half-pinned curls, already halfway through a monologue about the indecency of village shopkeepers who had the nerve to question whether Lord Ashford had indeed hired the likes of her to be his cook.

"How very rude," Cecily said, buttering a scone. "I hope you explained the situation."

"Trust me, they won't question me again." Mrs. Honeycutt grinned wickedly. "I might have scared the grocer with my fierce tongue. I heard him mutter something about redheads and the devil. Which I paid no mind to whatsoever."

"How you managed to get into the village before sunrise, I'll never know." Cecily yawned. "You're a wonder, Mrs. Honeycutt."

"I can't have my James going hungry," Mrs. Honeycutt said with obvious affection. "Or Lord Ashford, I mean. That's going to take some getting used to."

James, seated at the end of the table, gave a low chuckle. He looked rested and relaxed, his shirt sleeves rolled up to his elbows, hair slightly damp from washing. When he glanced up as she entered, something passed between them—a shared memory of their conversation by the fire.

"Good morning, Lord Ashford." Georgiana took the seat across from him, acutely aware of his presence.

"How did you sleep?" His eyes held hers for a moment longer than necessary.

"Very well, thank you." She felt warmth creep up her neck under his gaze. There was something different about him this morning—or perhaps something different about how she saw him. The harsh lines around his eyes seemed softer, and she found herself noticing details she'd missed before. The way his hands moved as he reached for his coffee. The small scar near his left temple.

He cleared his throat and addressed both sisters. "I've been thinking about your arrangements here. The inn is perfectly adequate, but with the work we're doing on the manor, it seems impractical for you to keep traveling back and forth. Especially with winter weather being so unpredictable."

The sisters exchanged a glance.

"What are you suggesting?" Georgiana asked carefully.

"Stay here. For as long as you're working on the restoration. Mrs. Honeycutt has plenty of room, and frankly—". He paused, seeming to choose his words with great care. "After last night, I realized how much I enjoy the company. This house has been too quiet for too long."

"Oh, yes, you must stay," Mrs. Honeycutt chimed in. "I'll be lonesome down here by myself. Besides, it's not proper for his lordship to be rattling around this big house with only me for company. People will talk."

"They're already talking," Cecily said with a grin. "About the mysterious sisters who've come to restore the manor."

"If you think we wouldn't be in the way?" Georgiana found herself hoping he'd insist.

"Nonsense. You're barely big enough to get in anyone's way," Mrs. Honeycutt declared.

James leaned forward slightly. "Mrs. Ellsworth starts today. Once she's settled and we've sorted out the staff quarters, we can move you to proper guest rooms upstairs. But for now, you're welcome to stay here with Mrs. Honeycutt."

"That would be wonderful," Cecily said, clearly delighted. "The inn is perfectly nice, but this feels more like…" She gestured around the warm kitchen.

"Home," Georgiana finished softly, then caught herself. "I mean, it's very kind of you. And it would help us manage our expenses."

"Then it's settled." James's smile was genuine, reaching his eyes. "I confess, I'm rather looking forward to more evenings like last night."

Before Georgiana could respond to that loaded statement, the back door opened and a woman stepped inside, removing her bonnet with one gloved hand and clutching a small parcel in the other.

"Well now, look at all of you." The newcomer delivered a wide smile. "It's been too long since this kitchen was full of hungry people."

James stood immediately. "Mrs. Ellsworth, welcome. I'm so glad you're here."

She patted his arm with obvious fondness before turning to the sisters. "You must be Mrs. Fairfax and Miss Linley. I've heard nothing but kind things about you in the village. You've created quite the stir with the young men, I'm told."

"We've heard wonderful things about you as well," Georgiana replied, rising to greet her. "James has just invited us to stay here at the manor instead of at the inn. I hope you won't mind. This will be your house to run, after all."

"I'll be delighted for the company," Mrs. Ellsworth said warmly. "It will be like the old days when this kitchen was filled with young people." She reached into her bag. "Speaking of which, on my way from the village, the postman asked me to deliver this. Apparently, word has spread that you're staying here. Like I said, everyone's talking about the two beautiful women who have come to save the manor from ruin."

She handed Georgiana a pale envelope with elegant, looping script.

Georgiana took one look at the handwriting and her face fell. "Oh no. It's from Mother."

Cecily groaned audibly. "Dear God, what does she want now?"

Georgiana broke the wax seal with the resignation of someone opening a bill she couldn't afford to pay. She read quickly, her expression growing more dismayed with each line.

"Well?" Cecily demanded. "Don't keep us in suspense."

"I'll read it aloud." Georgiana cleared her throat and adopted a theatrical tone:

"My darling girls, as I find myself in need of a change of scenery—and funds are temporarily tight—I shall arrive on Thursday, the twenty-eighth of January. Do make sure the village offers accommodations of suitable refinement. I expect to stay at least a fortnight. Longer if the mood strikes me or if I find the local society sufficiently entertaining. With love, Mama."

"That's in two weeks," Cecily said, calculating quickly. "What are we going to do?"

"She'll not be deterred once she's made up her mind," Georgiana said grimly. "Lord Ashford, I must warn you—under no circumstances should you invite her to stay here. She has a talent for making herself indispensable and overstaying her welcome. The last time she visited someone, she stayed for three months."

"And ate them out of house and home," Cecily added. "Not to mention rearranging all their furniture and criticizing their choice of servants."

"Now you'll have to pay for her lodging at the inn," Cecily continued. "On top of everything else."

Georgiana closed her eyes briefly. "God help us all."

James watched this exchange with growing amusement. "She sounds… formidable."

"That's one word for her," Georgiana muttered, folding the letter with more force than necessary.

Mrs. Honeycutt chuckled. "Well, this should make things interesting. I do love a good family drama."

"You won't once you meet her," both sisters said in unison, which only made James laugh harder.

A WEEK HAD passed since Mrs. Ellsworth's arrival, and Georgiana had settled into a comfortable routine at the manor. She was just finishing her sketches for the day when a soft knock came at the door. She looked up from her work as Mrs. Ellsworth entered, a familiar warmth in the housekeeper's expression that had developed over their days together.

"Mrs. Fairfax, this arrived in today's post. The village boy brought it up with the bread delivery." She held out a single envelope, cream-colored and crisply folded.

Georgiana frowned, setting down her pencil. "Was it forwarded from Brighton?"

"No. Addressed directly to you here. Which is strange, I thought."

Georgiana stood slowly and took the letter with cautious fingers. Her name was written in a looping hand, familiar and unwelcome. Her stomach turned to ice.

Julian.

No return address. No seal. But she knew. The way one knows when the air shifts before a storm. When poison slithers just out of sight.

She didn't open it.

Instead, she crossed the room with careful steps, lifted the brass poker from its stand, and nudged the fire until the flames leapt higher. Then, without a word, she tossed the envelope into the blaze.

Mrs. Ellsworth watched quietly, her concern evident. "Should I be worried?"

Georgiana's hands trembled as she set the poker down. "Just some unwanted correspondence. Nothing to concern yourself with."

The door opened before Mrs. Ellsworth could respond. James stepped in, still in his shirtsleeves from working on the estate accounts. Over the past week, these informal visits to check on her progress had become a treasured part of her day. He looked between her and the hearth where the last of the letter crinkled into ash, his expression immediately shifting to concern.

"What's happened?" His voice carried the protective note that had become familiar since she'd been living under his roof.

"Nothing at all," Georgiana said quickly, forcing a smile. "Just disposing of some old correspondence."

Mrs. Ellsworth cleared her throat. "I'll leave you both to your evening conversation then." She excused herself with a meaningful look, clearly recognizing the tension in the room despite Georgiana's deflection.

James watched the housekeeper go, then turned back to Georgiana, his eyes flicking to the fireplace. "You're pale as death, and your hands are shaking. That wasn't nothing."

"Truly, it's not worth discussing." She moved toward her usual chair by the fire, hoping to change the subject. "How were the estate accounts today?"

He followed her but didn't sit, instead studying her with the careful attention she'd grown to appreciate over their week together. "Georgiana."

The gentle use of her Christian name made her resolve waver, but she couldn't tell him. Couldn't burden him with her shame, couldn't risk him looking at her differently if he knew what Julian had done, what he threatened to reveal.

"Some correspondence from my past that I'd rather leave buried," she said finally. "Nothing that need concern you."

James was quiet for a long moment, clearly wanting to press further but recognizing her reluctance. Finally, he moved toward the sideboard. "Come, let me pour you a brandy. You look ready to collapse."

She sank into her chair gratefully. The flames consumed the last traces of ash from Julian's letter, but her hands continued to shake as she folded them in her lap.

"I don't like seeing you distressed," he said, returning with two glasses of brandy and pressing one into her hands. "If there's anything troubling you, anything at all..."

"You're very kind." She took a sip, letting the warmth steady her. "But some burdens are better carried alone."

His expression tightened with frustration, but he settled into the chair opposite her. "I disagree. But I won't force your confidence."

The comfortable silence that had developed between them over the past week felt strained now, weighted with unspoken things. Despite Julian's intrusion into her peace, she felt safe here with James—but she also felt the distance her secrecy created between them.

"I've been thinking about what you said," she said finally, desperate to recapture their usual ease, "about remaining alone."

"Have you?" He refilled both their glasses, though his movements were more careful now, more reserved.

"You spoke of not bringing a child into this world, of the world being too broken." She paused, gathering her thoughts. "But sitting here these past days, watching you with Mrs. Honeycutt and Mrs. Ellsworth, seeing how you care for the village—you're proof that there's still good in the world."

He was quiet for a long moment, staring into the fire. When he spoke, his voice held a new edge of doubt. "You see me through kind eyes, Georgiana. But perhaps you don't see me clearly enough to judge."

The words stung, and she sensed he was pulling away because of her refusal to confide in him. "I see you more clearly than you think."

"Do you? Because from where I sit, it seems you keep your true thoughts carefully guarded." His gaze flicked to the fireplace again. "You won't trust me with whatever troubles you, yet you speak of goodness and worthiness as if you know my heart."

"That's not fair—"

"Isn't it?" He leaned forward slightly, his expression earnest but guarded. "You ask me to believe in love, in connection, yet you burn letters and tell me some burdens are better carried alone. How can there be true intimacy without trust?"

She felt tears prick at her eyes. He was right, and it hurt. "Some things are too shameful to share."

"With anyone? Or just with me?"

The question hung between them, heavy with implication. She could see in his eyes that her secrecy had wounded him, made him doubt not just her feelings but his own worth.

"James..."

"The hour grows late," he said, standing abruptly. "And tomorrow your mother arrives."

The reminder brought her back to earth with jarring force. "Don't remind me. I'm still hoping she'll change her mind."

"From what you and Cecily have told me about her, that seems unlikely." His tone was polite now, distant.

"She'll take one look at this place and have opinions about everything. And she'll interrogate you mercilessly about your intentions regarding her daughters."

"I think I can handle one determined mother." But there was no warmth in his voice now.

Georgiana stood and smoothed her skirt, feeling the chasm that had opened between them. "Thank you for the brandy."

He nodded but didn't move closer as he usually did. "Good night, Georgiana."

"Good night."

As she made her way down the stairs to the room she shared with her sister, she felt the weight of what her secrecy was costing her. James's protection, his growing affection—all of it threatened by her inability to trust him with the truth about Julian. But how could she tell him? How could she risk losing what little respect he had for her?

The brandy had warmed her body, but her heart felt colder than ever.

CHAPTER SEVEN

James

BEFORE JAMES KNEW it, the first crocuses pushed through the cold dirt, bringing hints of spring, despite the bitter winds of late February. The workers, directed by Ben and Georgiana, had done splendidly. Last night before they retired, Georgiana had asked him not to look at the drawing room until she had everything ready. Now, standing outside the closed doors, he felt like a child on Christmas morning. Her careful and thoughtful work on his home touched his heart in ways that surprised him—a mixture of gratitude and admiration, along with the unfamiliar feeling of being part of a team.

They crossed the grand foyer together, Georgiana's excitement palpable beside him.

"Are you ready?" she asked.

"Show me."

With dramatic flair, she pushed open the doors to the drawing room.

He stepped inside and stopped abruptly. "Oh, Georgie. It's perfection."

"Is it how you remember?"

"It's better. You kept the essence of the past while updating it beautifully."

"Do you love it? Truly?" She bounced on her toes, looking absolutely adorable.

"I love it." He stepped farther into the room, turning slowly to take everything in.

Although it was nearing the end of January, they were experiencing a rare sunny day. Sunlight spilled through polished windows, illuminating pale blue walls adorned with gilded frames containing landscapes and classical scenes. A magnificent crystal chandelier hung from the ornately decorated ceiling, where pale blue paint showcased intricate white scrollwork and gold leaf detailing. The elaborate crown molding featured coral and gold patterns that created a harmonious frame for the entire room.

"We were able to preserve the original crown molding despite the water damage near the eastern corner." Georgiana moved beside him, speaking in her quiet, sure tone. "The plasterwork above the windows required complete reconstruction, but I followed the pattern from the surviving panel."

"Glorious," he murmured.

His gaze drifted to the elegant furnishings. The round mahogany table with its polished surface reflected the light, surrounded by delicate chairs upholstered in the same pale blue as the walls, their wooden frames highlighted with gold gilt. Against one wall stood a settee with cream fabric and ornately carved gold trim, flanked by matching side tables. A terracotta carpet with hexagonal medallion patterns in soft cream covered the floor, its colors warming the cool elegance of the room.

Snowdrops drooped gracefully over the sides of a crystal vase on the center table, their subtle fragrance mingling with the scent of beeswax polish.

"The blue and cream are soothing, don't you think?" Georgiana asked.

"I agree."

He turned slowly, absorbing more of the space. The settee was positioned perfectly for afternoon conversation. The paintings, restored to their former glory and depicting pastoral scenes and mythological figures, reminded him of happier times. There would be more of them—he felt more certain of that with every passing day.

"Are you ready to see your bedchambers?" she asked.

He'd been sleeping in the study so that she and her helpers could put the finishing touches on his bedroom. "Lead the way."

They headed up the newly refinished stairs, the scent of fresh stain filling the air.

"I'm nervous to show you this." She paused at a heavy oak door, her hand hesitating on the brass handle.

"But you must. I trust you completely."

The door swung open, and James fell silent.

Where there had once been peeling wallpaper and water stains now stood a room of commanding elegance. Deep slate-blue walls rose around him, paneled and adorned with gilded moldings that caught the afternoon light. Elaborate plasterwork panels featured intricate medallion designs, their craftsmanship unmistakable. His gaze traveled upward to the ceiling, where a circular medallion radiated outward in concentric patterns of carved plaster, centered by a brass chandelier with glowing globe-shaped lights.

"This is…" Words failed him entirely.

"Too much?" She watched his face carefully.

"No. Not at all. Extraordinary is the right word. It's fit for a king."

"Or perhaps a lord?"

The bed dominated the space, with an intricately carved headboard featuring metallic accents that echoed the room's gilded details. It was dressed in layers of midnight blue coverlets and pillows, a burgundy throw folded precisely at its foot. A wooden bench, carved with the same attention to detail as the bed, sat at the foot.

Tall windows that had been drafty and bare now wore sumptuous blue velvet curtains with gold tasseled valances. Beside them stood a blue upholstered armchair that looked the perfect place to read or reflect.

The herringbone-patterned wooden floor gleamed beneath

an oriental rug in blues and golds. Wall sconces cast a warm glow against the rich walls, complementing the soft light from elegant table lamps placed on ornately carved bedside tables.

"The writing desk was refinished and I'm pleased with how it turned out." She gestured toward a polished mahogany piece near the window. "The globe belonged to your grandfather, according to Mrs. Ellsworth."

"Yes, I remember it. And the desk. My father used to write his correspondence there." He could almost see his father's careful handwriting, the way he'd pause to consider each word.

James moved slowly into the room, awe washing over him. It was as if she'd looked directly into his soul and created his perfect sanctuary. "How did you do it? It's exactly what I wanted, even though I didn't know it myself."

"Would you like to know where I got my inspiration?" She stood framed in the doorway, her practical blue dress a stark contrast to the opulence surrounding them.

"I would indeed."

A slight flush colored her cheeks. "This will sound silly, but I thought of your eyes. Their blue is reflected throughout the room."

"Is this how you see me?" The words escaped before he could stop them.

"Yes. As I said when we spoke about the design initially—elegant yet masculine. Deep blue runs through the core of you, reflected in your eyes." She paused, her voice growing softer. "Blue's my favorite color."

"Is it?" He caught her gaze, his stomach fluttering in a way that had become familiar whenever she looked at him like this.

"I didn't know it was until I saw the particular hue of your blue eyes. They stir a soul, Lord Ashford."

The intimacy of standing in his private quarters, of hearing her speak about his eyes, about souls made his chest and other unmentionable parts tighten with longing.

"You stir my soul, Georgie. You've made a place for me that

feels safe. A room where I can think and dream and plan." His voice came out rougher than intended. "Thank you."

"Decorating your haven brought me much joy. I wanted to make it a place reflective of your goodness, your loyalty to those you love and the care you've given to the community in the short time you've been here." Her flush deepened. "That you see what I tried to do pleases me to no end."

"I see you, Georgie. In every part of this room."

The thought ambushed him, swift and undeniable. He wanted her here with him. In this room. In his bed. The desire was so sudden and fierce it nearly staggered him.

Was he falling in love with his architect?

No. Of course not. It was only that she was lovely and intelligent. He craved her company, but that wasn't love. Admiration, perhaps. Desire, certainly.

He did not do love. He must remember that, even as every fiber of his being seemed to argue otherwise.

BY THE TIME they'd made it downstairs to the kitchen, the air was rich with the scents of onion and rosemary, mingling with the yeasty aroma of fresh-baked bread.

Mrs. Honeycutt stood at the stove, ladling stew into bowls with practiced efficiency. Steam rose from the thick, fragrant liquid. James's stomach growled loudly. Cecily and Ben were already seated, discussing plans for a vegetable garden.

"The working boys have all been fed and are back on the job." Mrs. Honeycutt waved her ladle at James. "The way they can eat is almost alarming. Lord Ashford, you're too generous, feeding them a midday meal. They should bring their own dinner and be glad for a warm place to eat it."

"No man can work on an empty stomach." James took his seat at the head of the table. He would be sad when the dining room was complete and he no longer had an excuse to eat downstairs with the people he'd started to think of as family. Although he was now officially a lord, these were his people. Working people.

"It's generous of you, my lord," Ben said. "Everyone's talking about you in the village. Feeling hopeful about the future for the first time in a decade."

Cecily rose to help Mrs. Honeycutt bring food to the table.

"Does the lord have to save everyone?" Mrs. Honeycutt asked, though her tone was more fond than cross as she placed a bowl of stew before James.

"Not everyone. But I aim to do what I can to help put food in mouths. With privilege comes responsibility." His dear Papa had reminded them of that many times when he was a child. He hadn't thought he'd have privilege again and he had no intention of squandering the gifts that had befallen him.

"Mrs. Honeycutt, this smells like heaven." Georgiana slipped into her seat. "I shall miss your cooking when we leave."

When we leave.

He didn't like the sound of that at all.

"But we have a long time until that day comes," he said.

Georgiana caught his eye and held his gaze for a moment. He wasn't sure how to name the feeling that seemed to bind them together—something deeper than friendship, more profound than mere attraction, as if they'd been searching for each other without knowing it.

Mrs. Ellsworth entered, seeming flustered. "I'm sorry I'm late, Mrs. Honeycutt. I was interviewing girls from the village for our maid positions." She smiled with maternal satisfaction as she surveyed the assembled company. "It's nice to see people gathered around this old table again."

James lifted a spoonful of stew to his mouth—rich with tender meat, potatoes, and carrots. "Mrs. Honeycutt, you never cease to amaze."

"It'll stick to your ribs anyway," Mrs. Honeycutt said, her

eyes shining. No one loved a compliment about their cooking more than she did.

They'd barely taken three bites when a sharp knock thundered against the kitchen door. Three imperious raps, followed by an impatient, high-pitched voice that cut through the kitchen's warmth like a winter draft.

"Who could that be?" Mrs. Ellsworth jumped to her feet. "Are we expecting a delivery?"

"Not me," Mrs. Honeycutt said.

"Nor I," Georgiana replied, though James noticed her face had gone pale.

"I'll see who it is." Mrs. Ellsworth headed toward the kitchen entrance that led directly to the gardens.

A moment later, she returned with a tall, fashionably dressed woman in a traveling coat entirely unsuited to country roads. Her hair was perfectly arranged beneath her hat despite her journey, her lips stained the fashionable rose red of Town, and her hat bore three rather large purple plumes.

"Lord Ashford, may I present Lady Linley," Mrs. Ellsworth said.

Cecily dropped her spoon, the metal clattering against her bowl in the sudden silence.

"Lord Ashford, it is a pleasure to make your acquaintance." Lady Linley's voice dripped with condescension. "I've come to see my children. After a troublesome carriage ride from London, it's not the reception I anticipated. One would expect a butler or footman to answer the door, but no one came, so I took it upon myself to use the servant's entrance. Apparently, my daughters are no longer at the inn, which I had to learn from the barkeep."

James rose, his chair legs scraping against the flagstone floor. "We did not expect you, Lady Linley. My apologies." He glanced back at Georgiana, who had grown even paler.

"Well, that's obvious. My daughters have never been ones for details." Lady Linley removed her gloves with delicate disdain, one finger at a time, her eyes scanning the kitchen and everyone in it. She looked remarkably like Georgiana—the same light hair and blue eyes—but her expression held a calculating quality that her daughter's lacked entirely.

Lady Linley's gaze traveled from James's head to his feet. "Lord Ashford, how handsome you are." Her voice changed to more of a purr. "I didn't know what to expect. The things I've heard about you in the village were complimentary but you know how that is." Her gaze lingered on the breadth of his shoulders before sliding away with practiced nonchalance.

Georgiana and Cecily rose to greet their mother.

"We didn't expect you until this evening," Georgiana said, kissing her mother's cheek.

"Darling, you look positively mannish. This happens when one does a man's work, I suppose." Lady Linley turned to Cecily. "And you've more freckles than ever."

"Yes, I've been helping outside, planning the gardens." Cecily's voice sounded small and miserable.

"It shows on your face. One day you'll be sorry you didn't wear a hat at all times." Her voice held the sweetness of a mother's concern laced with just enough disappointment to sting.

James didn't care for it at all. Heat rose from his gut and flamed in his cheeks. Before he could stop himself, his voice an octave sharper than just moments ago, he said, "Your daughters have been working tirelessly to restore my estate to its former glory. You will show them respect in my home, or I'll be happy to escort you back to the village."

Lady Linley gasped. "I wasn't aware that commenting on one's own daughters required your permission. I'm simply concerned, as any mother would be. Though I confess I hardly recognize them anymore, having been so thoroughly forgotten in favor of… whatever it is that occupies them here."

Mrs. Honeycutt muttered into her apron, her reddened hands clutching the fabric as though it might shield her from the intruder.

"Would you care to join us for a meal?" Mrs. Ellsworth

wrung her hands, clearly distressed by the tension.

"How kind of you to offer. I've not eaten for hours. My daughter refuses to give me more than a pittance to live on."

Mrs. Ellsworth guided her toward the table while Mrs. Honeycutt returned to the stove to dish up another serving of stew.

Soon they had resumed their meal, though the comfortable atmosphere had vanished entirely.

Lady Linley glanced around the table, her eyes resting briefly on Ben and taking in his worker's clothes with dismissive swiftness before returning to James. Her smile was smooth as silk and just as insincere. "I had the most dreadful coachman from the inn. He kept asking questions, as if I were obliged to answer him. You've quite the reputation in the village, Lord Ashford."

James wasn't sure what she meant by that, so he decided to ignore it.

"How long will this restoration take?" Lady Linley poked at her bowl of stew as if afraid it contained something unpleasant.

"A few more months, at least," Georgiana said. "You'll want to return to London sooner rather than later, I assume? Now that you've seen the inn?"

"Yes, about that." Lady Linley set down her spoon with a delicate sigh. "My friend and I have had a little falling out, and I have nowhere else to go. So here I am, at your mercy. Surely there's a room for me here?" She smiled at James with calculated sweetness.

"Mother, you cannot stay here," Georgiana said firmly. "You'll have to remain at the inn."

James folded his arms across his chest. "That's correct, Lady Linley. I'm afraid we don't have any rooms appropriate for a lady. We're restoring one room at a time, and we've only just begun."

"Ah, I see." Lady Linley gave a tinkling laugh that never reached her eyes. "The inn will have to do, then. It's only important that I'm here to see my lovely girls." She turned back to Georgiana, who sat rigid as a statue. "Dearest, I shall be terribly lonely at the inn without you or Cecily. Surely you'll join me there?"

"We can discuss it later." Georgiana's tone was arctic.

James caught the slight tremor in her fingers as she set down her spoon with deliberate care.

No wonder they hadn't wanted their mother to visit. She'd been there five minutes and he already couldn't wait for her to leave.

CHAPTER EIGHT

Georgiana

THAT NIGHT, AFTER finally getting rid of their mother, Georgiana and Cecily sat with Mrs. Honeycutt and Mrs. Ellsworth in the kitchen. Both sisters had been quiet during supper. She couldn't speak for Cecily, but Georgiana felt completely drained by her mother's presence.

They'd all helped clear the table and assisted Mrs. Honeycutt in cleaning up. Someday soon, this would be a full working kitchen with maids to help the head cook, but for now the four women worked together to do whatever needed doing.

After supper, James had left them to enjoy their tea and biscuits.

The moment James had left, Georgiana had started missing him. She wished he'd asked her to join him upstairs. Ridiculous, she told herself. She would see him first thing in the morning. Still, she was distracted, thinking about what he was doing upstairs alone. In his newly decorated bedchambers, undressing for the night. Her mind conjured the image of his fingers working the buttons of his waistcoat, sliding his shirt from his broad shoulders. Perhaps he was having a glass of brandy while reading by the fire, firelight playing across his bare chest—

"Georgie?" Cecily's voice cut through her reverie. "Mrs. Honeycutt asked if you wanted more tea."

Heat flooded Georgiana's cheeks. "Oh, yes. Thank you." She

forced herself to focus on the women around the table, grateful for the dim lighting that might hide her blush.

It was a cozy scene, with the warm fire crackling in the hearth and good company around the table. But Georgiana's gaze kept drifting toward the ceiling, as if she could see through the floorboards to where James might be moving about his room.

Cecily had spent much of the afternoon looking at the glass-house in one of the gardens where they had once grown vegetables and fruits for the manor. Ben had made suggestions for how to bring it back to life, and Cecily had not been able to contain her excitement as she described the plans during supper. James had been clearly pleased with the ideas and had promised Cecily a few workers to create her vision.

"You're distracted tonight," Cecily observed, studying her sister's face. "More than usual."

"Am I?" Georgiana attempted a light laugh. "I suppose I'm tired."

"Mmm." Cecily's knowing look suggested she wasn't fooled. "Tired from Mother."

"Yes, I suppose so." Georgiana and Cecily exchanged a knowing glance. No one understood the trial that was Lady Linley more than the two sisters.

Georgiana had adored her little sister from the moment she was born. She'd been a little mother to her, even though there were only four years difference in age between them. With a mother like Lavinia, it had been left to Georgiana to make sure Cecily felt loved and cared for. They were unusually close, even now that they were grown. But that closeness meant her sister could untangle her secrets as easily as unknotting embroidery thread. And, she, in turn could do the same with Cecily.

Georgiana had never seen her sister so engaged or enamored with a project as she was about the gardens. She had spent evenings drafting her ideas on paper. James had found her a book in the library about plants, which she had pored over to learn what she could.

Georgiana had assumed Cecily would be an excellent assistant, but the more they worked together, the more impressed she became. Her little sister was a woman of many talents.

"What I wouldn't do for a good wash." Cecily ran a hand through her tangled curls. "I think I've still got half the garden soil hiding in here."

"I would love one too," Georgiana said. "Mother may have had a valid point about my appearance."

"Nonsense. You girls are beautiful," Mrs. Ellsworth said, sounding loyal.

"I can heat water for you," Mrs. Honeycutt said. "We have a tub in the scullery. You can take turns."

Mrs. Ellsworth, smoothing down her apron, gave a fond smile. "With your permission, I'll assist you. I used to be a lady's maid back before I was promoted to head housekeeper. I can still remember how to wash and fix a lady's hair."

Georgiana raised a brow. "Are you sure it's not too much trouble?"

"Not at all," Mrs. Ellsworth said. "It will be my pleasure."

Cecily jumped to her feet. "I'll get our nightgowns to change into afterward. Georgie, you can go first, since you're the oldest. That's how we always did it at home, remember?"

After Mrs. Honeycutt and Mrs. Ellsworth had filled the tub, Georgiana slipped into the warm water, sighing with pleasure. She scrubbed her body with soap that smelled of lavender, but even the simple act of washing herself made her think of other hands on her skin. Stronger hands. James's hands.

A few minutes later, Mrs. Ellsworth came in to wash her hair.

Mrs. Ellsworth used a pitcher to wet Georgiana's hair, then scrubbed her scalp with strong fingers. The touch was firm and sure, and Georgiana's treacherous mind immediately wondered what it would feel like to have James's fingers threading through her hair, his palms cupping her head as he—

"Goodness," she breathed, her voice catching.

"Are you all right, dear?" Mrs. Ellsworth paused.

"Yes, that just... feels very good," Georgiana managed, her pulse quickening at her own wayward thoughts.

"You have lovely hair. The color of a corn tassel," Mrs. Ellsworth said.

"Thank you." Georgiana's voice sounded strained even to her own ears as Mrs. Ellsworth poured one final rinse over her hair.

When she was done, Mrs. Ellsworth left her alone to step out of the tub and dry herself with a towel before getting into her nightgown. She felt anything but relaxed, her body humming with an awareness she couldn't shake.

Cecily went next, while Mrs. Ellsworth had Georgiana sit by the stove in the kitchen and went to work on Georgiana's damp hair, using a brush to untangle knots.

"Did you have a maid when you were married?" Mrs. Ellsworth asked.

Georgiana hesitated. The question felt like stepping onto unstable ground. "We had a modest household. Robert preferred things simple."

"He sounds like a sensible man."

"He was." The words came easier now. "Very sensible. Very kind. He was... he was my dearest friend. Other than Cecily, of course."

Mrs. Ellsworth paused her brushing. "A friendship marriage can be a blessing, in its own way. But passion is also a wonderful thing."

Georgiana found herself at a crossroads. She could leave it at that, keep the full truth buried as she had with everyone except Cecily. However, Mrs. Ellsworth's gentle, motherly manner made her want to tell her about her marriage to Robert. Perhaps it would be a relief to share it with someone who might understand.

Yet what if Mrs. Ellsworth was shocked? What if she thought less of Robert's memory, or worse, what if she thought less of Georgiana herself?

"Was it a love match?" Mrs. Ellsworth asked softly.

Georgiana hesitated another moment before making her choice.

"We both required a spouse. Me, for security. And him—for respectability." She paused, then took the leap. "He had… particular friendships. With gentlemen. He was very discreet, but I knew. He was honest with me about everything. And I didn't mind."

Mrs. Ellsworth's hands went completely still. The brush stopped mid-stroke. Georgiana could almost hear the older woman absorbing this information. She was shocked. Of course she was.

"Oh," Mrs. Ellsworth said finally, her voice barely above a whisper. "Oh dear."

Georgiana's stomach clenched. Had she made a terrible mistake? "I shouldn't have said anything. Please, you mustn't think poorly of him. He was a good man, truly. He never hurt anyone, and he was so careful to keep everything quiet."

"Hush, child." Mrs. Ellsworth's voice was gentle but firm. "I'm not judging him. Or you. I'm just… surprised. In all my years, I've heard whispers of such things, but I've never known anyone to speak of it so openly."

"Cecily knows. But no one else." Georgiana's voice trembled slightly. "I hope my mother never learns the truth. She might suffer an attack of some kind if she knew."

Mrs. Ellsworth resumed brushing, her touch even gentler than before. "It must have been lonely for you though."

"It was. But also… freeing, I suppose. There was no pretense between us about passion or romance. We simply cared for each other. He was willing to treat me as an equal, teaching me his craft and allowing me to flourish in that way. Most women do not have that."

"And now?" Mrs. Ellsworth asked.

"Now I find myself wondering what it would be like to be married to someone who truly desired me. Someone who wanted me in every way." The admission came out in a rush, and

Georgiana felt heat flood her cheeks. "I know it's foolish. I should be grateful for what he taught me."

"There's nothing foolish about wanting to be desired, dear one. You're a young woman with a full life ahead of you."

Now that she was sharing all her secrets, they continued to spill out. "Robert left everything to me, but I knew Cecily would need a proper dowry for her season. The sale of the house has provided her with enough to make a good match." Georgiana's hands twisted in her lap. "I've been living off the remainder, but it won't last much longer. That's why this position is so important. The wages will help us get by until Cecily marries."

"And then?"

"I have not gotten that far in my planning." The future stretched before her, gray and lonely. "I hope to keep working but most men will not be as gracious as James when they learn I'm a woman."

"But you should marry again. You're young and beautiful."

"No gentleman wants a widow with no fortune," Georgiana said. "I shall have to accept my fate. I am a woman of passion without hope for a love of my own."

"You might be surprised." Mrs. Ellsworth resumed brushing her hair. "Especially if the right gentleman sees past a fortune to the woman herself. Perhaps a certain newly restored lord."

Heat bloomed low in her stomach, swift and alarming. Was it possible James could love her? "What kind of boy was James?" She knew it was dangerous to ask, but her curiosity outweighed caution.

Mrs. Ellsworth chuckled under her breath. "There was never a more precious little boy. All golden haired and those big blue eyes. He was a mischief maker, always up to something. His brother Sebastian was the steady, serious one, whereas James was fun and spirited. That was taken from him the day they hanged his father. I was there. I saw the light go out of my dear boy's eyes. Replaced by rage, I'm afraid. I hated to send them off, but I'd hoped the cousin would look after them."

"From what Lord Ashford's told me, the rest of their childhood was violent and chaotic."

"I fear you're correct." Mrs. Ellsworth separated Georgiana's hair into three sections. "But I believe the light's returning to his eyes. Especially when you're in the room."

Her pulse quickened with a longing she had no right to feel. "Really?"

"You make a good team. I hope you'll not shy away from whatever is brewing between you."

Her heart gave a treacherous leap. Whatever was brewing between them? Could Mrs. Ellsworth see the desire Georgiana had been trying so desperately to hide?

"He doesn't want to marry," she said quickly, as if speaking the words aloud could protect her from her own feelings. "He told me so himself. He thinks he's not capable of love. He sees himself as broken. Too broken to love or be loved."

"If we were to search back in time, we'd find a lot of happily married men who claimed they never wanted to wed."

She felt herself teetering on the edge of a precipice she'd sworn never to approach. Georgiana's breath caught as she imagined James changing his mind, imagined him looking at her with real desire, real want. The kind of passion she'd only read about in books, the kind Robert had never been able to give her.

The kitchen door creaked open.

"Forgive me, I forgot my—" James's voice cut off abruptly.

Georgiana's mouth went dry as dust. There he stood in the doorway, his shirt partially unbuttoned, his hair mussed as if he'd been running his hands through it. His gaze found hers immediately, and she saw his eyes widen as he took in her appearance— hair loose and damp around her shoulders, wearing only her thin nightgown, the firelight playing across her face.

For a heartbeat, neither of them moved. The moment stretched taut as a bowstring between them. The very air seemed to hum with awareness. His gaze dropped to her lips, then lower, and she felt her body respond to that look in ways it never had during her marriage.

"I… my book," he said, his voice raspy. "I left it on the table."

"Yes, it's there, my lord," Mrs. Ellsworth said.

He blinked, almost as if he'd forgotten his loyal housekeeper stood just behind Georgiana.

"Thank you. Sorry to interrupt. I didn't realize…what was happening down here."

"It is of no consequence," Georgiana said. She couldn't seem to look away from the triangle of skin visible at his throat, couldn't stop imagining what it would feel like to press her lips there.

James grabbed a leather-bound volume from the far end of the table, his movements quick and almost clumsy. "Good night, ladies." His eyes lingered on Georgiana for just a moment too long before he retreated.

The door closed behind him with a soft click, leaving the kitchen in charged silence.

Mrs. Ellsworth cleared her throat delicately. "Well then."

Georgiana's face burned. Her hands were shaking now, and she gripped them together in her lap to still them. Understanding crashed into her with startling clarity—she wasn't just falling for James. She was already gone, completely and utterly lost to feelings sure to break her heart in the end.

For the first time in her life, she understood what it meant to truly want someone. Not just companionship or security, but real, consuming desire. The kind that made her breath catch and her skin burn.

"I had not anticipated him coming down here," Georgiana said. "Or I would not be in my nightgown."

"I shouldn't worry too much," Mrs. Ellsworth said. "He seemed as flustered as you."

"I seemed flustered?"

"Dear one, surely you cannot imagine otherwise? Even I could feel the heat between you."

"Mrs. Ellsworth!" But Georgiana couldn't help but laugh at

her perceptive new friend.

"These old eyes have witnessed much in their time, child. It takes a lot to fool me."

As Mrs. Ellsworth finished braiding her hair, Georgiana couldn't shake the image of the way James had looked at her, or the way her own body had responded to that look. She was frightened by the intensity of her own feelings, by how much she wanted something she could never have.

And she was even more terrified that she was already in too deep to save herself.

THAT NIGHT, FEELING good from their baths, the sisters slipped into freshly made beds. Mrs. Ellsworth had been busy. The sheets and blankets were clean and smelled of soap.

"This is a wonderful bed," Cecily said, sleepily. "Mrs. Ellsworth has been too good to us today."

Georgiana snuffed out the lamp on the table between the twin beds and pulled the covers up to her chin. She always slept on her back, whereas her little sister curled into a ball like a cat. Georgiana could remember many times during their childhood when Cecily had climbed into bed with her big sister, claiming she was cold, but Georgiana suspected she was lonely or frightened. Their childhood had been fraught with their parents' cold and silent arguments, their mother's volatile behavior and their father's drinking and gambling. They'd clung to each other and still did.

"She has indeed." Georgiana closed her eyes, hoping sleep would come quickly. Instead, an image of James from earlier in the day played before her eyes. He'd been at his desk in the study, poring over her suggestions for the library. His golden curls fell over his forehead and his jaw was set with determination. His eyes, however, had glittered with pleasure at her proposal for saving the books from mold and the suggestions for furnishings now that the roof had been repaired.

She must have sighed because Cecily asked if she was all right. "Are you worried over something?"

Her sister knew her too well.

"A little, yes."

"Do you want to talk about it?" Cecily asked in her sweet, patient voice.

"I'm afraid to. Saying the words out loud might make them seem even truer."

"Is it about Lord Ashford? Your feelings for him?"

Her sister's keen insight might have made her laugh if her stomach hadn't been clenched with worry. She should have known Cecily would guess her secret.

"Why must I feel this way? Again?" Georgiana asked. "Setting myself up to be rejected is horrifying."

"It's not the same. Not really. Robert didn't reject you. He simply didn't feel that way about women. There's nothing you could have done. Seeing as how things have turned out, his willingness to train you in interior design and architecture have been a great gift. It brought us here. Where you might actually find true love."

"No, it's impossible. James told me himself he won't marry. He's too broken."

"Aren't we all broken, in one way or the other?" Cecily asked.

"Regardless, if he were to marry, it would not be to someone like me. He'll choose someone without scandal attached to her name. Someone with a dowry and family that will be helpful to his reputation instead of the opposite. He has enough of a battle waiting for him without another burden."

"What do you mean?"

"He will have to fight to gain the respect of his peers. They might continue to see him as a ruffian who ran a tavern instead of a lord."

"Yes, but there is the way he looks at you," Cecily said. "We mustn't discount that."

Was it true? Was there a reason to hope? In her experience, hope was dangerous. It led to eventual heartbreak. Whatever Georgiana had ever wanted had been denied her other than Robert's gift of apprenticeship. As Cecily had said, without that, they would not be here.

THE DREAM CAME without warning.

She was back in their London apartment. The one she'd shared with Robert. The sitting room was too quiet, the light wrong—yellow and thick like oil. And Julian was there.

He stepped into the room like a shadow that had always belonged, smiling as if nothing had ever happened. The scent of his cologne filled the air, that cloying bergamot she'd once thought sophisticated.

"You're even prettier now that he's gone," he said, running his eyes over her like he owned her. "Grief suits you."

"No," she whispered. "Leave."

He closed the distance in three strides, his breathing heavy and deliberate. "You didn't say no last time. Not really. Not at first."

"That's not true."

But her voice was soft. Weak. Her arms wouldn't move.

Then his hands were on her—rough, urgent—fisting the front of her dress, yanking at the fabric until it gave with a sickening tear. She felt the sharp drag of stitching snapping across her skin. His breath was on her neck, hot and sickly sweet.

She screamed—but no sound came. She shoved him— nothing moved. She was frozen, trapped in her own memory.

"Georgie! Wake up."

A hand touched her shoulder, gentle but firm. Her eyes flew open, breath heaving. She sat bolt upright, tangled in the quilt, gasping for air. Her heart hammered so violently she was certain it would wake the entire house.

In the darkness, she could barely make out Cecily's silhouette kneeling beside the bed. Her sister's voice came soft and steady. "It's all right. I'm here. You're safe. It was a dream."

Georgiana pressed her palms against her face, sweat cooling on her skin, her chest tight. "I—yes. Just a dream."

Her hands trembled as she tried to smooth back her hair.

Without a word, she felt the mattress dip as Cecily climbed up beside her, the blanket rustling as her sister pulled it back over both of them. Cecily's warmth settled against her side.

"When we were children, it was I who had the nightmares," Cecily said. "Do you remember how I used to climb into bed with you?"

Georgiana gave a shaky laugh, still half-caught in the dream's grip. "You shouldn't have to take care of me like this. I am a grown woman."

"Who cares?" Cecily's head found her shoulder in the dark. "You're my sister. And, anyway, it is you who takes care of me. I can feel the burden you carry. For me. For Mother. I hope someday to repay you."

"You mustn't think of it that way. I do not. You are my family."

"And you are mine."

They lay in silence, the house occasionally creaking. Gradually, Georgiana felt her breathing steady, her pulse slowing to something approaching normal. Soon, she fell asleep, nestled against the warm body of her sister.

THE NEXT MORNING, even though neither of them wished to do so, duty toward their mother swayed them to go into the village to visit with Lady Linley at the inn. Georgiana wished to ask her mother about exactly what had transpired in London that had caused her to come searching for them. Her mother's friend, Mrs. Cline, and her husband had generously offered Lavinia a place to stay. Mrs. Cline was a kind woman, the type who saw the good in everyone. Which meant she was easily manipulated by Lavinia. They'd been friends since childhood and Mrs. Cline had a soft heart for Lavinia. Or at least she'd had one. Her mother had obviously done something terrible for Mrs. Cline to send her away.

What was she to do with Mother now? None of them had homes or husbands. There was nowhere for Lavinia to go. Other than to her daughters.

Before she and Cecily set out, Georgiana went to see James in his study. He was at the desk, poring over ledgers of some sort.

"Georgie, how are you this morning?" He stood, smiling. "Are you going out somewhere?"

She was wearing her best day dress. Leave it to him to notice.

"I'm well, my lord. Thank you. I've come to inform you that Cecily and I are going into the village to see our mother this morning. It is necessary that I figure out what she's really doing here and how to get rid of her."

He gestured toward the chair closest to the desk. "Please, sit. I want to hear more about her situation. Perhaps I can be of some help."

Why was he so kind? Why did he make her feel so safe?

She did as he asked, sitting and clasping her hands together on her lap. "Mother has clearly done something to offend her benefactor, Mrs. Cline." Georgiana explained their history and how Mrs. Cline had offered her a place to live. "I don't know why Mrs. Cline has been so generous. Mother always treated her like a maid rather than a trusted friend. Mother's love of herself leaves little room for anyone else."

"Yes, I confess to noticing that myself."

"She never forgave Mrs. Cline for marrying well. Her husband is a good man and also a clever businessman who has done very well for himself, albeit untitled. Whereas my father was titled but decidedly without cleverness. In fact, he was weak and irresponsible. Mother never forgave him for not being who she thought he was when they married. Things only got worse when he proceeded to gamble away any sense of security.

"Mother's vain and status-conscious above all else. She wants to be admired and sought after. Instead, invitations stopped coming to balls and parties. She was shunned at the park and at social functions. To have such a public humiliation only made her self-absorption worse." She found herself telling him more about their childhood. How she and her sister had not felt love from either of their parents. While her father was distracted and distant, their mother was manipulative and controlling. "She was only happy with us if we did something to make her look good."

"You and Cecily are very close because you only had each other."

"That's correct. My sister is an angel. If not for her, I would not have made it through my childhood."

"And now you must decide what to do with your mother?" James asked. "With little funds to support her."

"Especially how she likes to live. Her dresses alone could bankrupt me."

He tilted his head in that way he did when he was thinking through a problem. "You have too much responsibility. Taking care of your mother and sister. And yet you must."

"Because they are family. I would do anything for Cecily and she for me. But Mother? She's frustrating and impossible. Try as I might, I easily lose my temper when I'm with her."

"Perhaps I spoke too hastily yesterday," James said. "We can make a room for her here."

She nearly groaned with dread at the idea of her mother being underfoot day in and day out. "She has this way of making me feel badly about myself. I fear she'll derail our plans here. Please, I beg of you, do not offer. You will regret it, I can assure you."

"I understand." He tapped his index finger against his chin. "What if we were to give her some kind of job. Something to keep her busy enough that she stays out of your way?"

"What would that be? She has no skills. Other than to drive me mad."

"What are her interests?"

"Clothes and other vanities. Going to parties and balls give her great joy. She's not invited any longer but when we were children, she was never happier than when she was dressing for a social event."

"Ah, yes, I've got it." James leaned forward, blue eyes sparkling. "I'll ask her to plan our first ball. A debut for the manor's grand reopening."

Her chest tightened. "No, you shouldn't. It's a terrible idea."

"But why? She'll be good at it. She knows all the right people to invite, would you not agree?"

"She does keep up with gossip," Georgiana said, somewhat reluctantly. "She'll advise you well in that regard. And she's actually very talented at planning social events. Especially now that she has no outlet for such a thing. But please, you must keep a close watch on her. She'll not hesitate to spend your money unwisely. I wouldn't put it past her to pocket some for herself if she thinks she can get away with it."

"I'll keep a close watch on the spending. Nothing will be ordered without my approval."

"Yes, all right. It will keep her occupied, which will mean more peace for me and Cecily. She's going to be painfully focused on finding Cecily a husband. I shudder to think of the trouble she might cause my sister."

"In my experience, it is best for women like your mother to have something to focus on, especially if it interests them. I have another idea as well. My need for a gentleman's wardrobe has been weighing on me. I fear I'm the opposite of your mother. Anything to do with fashion puts me right to sleep. But we must admit, I'm rugged looking and in need of help. What if we were to task her with working with a tailor to put together an entire closet fit for a gentleman?"

"She does keep up with the latest fashion. I'm loath to admit it, but she would be very helpful in that regard."

"Yes, and she'll be flattered that I'm looking to her for advice."

"She loves being the savior," Georgiana said. "Even though she's usually more like the villain."

"When you see her, ask her to join us for supper. We'll present these ideas to her."

Georgiana managed a weak smile. "God help us all."

WHEN THEY ENTERED their mother's room at the inn, Lavinia sat draped across the faded settee as if it were a chaise in a Mayfair salon, a silk dressing gown tied loosely at the waist. A tea tray sat untouched on the table beside her, the porcelain cup cooling at her elbow.

"My darlings. At last. I feared you wouldn't come."

"We said we would," Cecily said gently, pulling off her gloves.

Georgiana remained standing, hands folded at her waist. "Mother, what happened at Mrs. Cline's? She was so generous to offer you a place to live. What did you do to her?"

Lavinia let out a tragic sigh. "Why do you think it's something I've done? You know how other women can be. Jealous. Spiteful. Especially given how I've aged compared to her."

Cecily glanced at Georgiana. "What did you do, Mother? Mrs. Cline is the nicest woman in all of England."

"She certainly plays that role." Lavinia gave a brittle laugh. "But you don't know her as I do."

Georgiana's brows lifted. "Go on."

Lavinia leaned forward slightly, as if letting them in on a

secret. "It's him she should be angry with."

"Who?" Georgiana asked.

Lavinia rolled her eyes, as if it should be obvious of whom she spoke. "Charles. Caroline's husband. He behaved very badly and now I'm to blame. It's devastating to be betrayed in this manner."

"What are you saying?" Georgiana asked.

"I should preface this to say—Charles Cline has always admired me. Even as a young man, he followed me around like a puppy. Of course I married someone else. And so did he. But old affections? Apparently, they linger."

"What did he do?" Cecily asked, eyes wide.

"He tried to kiss me, which I absolutely did not want." Lavinia reached for the teacup but didn't drink. "We were alone in the library when he suddenly yanked me to him and planted his mouth right on mine. I pulled away immediately, but not before Caroline walked in and saw enough to draw her own conclusions. Of course she blamed me."

Georgiana said nothing. Her mother's tone was too polished, the story too conveniently staged.

"She accused me of trying to steal him," Lavinia continued. "Me! After everything I've done for her."

"What exactly have you done for her?" Georgiana asked sharply. "The Clines were kind enough to bring you into their home. I'm not sure what you've ever done for them."

A flicker of annoyance passed across Lavinia's face but only for a moment, just a tiny crack in her composure.

"She lorded it over me too. Day in and day out. As if I weren't grateful enough. She has always been insecure. Ever since we were girls. She always tried to steal whomever I liked away. I don't know why she does it, but it's true."

Georgiana felt quite sure it was the other way around.

"Anyway, she wouldn't listen to reason," Lavinia said with a wan smile. "She flew into an absolute rage. Demanded I leave at once. Which is cruel, seeing as my own daughters don't want me."

Cecily shifted uncomfortably. Georgiana watched her mother closely, noting the way her fingers played with the edge of her sash, the way her eyes flicked toward the mirror behind them. She was always aware of herself, even in performance. Or, perhaps, especially in performance.

"What is your plan, Mother?" Georgiana asked. "Because it cannot be living here indefinitely. I'm saving money for Cecily's Season, not your rent."

Lavinia gave another sigh, this one practiced to the last breath. "I have nowhere else to go, as you well know. You and Cecily seem quite cozy at the manor. Perhaps Lord Ashford would take me in too? Just until I can get back on my feet."

"We're working," Cecily said. "Not living with him out of charity."

"He's been generous to us and I won't have you taking advantage of him," Georgiana said, choosing her words carefully. "However, he's asked if you'd like to join us for supper next week. The dining room will be ready for guests by then."

"How lovely," Lavinia said, setting the teacup aside with an audible clink. "He must be interested in our Cecily if he's inviting me to dine at the manor."

"He is not interested in me," Cecily said quickly. "And please, do not interfere or try and matchmake. I would be mortified if you were to do so."

"As would I," Georgiana said.

"Fine. I'm only trying to help." Lavinia sniffed. "But clearly you don't want it."

CHAPTER NINE

James

BY EARLY MARCH, the dining room of Ashford Manor had been brought back to life. Georgiana and Ben's team had produced a miracle. Light from the newly restored chandelier spilled across the table, the cascade of crystal prisms catching fire with each flicker of candlelight. Above, a stunning ceiling medallion crowned the fixture, its plasterwork sunburst pattern elegant and proud.

Walls once faded and cracked now gleamed with hand-painted wallpaper in muted olive and gold tones, delicate vines and flowering branches curling up the surface. Twin gilt sconces flanked the carved white mantelpiece, their flames dancing beside a grand oval mirror whose gold frame had been polished until it glowed.

The fireplace below stood cool and formal, its surround a polished green marble that mirrored the garden glimpsed through tall windows behind billowing drapes of mossy velvet. A gleaming mahogany table stretched nearly the length of the room, its surface so perfectly waxed it reflected the sparkle of cut crystal goblets. Porcelain chargers ringed each place setting, and bowls of jewel-toned flowers in deep crimson, violet, and green anchored the center like bursts of life.

Mrs. Honeycutt had managed a miracle with roast duck, and Mrs. Ellsworth had set the table with crisp linens and polished silver that hadn't seen light in over a decade.

The team of workers had labored all day to get the dining room ready for their first visitor. James had assumed they'd eat downstairs but they'd finished in time. He supposed he had to begin life as a gentleman, even though he preferred the cozy kitchen to the massive dining room. Regardless, here they were.

And here he was, having trouble focusing on anything about how lovely Georgie looked that evening. Her deep plum gown had a modest neckline and the faintest sheen of lace at the cuffs. She wore no jewels but the locket at her throat, yet somehow she looked regal anyway. True beauty like hers needed no adornment.

Lavinia Linley perched at the far end of the table, a glass of claret in hand and her silk sleeves rustling with every affected movement. She wore a gown of peacock blue. James didn't know anything about fashion but he was slightly worried about his own wardrobe when he saw the color. He must remember to tell her he wanted nothing garish. He might be back in Society but he didn't want to look like a dandy. That was going too far.

Lavinia had not stopped talking since they took their seats. "It truly is a lovely old house. So much potential. I've always had an eye for these things. That's where my daughter gets her talent. When I had a fine home, before my late husband ruined our lives, I was known in my social circles as someone with exquisite taste. Alas, all that was lost when Edmund decided to gamble away our livelihood."

James speared a potato and gave her a benign smile. "That's fortunate. We could use someone with vision."

Across the table, Georgiana lifted her eyes at him and they exchanged a brief moment of humor.

Cecily, dressed in a sage green silk frock that complemented her fair skin, focused intently on her peas.

Lavinia leaned in, mistaking interest for invitation. "Of course, had you brought me in earlier, I might have helped with the drawing room. My daughter's design, while nice, is a touch…outdated. Poor dear. She should have been born in the last century."

"I disagree," James said. "She restored it perfectly. I couldn't be happier with everything Georgie's done."

Lavinia blinked, then laughed, as though he were joking. "Aren't you a gem? You must tell me the story of your first meeting. Did you know it was a woman who offered her services?"

The question was obviously meant to stir up trouble. This woman was good. That is, if slithering, poisonous snakes could be good.

"I was surprised but quickly understood that she was the best around, regardless of gender." James smiled brightly at Lavinia, even though he wanted to strangle her.

"Isn't that nice?" Lavinia asked. "At least I have Cecily. My last hope for grandchildren."

Georgiana caught his eyes again, raising one brow.

"On another matter," James said. "I am in need of your expertise, Lady Linley."

"Whatever could you need from me?" Lavinia giggled like she was a schoolgirl instead of a woman in her forties.

"I have two tasks for which I feel ill-equipped." He set down his fork and folded his hands. "I've decided to host a ball once the estate is fully restored. Something to mark the manor's return to Society."

Lavinia brightened like a chandelier. "A ball? How deliciously ambitious. But dear me, will your staff know what to do?"

"Mrs. Ellsworth helped plan many balls and parties when my father was still alive," James said mildly. "But she has her hands full with running the house, hiring staff and all, so I was hoping I might hire someone to assist her. Someone schooled in the fine art of hosting such an affair? Someone tasteful and well-connected. Can you think of anyone?"

He let the words hang there, and Lavinia devoured them like sugar cubes.

"My dear Lord Ashford." She set down her glass with a flutter. "You can count on me. I shall be honored to help."

"Are you certain? You're probably much too busy." James picked up his fork, biting the inside of his mouth to keep from laughing.

"I am busy, of course, but never so much so that I would turn you down in your time of need. In fact, I am the perfect choice for such a momentous occasion. I know who to add to the guest list and how to decide a theme. It would keep me here for another few months, of course, but I don't mind sacrificing my time for you."

"Really?" James asked. "That's awfully generous of you. I'll pay, of course."

"How distasteful to discuss money at the dining table," Lavinia said. "But we can talk about all of that tomorrow. For now, I can assure you there's no one better to plan a ball than myself. Oh, you should have seen some of the parties I threw when I was younger. They were always the talk of the Season."

"I'm sure they were," James said. "I'd be grateful if you can keep me from looking a fool in front of Society. This will be my first venture out and it must be perfect."

Lavinia's smile spread, victorious. "Well, then. I will rise to the occasion."

"I could use your help with another matter," James said.

Lavinia arched a brow. "Oh?"

"My wardrobe. As of now, I have nothing worthy of a gentleman. I need to be dressed from head to toe for day and night and everything in between. Since I have yet to hire a valet, would you be willing to help me? I can't think of a finer choice than to use a woman of your exquisite taste."

"I'd be thrilled," Lavinia said at once, her voice an octave higher suddenly. "You are naturally handsome but a true gentleman must look the part. It is only a matter of refinement. Do you have a tailor?"

"There is one in town. I've already spoken to him and he

knows a tall order's coming," James said.

"I'll need a significant budget," Lavinia said. "For the right fabrics and accessories."

"I ask only that you do not dress me up as a dandy."

"I wouldn't think of it," Lavinia said. "Nothing but pure elegance for you."

"Thank you, Lady Linley. I can't tell you how delighted I am." James was a better actor than he'd figured himself to be. It was actually kind of fun, playing her like this. She would be too worn out to cause trouble for her daughters.

Lavinia positively beamed. "Isn't it fortuitous that I showed up at just the right moment to offer my services?"

"I couldn't agree more," James said, nearly laughing at the sight of the two younger women at the table hiding smiles under their napkins.

THE FIRE HAD burned low by the time they entered the drawing room after supper, but the warmth lingered. James crossed the space and added a log with the toe of his boot, watching the embers glow red and gold.

Behind him, Cecily sank into the velvet settee with a relieved sigh, her hair slightly loosened from the evening's formality. "Mother's gone. I thought she might dig in and refuse to go back to the inn."

"She asked me twice if I really wanted to send my poor mother off all alone." Georgiana pulled off her gloves one finger at a time.

James found himself watching the deliberate movement, the slow revelation of her slender wrists.

"But I stayed firm," Georgiana said.

"Which is nearly impossible with her," Cecily said.

James turned, suppressing a smile. "You did not exaggerate

when describing her disposition."

Georgiana arched a brow. "No, we did not. Today, at the inn, she told us that Mrs. Cline's husband tried to seduce her and that Caroline caught them and blamed Mother. That's the story she's come up with, but I don't believe it for an instant."

"Me either," Cecily said. "I feel certain she was the failed seducer, not him."

"I feel terrible for Mrs. Cline," Georgiana said. "The woman's been nothing but kind to all of us."

"Yet Mother betrayed her. It's horrible." Cecily tucked a loose curl back into her bun. "We should write to her."

"I plan to. If only to thank her for taking Mother all these months. I have no idea what we are to do with her."

"We have some time," James said. "The next few months will keep her busy."

"Meanwhile, she'll run up the bill at the inn," Cecily said.

"Not to worry about that," James said. "I stopped by this afternoon to speak with the proprietor. I assured him that I would pay the bill for her room and board, but requests for anything out of the ordinary should be denied."

"You're a smart man," Cecily said.

"A quick learner too," Georgiana said with a laugh. "How can we thank you? You're much too generous."

"Consider it a token of my appreciation. You're bringing back my home. Handling your mother's bills is the least I can do." James leaned against the hearth, arms crossed, savoring the feeling that had taken root in his chest over the course of the evening. It was fun to be part of something. These sisters reminded him of the relationships he shared with his own siblings. But they were off, living their own lives, and he missed them. He missed being part of a family.

"It was almost too easy," Cecily said. "You two were absolutely correct that she would fall right into our trap."

"Oh, she'll throw herself into all of it." Georgiana eased into the wingback chair beside the hearth. The firelight caught in her light hair, turning the edges to gold. She was beautiful in any light, but never more so than now. "She's been starved for relevance since our father's suicide. This gives her just enough illusion of control to keep her from meddling somewhere worse."

"I certainly hope so," Cecily muttered. "If she does anything to wreck my Season, I shall never forgive her."

Georgiana stilled for a moment, then looked away, a faint color rising in her cheeks. "I swear to you both, if she causes one iota of trouble for either of you, I shall take care of her myself and it won't be pretty."

"She won't have time," James said. "She'll be busy creating guest lists and planning the theme for the ball. I do worry a little about Mrs. Ellsworth."

"I do as well," Georgiana said. "Mother will be high-handed and demanding."

"Mrs. Ellsworth has enough grit to withstand whatever Mother does," Cecily said. "I've no doubt at all that she'll be the one in control, not Mother. And anyway, we've warned her. She'll be ready for whatever antics Mother employs."

"And we've got Mrs. Honeycutt for backup," James said. "She's dealt with drunks, charlatans, ladies of the evening—you name it and we had them come through the tavern. A vain, middle-aged member of Society won't worry her at all."

That made Georgiana laugh. The sound struck him low in his chest.

"I must say," Georgiana shifted to face him fully, "I never thought I'd find myself plotting with a lord to contain my own mother."

"Yes, it is rather unusual. But we must approach it as an adventure," James said.

She didn't look away, and James felt his breath catch despite himself. He found himself cataloging details he'd never consciously noticed before—the precise shade of her eyes in firelight, the small scar at the edge of her jaw, how her fingers absently traced the arm of her chair. Each observation felt dangerous, like stepping onto untested ice.

Cecily yawned and stretched, rising from the settee. "I'm going to bed. I have to be up early. Mrs. Ellsworth asked if I'd help interview a gardener. Good night to both of you and thank you for a most enjoyable evening." She paused in the doorway and added with a sly grin, "Who knew this job would be so much fun?"

When she was gone, silence settled in the room, softened by the crackle of the fire and the subtle scent of smoke. The room seemed smaller suddenly, more intimate without Cecily's bright presence.

Georgiana stood, smoothing her skirts. "You did well tonight, Lord Ashford."

"You're not going to call me that any longer," James said. "I have begun to call you Georgie, as Cecily does. Which means, you should call me James."

"I suppose we are conspirators, which gives us an intimacy of sorts."

"I couldn't agree more." Firelight made shadows dance across the hollow of her throat. "I don't feel like Lord Ashford anyway. I'm James and I always will be."

"But you're meant for greatness," Georgiana said huskily. "You're kind and compassionate and thoughtful. All qualities of a true gentleman."

"Why, thank you. That's very nice of you to say." He looked away, embarrassed by her compliments, yet pleased too.

"I should retire as well," Georgiana said. "Tomorrow will be here before we know it."

"Yes, I suppose it will."

"Good night, James." She flushed, tugging at her ear. "It might take time to grow accustomed to calling you James."

"You'll think of me as James soon enough." He smiled back at her. "Good night. Sweet dreams."

As she moved toward the doorway, her glove slipped from her fingers and fluttered to the floor. They both reached for it at the same time, James taking an instinctive step forward. Their hands met over the scrap of fabric, his fingers closing over hers for just a heartbeat. The contact sent heat racing up his arm, and he felt her slight intake of breath.

He straightened slowly, the glove in his palm, acutely aware of how close they stood. Close enough that he could see the flecks of silver in her eyes, close enough to catch the faint scent of rosewater in her hair.

"James," she said again, softer this time. "Yes, that sounded better, did it not?"

"Indeed." In fact, the sound of it nearly undid him. His pulse hammered in his throat, and every instinct urged him to close the remaining distance between them, to discover if her lips were as soft as they looked. The urge was so powerful it took all his willpower to step back, to place the glove carefully in her outstretched palm without allowing their skin to touch again.

"Good night, Georgie."

She lingered in the doorway for a moment longer, as if she too were reluctant to break whatever spell had settled over them. Then she nodded and disappeared into the hallway, leaving him alone with the dying fire and the thundering of his own heart.

James clenched his hands at his sides, fighting the urge to follow her, to call her back. The sweet scent of rosewater still lingered in the air, and he closed his eyes, breathing it in like a man starved.

For the first time, he wished desperately that the manor required more work than it actually did, that he could find some excuse to keep her here indefinitely. But he knew that was impossible. Someday—too soon—he would have to say goodbye for good.

The realization stole the air from his lungs and left him hollow and aching. Her disappearing from his life wouldn't just break his heart. It might destroy him entirely.

This was a most unwelcome discovery.

CHAPTER TEN

Georgiana

TWO DAYS AFTER she'd agreed to help plan the ball, Lavinia swept into the drawing room as if arriving on stage, her green satin sash trailing behind her. In her gloved hands, she carried a thick notebook bound in marbled paper, which she laid ceremoniously on the center table between them.

James, Cecily, and Georgiana had been poring over the plans for the library's restoration when she arrived. Without warning. Georgiana's heart sank. She'd hoped they'd have a little more time without her presence, figuring it would take some time to plan a ball. However, as usual, she'd underestimated her mother's desire for attention.

"Hello, Mother," Georgiana said. "What brings you by? Un-announced?"

Lavinia dropped into a curtsy before James. "Good morning, my lord. Daughters." Lavinia straightened, gave a regal nod, pausing just long enough for dramatic effect before continuing. "I am here to present the theme for the Ashford Manor Ball."

Cecily and Georgiana, who were sitting together on the set-tee, designs between them, exchanged a wary glance. God only knew what they were about to see. She really hoped James held onto his purse strings.

James, across the room near the fire, leaned an elbow on the mantel and raised an eyebrow. "You've chosen already?"

"How could I not?" Lavinia asked. "Something of this import must not be delayed. Prepare to be amazed by my work. It's clever, elegant, and perfectly in keeping with the tone I intend to set."

I intend. Everything with her mother always started with her in the starring role.

Lavinia sat across from her daughters, motioning for James to sit beside her by patting the cushion as she set her notebook on the coffee table. She then flipped open the notebook with a flourish, revealing a hand-colored sketch of a ballroom adorned with draping vines, golden lanterns, and what appeared to be olive branches cascading from the chandeliers.

"The theme will be—Much Ado About Nothing. The Shake-spearean comedy. Much like the unforgettable ball thrown by the Wentworths last year. I'm sure your brother and sister-in-law have told you about that night."

"Go on," James said, sounding impatient.

Lavinia seemed not to notice, smiling sweetly, like a cat just before the pounce. "I wasn't invited, of course. A travesty of an oversight, I'm sure. But I heard it was absolutely breathtaking. And then, of course, chaos ensued. Luckily for you, am I right, my lord?"

James's expression hardened, a shadow passing behind his eyes. The muscle along his jaw jumped once, twice, as his shoulders drew back with the rigid control of a man containing a storm. His knuckles whitened against the mantel. "I'm not certain that night is something to emulate."

Georgiana glanced at him. His voice carried no particular inflection, but she knew the story. Everyone knew the story. The night Sebastian Ashford's identity was exposed. The night Rose nearly died at the hands of her would-be fiancé. The night that had ended with two men in custody.

Lavinia, oblivious or choosing to be, continued. "Of course, we'll avoid the melodrama. But I thought the literary homage was rather inspired."

Georgiana folded her arms. She felt James's gaze shift to her, brief but intent. An unspoken alliance against Lavinia's obliviousness that stirred something deeper than mere solidarity.

"And what does Much Ado entail, exactly?" James asked.

"Everything wonderful," Lavinia said, clearly delighted with herself. "Wit, elegance, a touch of mystery. We'll recreate the atmosphere of a Sicilian villa, with candlelit arches, garlands of lemon and olive, dark velvets. Evocative. Sensual, but tasteful."

James cleared his throat softly. "Let's aim to keep scandal to a minimum. My family's had enough of that."

"Oh, absolutely." Lavinia's dismissive wave of her hand belied by the calculating gleam in her eyes. "Nothing ruinous. Just enough romantic tension to be remembered. After all, what's a ball without at least one broken heart?" She turned the next page to reveal a diagram of the ballroom divided into scenes: dancing, quiet corners for overheard dialogue, and a garden nook complete with seating and mock hedge walls.

"Guests will be instructed to dress in jewel tones. Sapphire, amethyst, garnet. Venetian masks for a brief interlude—enough to play with mistaken identity, but not a full masquerade. I wouldn't dare copy your sister-in-law. Although, I've no doubt our ball will be spoken of for years to come. We will dazzle the guests. Leave them breathless. Just as they would be after a performance of a play, only they get to be participants. Isn't it divine?"

Georgiana exchanged a glance with Cecily, who simply shook her head.

"And the guest list?" James asked, mostly because he had to. "Have you spoken with Mrs. Ellsworth about who should be invited?"

"Oh yes, between the two of us we know exactly who should attend." Lavinia turned another page. "I've written our suggestions for your approval. You may add whomever we've missed. Your brother and his wife will come, I hope?"

"We'll see." James wasn't sure Rose and Sebastian would be

excited to attend another Shakespearean themed ball, considering what memories it might bring up for them.

"Naturally, there will be dancing." Lavinia turned yet another page to reveal a rough sketch of the ballroom. "But as I've mentioned, a proper ball is like a play. You need mood, rhythm, mystery, a climax."

She tapped the diagram. "The ballroom shall be draped in midnight blue silk and gold garlands. Hanging lanterns, not chandeliers. Candles at every table. Between sets, there will be a masked interlude, brief, just enough for mistaken identity. The drawing room will be transformed into a garden at night. Think trellises, lemon trees, soft music from a hidden quartet. Low seating. Places for whispers.

"And the library—oh, the library will be my masterpiece. It shall be the Whispering Gallery. Curtained alcoves, candles, and little trays of note paper. Guests may pen secrets, compliments, mischief or whatever they fancy, then fold them and leave them where others might find them. It will be deliciously dangerous."

"I've drafted the supper menu," Lavinia declared. "It's sweeping and ambitious, but if we do it right, no one will be able to stop talking about it long after the night's complete."

Georgiana braced herself as Lavinia cleared her throat and lifted a page with the gravity of a clergyman about to deliver a eulogy.

"To begin, we'll offer guests a light selection of canapés: smoked salmon on rye with dill cream, quail egg tartlets with cress, and miniature beef wellingtons. Passed on silver trays by footmen."

James raised an eyebrow. "Go on."

Lavinia's eyes gleamed. "We'll present a buffet of main dishes. Glazed duck with orange and clove. Roast beef carved to order with horseradish cream. Poached salmon chilled over watercress, and lamb cutlets with a mint and pistachio crust."

She turned the page. "The vegetable offerings shall include green peas in cream, buttered asparagus with toasted almonds, and a savory mushroom tart for those inclined toward rusticity."

"Mother, this is extravagant," Georgiana said, her stomach in knots. James was a patient man but this might anger him. She consoled herself only by mentally noting that James had been the one to suggest this task for her mother. "Perhaps we might scale it back a little?"

Lavinia smiled sweetly. "Darling, what is a ball if not a declaration of wealth, taste, and restrained theatrical excess? This will be a night of triumph for Lord Ashford."

James crossed one leg over the other, looking pensive. "This would certainly make a statement."

"That's right, Lord Ashford," Lavinia said. "Think of it as your debut into Society. It must be perfect, if not a little extravagant."

"My worry, however, is Mrs. Honeycutt and her staff," James said. "This is a tremendous amount of work and I'm not sure any of this is in her repertoire."

"I've taken the liberty of inquiring after a chef in Brighton," Lavinia said. "One must have vision, my lord."

"And bottomless coin," James said with a wry smile.

Lavinia went on, undeterred. "Also, we'll have a cold table. Stilton, Wensleydale, oat cakes, sugared almonds. Though not the pink ones. They're simply vulgar. A towering trifle. Lemon syllabub. Pistachio macarons. Plum cake with sugared violets. And finally, a centerpiece sculpted from spun sugar. I was thinking something allegorical. Perhaps a laurel wreath or Cupid's bow. Depends on what the sugar artist can manage in winter."

Georgiana blinked. "Sugar artist? Is that really a profession?"

"Georgie, dearest, where have you been?" Lavinia asked. "They're quite the rage. I've narrowed it to three artists, all of whom have good reputations." She closed the folio with a satisfied sigh. "The entire evening shall be exquisite. A feast for the eyes and the appetite."

James leaned back, looking a bit like someone had run over

him with a carriage. "It's certainly well-thought out, Lady Lavinia. You've done well."

"I knew you would understand my vision," Lavinia said. "You're a man of exquisite taste."

Georgiana met James's gaze and tried very hard not to laugh.

"I suppose what you say is true. This is my debut into Society. I believe we should do it exactly as you've suggested, Lady Lavinia. However, we must also plan a party for the villagers and tenants to attend. Later in the year. Perhaps in the fall?"

Lavinia looked at him with a blank expression, as if she couldn't understand why he would contemplate such a thing. "Mrs. Ellsworth will do an adequate job of that type of event, I'm sure."

Cecily choked on a laugh. James didn't look away from Lavinia.

"Shall I proceed as planned?" Lavinia asked. "I can begin as soon as you are ready."

James rubbed a thumb along the edge of the mantel and said mildly, "It would be foolish to deny your talents, Lady Linley. Yes, I say we go forward with the plan. The house will be complete by late spring. We will plan it for the end of May."

Lavinia preened. "I do try. And yes, that's a fine idea. I'll have plenty of time between now and then to ensure every detail is perfect."

She paused, her expression shifting to something more serious. "Speaking of details, there is one tiny matter we must address before we can proceed with all these wonderful plans."

Georgiana felt her stomach clench. She knew that tone.

"Oh?" James asked.

"Well, it's really nothing more than a minor inconvenience." Lavinia waved her hand dismissively. "You see, I've had some rather pressing expenses lately—maintaining appearances, you understand. One simply cannot economize when representing the family name."

"What kind of expenses, Mother?" Georgiana's voice was

tight with dread.

"Oh, the usual things. Proper clothing for my stay with dear Caroline, travel expenses, a few necessary accessories. And of course, the gowns I had made for last Season's balls, naturally. We can't have people thinking we've fallen on hard times."

Georgiana's hands clenched in her lap. "How much, Mother?"

"Really, Georgiana, you needn't look so severe. It's not as if I've been frivolous." Lavinia arranged her skirts with practiced elegance. "Though I will admit, Mr. Craven has become quite unreasonable about the timeline for repayment."

"Mr. Craven?" James's voice carried a warning edge.

"A gentleman who provides financial assistance to people of quality when banks are being tedious about paperwork," Lavinia said airily. "Very discreet, very accommodating. Though he has developed some rather rigid ideas about when loans should be settled."

Ice flooded Georgiana's veins. "How much do you owe him?"

"Well, with the interest that's accumulated..." Lavinia paused, as if calculating something trivial. "I believe it's come to roughly twelve hundred pounds."

The silence that followed felt like the moment before lightning strikes. Georgiana's vision blurred at the edges, and she gripped the arm of the settee to keep from swaying.

"Twelve hundred pounds?" The words came out as barely a whisper.

"Give or take a few pounds," Lavinia said cheerfully. "Really, it's not so very much when you consider what we'll need for Cecily's Season anyway. And Mr. Craven has been quite patient, though he did mention something about reputation and consequences if the matter isn't resolved soon. Dreadful man, really. I'm sure he didn't mean anything serious by it."

Beside her, Cecily made a small, choked sound. "Mother, that's more than Georgiana got from selling Robert's townhouse."

"Oh, surely not. That lovely house must have brought in at least—" Lavinia stopped, finally seeming to notice their stricken expressions. "Well, perhaps we'll need to be a bit creative about funding."

The room tilted around Georgiana. Everything she'd sacrificed—Robert's townhouse, her jewelry, her home furnishings, sleeping in cramped rooms in Brighton—all of it had been for Cecily's future. And now it was gone. Not just gone, but they owed money they didn't have to a man who made veiled threats.

"There is no funding, Mother." Georgiana's voice was as hollow as she felt. "Cecily's dowry is gone. All of it."

"Nonsense," Lavinia said briskly. "We'll simply have to find another solution. Perhaps Lord Ashford would be willing to advance—"

"Absolutely not." Georgiana spoke sharply, then glanced apologetically at James, before looking down at her clasped hands. "I mean, we cannot possibly impose. Anyway, my fees don't come close to covering what we need for the dowry."

"Actually." James's expression was thunderous as he glared at Lavinia, but when his eyes met Georgiana's, they softened with something that made her breath catch. "I have a proposition."

Knowing what he was about to say, Georgiana bit back tears. "James, no. It's too much."

"I'll cover your mother's debt to Mr. Craven," James said, ignoring her protest. "So that you may keep the dowry you sacrificed your home for." He directed a pointed look at Lavinia, which had little effect. "And I'll sponsor Cecily's Season in London. All expenses—gowns, parties, everything she needs. Including her dowry, so that Georgie will not have to worry so much about the future."

The world seemed to stop spinning. Georgiana stared at him, unable to process what he'd just said.

"James, we can't accept such generosity."

"We most certainly cannot," Cecily said.

"You can, and you will." His voice brooked no argument.

"Consider it an investment in having the finest staff at Ashford Manor. Your work here has changed my life. It has meant everything to me."

Lavinia clapped her hands together. "Oh, how marvelous! I knew everything would work out perfectly. Lord Ashford, you are truly a gentleman of the highest order."

But Georgiana barely heard her mother's exclamations. She was drowning in James's steady gaze, in the certainty she saw there, in the way he was looking at her as if she mattered more than propriety or money or any of it.

"This is far too much," she said softly.

"It's exactly what's needed." His gaze never left her face. "And it's my pleasure to provide it."

The look that passed between them sent heat spiraling through her chest—gratitude and longing and desire. Something that had nothing to do with charity and everything to do with the way his voice had roughened when he said her work meant everything to him.

Cecily had tears streaming down her face. "Thank you," she whispered. "Thank you both."

But Georgiana couldn't look away from James. In his eyes, she saw not pity but something that looked terrifyingly like the feelings growing in her own heart. Good God, it was true. She was completely, irrevocably in love with him.

And for one breathless moment, she thought she saw the same revelation reflected back at her.

CHAPTER ELEVEN

James

THE NEXT MORNING, James followed the aromas of toasted bread and sizzling ham downstairs to the kitchen. Mrs. Honeycutt bustled past with a tray of perfectly boiled eggs, while Cecily poured tea. The atmosphere felt lighter somehow, as if a weight had been lifted from the household.

James settled into his usual chair at the long oak table, his dark hair still damp and tousled from washing. Soon, the ladies were seated as well, though he noticed Georgiana seemed quieter than usual, stealing glances at him when she thought he wasn't looking.

They were all about to dig in when Cecily set down her teacup, her hands trembling slightly. "Mrs. Honeycutt, Mrs. Ellsworth, I have something wonderful to share with you both."

The two women looked up expectantly.

"Lord Ashford has made the most generous offer. He's going to sponsor my Season. Everything—gowns, presentations, even a dowry. I'm to have my debut this spring."

Mrs. Honeycutt's mouth fell open. Mrs. Ellsworth pressed both hands to her heart.

"What? My lord, truly?"

James shifted uncomfortably in his seat, heat rising in his cheeks. "It's nothing extraordinary. Miss Cecily deserves her chance."

"Nothing extraordinary?" Mrs. Ellsworth's eyes filled with tears. "Oh, my dear boy, this is absolutely brilliant."

Mrs. Honeycutt abandoned all pretense of propriety and rushed around the table to envelop James in a fierce hug. "Bless you. Bless your generous heart."

"Mrs. Honeycutt, please." James's face burned. "It's really not—"

"Don't you dare diminish this." She pulled back to look at him sternly.

"I agree," Mrs. Ellsworth said. "This is the kind of thing your dear father would have done. He'd be so proud."

James's eyes pricked with tears. He glanced at Georgiana, who was watching him with such warmth that he had to look away.

Mrs. Ellsworth had moved to Cecily's side and was stroking her hair like she would a daughter. "A Season, my dear girl. You'll be the belle of every ball. Those London gentlemen won't know what hit them."

"And with a proper dowry, you'll have your pick of suitors." Mrs. Honeycutt returned to her seat but seemed unable to stop beaming. "Oh, the shopping you'll need to do! Gowns and gloves and dancing slippers…"

James found himself smiling despite his embarrassment. The joy radiating from the women was infectious, and seeing Cecily's face light up with hope made the tightness in his chest ease.

But as he watched the celebration unfold around him, his thoughts turned inward. Why had he really made the offer? Yes, seeing Georgiana's devastation when her mother announced the debt had been unbearable. The way her face had crumpled, the way she'd gripped the settee as if the world were tilting beneath her—it had stirred something fierce and protective in him.

He couldn't stand the thought of either sister suffering. Not Cecily, who deserved every chance at happiness, and certainly not Georgiana, who had already sacrificed so much for her family.

But if he was being honest with himself, there was more to it than simple compassion.

The moment Lavinia had casually destroyed their future, James had felt something crystallize inside him. Not just anger at the woman's selfishness, but a desperate need to fix it, to protect them, to keep them safe and close.

To keep Georgiana close.

Because somewhere between her first day at Ashford Manor and last night's revelation about her marriage, he'd fallen hard. His heart belonged to Georgiana. In fact, a future without her seemed impossible. Yes, it was all true. He couldn't imagine spending his life with anyone but her.

The realization should have terrified him. He'd spent years convinced he was too damaged for love, too broken by his childhood to offer anyone a whole heart. But watching Georgiana bring his home back to life, seeing her strength and grace and kindness, had changed something fundamental inside him.

He was in love with her laugh, with the way she tucked a strand of hair behind her ear when she was thinking, with her fierce protectiveness toward Cecily. He was in love with her courage and her vulnerability. With the way she made him want to be the man his father had raised him to be.

"Lord Ashford?" Mrs. Ellsworth's voice pulled him from his thoughts. "I asked if you'd like me to arrange for accommodations in London?"

"Yes, of course." He was grateful for the distraction. "Whatever arrangements you think best. A rental for the Season somewhere appropriate."

"And we'll need to plan shopping expeditions and hire a dressmaker." Mrs. Honeycutt's excitement was palpable. "A proper wardrobe takes time to assemble."

Georgiana finally spoke up, her voice soft. "I still can't quite believe it's real."

Their eyes met across the table, and James felt that familiar jolt of awareness. He wanted to tell her it wasn't just generosity driving him. He wanted to confess that the thought of her leaving once Cecily was settled made him feel hollow inside.

But he couldn't. Not yet. She saw him as a benefactor, a kind friend. The last thing she needed was the complication of his feelings.

"It's very real. And Cecily is going to take London by storm."

Cecily blushed prettily. "I hope I don't disappoint you, my lord."

"Impossible. Any man would be lucky to have you."

But even as he said it, his gaze drifted to Georgiana. Because while any man would indeed be lucky to have Cecily, there was only one woman James wanted for himself.

And she was sitting just out of reach, looking at him like he'd hung the moon, completely unaware that he was already lost to her.

"Well then, we'd best finish breakfast. We have a Season to plan!" Mrs. Honeycutt clapped her hands together.

As the conversation turned to practical matters—dressmakers and dancing masters and presentation gowns—James allowed himself to imagine, just for a moment, what it might be like if Georgiana looked at him not with gratitude, but with love.

The thought was dangerous, and wonderful, and utterly terrifying.

But for the first time in his life, James Ashford found himself hoping for something he'd never thought he deserved.

THE TAILOR'S BELL jangled softly as James stepped into the narrow shop. He'd not visited since his return but he had vague recollections of accompanying his father at one time or another. The scent of the place tugged at his memories, the distinctive scents of beeswax candles, wool, and the faint tang of heated pressing irons, reminding him of a time long past. Although the weather remained dreary, good light came in from the large front windows. Rolls of fabric were stacked on wooden shelves. Behind a worn oak counter stood Mr. Drayton himself. He straightened at the sight of James, a grin breaking out on his face.

"Lord Ashford, how delightful to see you again." Mr. Drayton bobbed his head. "Is it time for your wardrobe? I've been praying every night you would come to me."

"There is no one I'd rather have than you, Mr. Drayton. In fact, I am here to order an entire wardrobe."

"Much obliged, your grace. Having your order will allow me to keep food on the table."

Through the partially open door to the back room, James glimpsed a large cutting table strewn with pattern papers and the glint of shears hanging on the wall alongside measuring tapes and other implements of the tailor's craft. "I have a friend joining us. She knows how a proper gentleman dresses, whereas I cannot confess to caring much about clothes."

"But now, you must look your part. Here in the village, we couldn't be more delighted about your return. You've put a lot of young men to work who were facing hard times."

"It's my hope that at some point, our village and farms will thrive as they did during my father's leadership."

"I've no doubt they will," Mr. Drayton said. "No doubt at all."

From behind him, the front door opened and in came Lavinia, cheeks flushed from the chilled air and the feathers of her hat quivering as if to indicate their excitement.

"Lord Ashford. How delightful this is." Lavinia clasped her hands and gave a dazzling smile. Despite being middle-aged, the woman was beautiful. Looks she'd passed onto her daughters. Fortunately, that was all she'd given them. "I never thought I'd have the chance to help another man with his wardrobe. It was one of the only joys of my marriage."

"Good morning, Lady Linley." He caught a whiff of her jasmine perfume. She must have poured the whole bottle over herself.

He introduced her to Mr. Drayton. "This is the friend I mentioned earlier."

"It's an honor to serve you," Mr. Drayton said.

"Mr. Drayton, we are going to keep you quite busy." Lavinia whipped out a piece of paper and laid it on the counter. "I took it upon myself to write up a list of what we need. However, if I've missed anything, please let us know. The lord must be the best dressed at whatever event he attends."

James glanced at the list, unable to disagree with Lavinia's suggestions. His current attire fell so far short of a gentleman's requirements that outfitting him properly would surely constitute Mr. Drayton's largest and most lucrative commission in decades. James took comfort in that.

Lavinia wanted him to order impeccably tailored white linen shirts to be worn beneath superfine tailcoats in blue or brown, paired with buff or fawn-colored pantaloons and waistcoats that would range from striped satin to plain cream. Multiple cravats—some plain muslin for everyday wear, others embroidered silk for making calls—would need to be tied with the precision that marked a true gentleman. For evening entertainments, the requisite black tailcoat and knee breeches would be accompanied by an ivory silk waistcoat and white silk stockings. Whether braving London's unpredictable weather in a greatcoat with triple shoulder capes or riding through his estates in waterproof wool, James would finally appear as his station demanded. However, he suspected Lavinia's ambitious plans would ensure his wardrobe commanded far more attention than he preferred.

James stifled a sigh. This was going to be a long morning.

Mr. Drayton adjusted his spectacles nervously as he read through her requests. "This is extensive, Lady Linley."

"I realize some of these items will have to be purchased in London," Lavinia said. "But we'll expect you to make the clothing. Lord Ashford has insisted we have those done locally." She said this in a tone that expressed disapproval but resignation, as if she were an embattled soldier accepting the faulty missive of her superior.

"Yes, my lady," Mr. Drayton said.

"Shall we get him measured? Up you go, my lord." Lavinia flicked her fingers toward the pedestal.

James stepped onto the platform, watching Lavinia through the triple mirror as she circled him with narrowed eyes before taking it upon herself to step behind the counter to look at the various fabrics.

Mr. Drayton coughed and stepped in with the measuring tape. Lavinia continued dictating fabric weights and lapel shapes with the precision of a general planning an invasion. James stood stoically as the tailor's cool fingers pressed the tape against his inseam, his chest, his neck.

Lady Lavinia continued without seeming to take a breath with instructions about materials and colors.

"Yes to ivory, pale blue, and burgundy. No to lemon yellow. It drains the color from Lord Ashford's face."

"I wasn't aware I owned a lemon-yellow cravat from which you gathered this opinion," James said, smiling.

"I don't need to see it. I have an excellent sense for these things. Trust me when I say no yellow for you. Waistcoats should be one gold-threaded, one black brocade, and a third in deep green velvet. It sounds daring, but trust me. With your wide shoulders, you can carry it."

James looked at the ceiling and counted to ten.

She moved closer to the tailor, lowering her voice to a theatrical whisper. "Ensure the jackets accentuate his height, Mr. Drayton. A man should look imposing in evening wear." In a normal tone she said, "Should you have a walking stick, I wonder? Perhaps with the head of a lion?"

"A lion?" James asked, meeting her gaze in the mirror.

"You are, after all, being reintroduced to Society. We must create an impression."

He gave a tight smile. "I don't need a walking stick, Lady Linley."

"Fine. We can discuss it at a later time," Lavinia said.

"That will do for now, my lord." Mr. Drayton stood.

"Thank you, Mr. Drayton," James said.

When they finally exited into the crisp village air, he exhaled deeply, loosening his cravat with one finger.

"I am very pleased." Lavinia adjusted her gloves with practiced elegance as her hat plumes fluttered in the breeze. "You will cause quite a sensation this Season."

"I was hoping to avoid sensation and simply blend in," James said.

"Too late for that. Your return alone is sensation enough. You'll be the talk of the Season."

At that moment, the door of the seamstress's shop next door opened and out stepped Cecily and Georgiana, heads bowed together as they adjusted their bonnets.

James straightened instinctively, a tension of an entirely different sort claiming his body. Georgiana's smile was still lit with joy as she glanced at her sister, sunlight catching in her light hair where it escaped her bonnet.

Lavinia paused beside him, her entire body going still in that way predators do when sensing competition. Her eyes narrowed slightly.

Cecily spotted them and froze, her laughter dying mid-breath.

Georgiana's gaze met James's across the cobblestones. His stomach fluttered and his thoughts went fuzzy. She was so pretty standing there that he could scarcely breathe.

"Perfect timing, girls." Lavinia's voice carried a calculating edge. "I trust you've ordered everything Cecily needs for her debut? Though of course, we'll need to discuss my wardrobe as well."

James hesitated, watching color rise in Georgiana's cheeks as she looked down, straightening her gloves with careful precision.

"Your wardrobe, Mother?" Georgiana asked carefully.

"Naturally. I'll be accompanying Cecily to London as her chaperone. One cannot simply send a young girl into Society unattended." Lavinia's eyes were calculating, darting between James and Georgiana with dangerous intelligence. "And since Lord Ashford has been so generous in settling my little difficulties with Mr. Craven, I'm sure he understands that a proper chaperone must be appropriately dressed. I can't accompany my daughter looking like someone's poor cousin."

"I'll be her companion," Georgiana said quickly. "We've already ordered dresses for me."

Lavinia continued on, as determined as a hawk driving for prey. "Don't be absurd. You wouldn't send a girl into the lion's den of Mayfair without her mother's guiding hand. A chaperone is required, and I am her mother. Who better? Georgiana isn't educated in the ways of the *ton*. I've already begun thinking of where we'll stay in Town. Somewhere fashionable, obviously."

Georgiana shook her head. "No, Mother. I'll be with her. This is not about you."

"And we know you'll take over and make it all about you," Cecily said, flushing. "I want Georgiana."

Lavinia waved her hand dismissively. "Your sister will be working."

"I'll take whatever time I need to ensure Cecily's safety," Georgiana said.

James could see by the worried dip of her chin that it would indeed be a sacrifice. How was she to earn a living if she spent months in London with Cecily? Then, the solution popped into his head. It required a fib, but this was war. "In fact, I believe it's the perfect time for Georgiana to be in Town. I'll be able to make introductions, sharing with everyone that she's the one who restored my family's country home. We'll make it a mission to find the next client."

Lavinia tilted her head. "That will hardly be helpful to Cecily. A proper debut requires presence, style. Influence. Not the older sister selling her wares."

James spoke softly but firmly. "Lady Linley, since I'm the one paying for her Season, I get to decide how it's all to go. Georgie will be the one to accompany Cecily. That's final."

"You just called her Georgie." Lavinia stared at him, a glint in her eyes that made it all too obvious what she was thinking.

"We're working closely together, Mother," Georgiana rushed to say. "We call each other by our first names. It's nothing to be concerned over."

"Oh, is that right?" Lavinia asked, brows raised. "Because to me, it tells an entirely different story. Lord Ashford sponsors your sister's debut, settles my debts without question, and you address each other with such… familiarity. You're together day in and day out. Only a fool wouldn't see what's going on here."

"Lady Linley, consider yourself lucky to have daughters looking after you," James said, heat rising in his voice. "You are not to criticize them or manipulate this situation to your own benefit. If you continue in this way, you will no longer be welcome in my home. As far as your accusations about the nature of our relationship, frankly, it's none of your concern. We are colleagues working together. That's all."

Even as he said it, he knew it was not so. If he thought his reactions were that of a colleague, he was the fool.

What was he to do now? He was falling in love with his architect.

Lavinia's lips parted, but no sound came out. For one sharp second, she looked stunned. Then she gave a brittle laugh. "Well, I guess you've put me in my place, Lord Ashford. As usual, my daughters think of no one but themselves. As far as the pair of you goes, I'm not an idiot. It's perfectly clear what's going on here."

Georgiana's cheeks flushed, but she held her mother's gaze. "This is about Cecily's future. Not yours. Not mine. The sooner you understand that, the better."

Lavinia didn't respond immediately. Instead, she smoothed her gloves as if the gesture gave her control. "Go on, then. If it's already decided, I'll simply have to find a way to amuse myself in the country. Alone. Excluded from my own daughter's debut while you three are off to London. I'll wilt away out here in the middle of nowhere."

James raised an eyebrow. "I'm sure you'll manage."

Lavinia huffed, gave them all a withering look and then swept down the street like a wounded duchess, her plume bobbing indignantly with every step.

The village street was oddly quiet in her wake. A dog barked in the distance. Somewhere, someone was chopping wood.

"Well. That went about as expected." Georgiana exhaled, closing her eyes for the briefest second.

James glanced at her, arms folded. "She really is something, isn't she?"

A corner of Georgiana's mouth twitched before she sobered. "I have a bad feeling about this."

"I do as well," Cecily said, sounding near tears. "She'll ruin it somehow."

"No, I won't allow that," James said. "Please, both of you, try not to worry. Everything's going to be all right in the end."

Was that true? Or was this whole thing ending with his heart broken over a woman who would never want him and sweet Cecily without a husband?

CHAPTER TWELVE
Georgiana

THE FIRE HAD been laid, supper cleared, and Georgiana had just settled into her chair near the window with a cup of tea when the sharp echo of knocking rattled the manor's front door.

Cecily looked up from her embroidery. "We're not expecting anyone, are we?"

James, standing near the hearth, frowned. "Not that I know of."

Mrs. Ellsworth entered a moment later, looking slightly windblown and very displeased. "It's your mother, miss. She wants to speak with all three of you."

Georgiana barely had time to sigh before Lavinia swept into the drawing room in a rustling cloud of plum-colored silk and indignation disguised as graciousness.

"My dears." She paused just inside the doorway as if waiting for applause. "I come not in anger, but in resolve."

Georgiana set her cup down carefully. "Good evening, Mother."

"Lord Ashford," Lavinia added with a small, elegant nod. "I hope you'll pardon the late hour, but I felt it best we clear the air sooner than later."

James folded his arms across his chest. "Go on."

Lavinia laughed just this side of brittle. "Truly, my darlings, you must listen to me. A young debutante cannot, must not, enter Society without her mother beside her. It would cause speculation. There would be gossip about her sponsor and perhaps the nature of his relationship with Cecily's older sister. It's ripe for scandal."

Georgiana really hated to admit it, but her mother's arguments had merit. Since their altercation earlier, Georgina had not been able to set another fear. What kind of trouble would her mother cause should she not be with them? Wilting away in the country as she'd so delicately put it earlier?

Lavinia lifted her chin. "In addition to the threat of gossip, a true debut requires a mother's touch. The right whispers in the right ears. You've already almost blundered by leaving me behind. What will you do without me there to ensure our reputations are intact? You've said yourself, my lord, that you have much to learn about being a gentleman. Please, let me help."

"And your wardrobe?" Georgiana asked, too tired to be subtle.

Lavinia's eyes sparkled. "I'm so glad you brought that up. It would be an embarrassment to my daughters and to you, Lord Ashford if I were seen in last year's gowns. I've already drawn up a modest list. Three evening ensembles, two for daytime appearances, and a walking dress or two for Hyde Park."

"A modest list," James said wryly.

Cecily bit her lip. Georgiana rubbed her temple.

"I know I've been misunderstood lately," Lavinia continued with a tremble in her voice that fooled no one. "But surely you don't mean to deprive me of seeing my youngest presented? It is, after all, *my* triumph as well."

There it was. Not Cecily's future. Not Georgiana's labor. *Hers.*

James raised a hand, echoing Georgiana's thoughts by saying, "It would reflect poorly if we left her behind. She's right about that."

Georgiana stiffened, wanting to fight, but knowing it was

futile. Her mother *was* right. It would cause talk if they were to arrive without her.

Lavinia smiled like a queen receiving tribute. "I knew you'd see reason. I'm so relieved."

"And the gowns?" Georgiana asked.

"I'll keep expenses within reason," Lavinia said. "I do know how to be practical when I must."

"That would be a first," Cecily muttered.

James glanced at Georgiana, then back at Lavinia. "Very well. You make good points. We shall bring you. But understand this, if you cause any trouble to either of your daughters, you will have me to answer to. I've fought in wars, Lady Linley, and right now you feel very much like the enemy."

Lavinia gasped, her cheeks paling. "How dare you speak to me that way. I'm their mother. They may not like that fact or me but it's true just the same."

"I'll speak to you any way I wish, Lady Linley," James said. "That's the privilege one has when one is paying the bills. Do see that you keep your dress expenses to a minimum. Whether you can admit it or not, your time as the center of attention is long gone. This is about Cecily. I hope you'll remember that."

Lavinia pursed her lips. "Fine. When will we depart?"

"Late April," James said. "Our wardrobes should be finished by then. Mrs. Ellsworth is finding a suitable rental in London."

"Mayfair, darling. It must be just right for my Cecily." Lavinia brightened, clasping her hands together. "Think of all the callers she'll have. Oh, it's simply too wonderful."

Lavinia kissed Cecily's cheek, floated past Georgiana and flounced from the room as dramatically as she'd entered.

They all sat in stunned silence for a moment.

"She is right," James said. "We really have no choice. We were kidding ourselves to think otherwise."

"Yes, you're correct," Georgiana said. "But regardless, I need a brandy."

This set them all laughing, breaking the tension.

"Whatever comes our way, we shall face it together," James said as he headed to the liquor cabinet to pour them all a drink.

GEORGIANA'S HEART GAVE a strange little flutter at the sight of the gowns displayed on dress forms at the far end of the room. Gowns made for her. After a year of mourning, wearing black and dark gray, it was surprising how charmed she was by the thought of dressing for fashion instead of function. Not that anyone would be looking at her. Cecily would shine too brightly for that. As she should.

Georgiana stepped forward to take in what the talented seamstress had made for her. The day dresses were modest but elegant, in soft grays and pale mauves made of fine muslin and dimity. For evening, there were two gowns: one in dove gray silk with a silver underskirt and pale blue sash, and the other in iris-colored satin, high-waisted with embroidered sleeves and a delicate lace collar.

She touched the fabric of the iris gown, her fingers trembling slightly. The color reminded her of the wild irises that grew in the local meadows. Her throat tightened. It was the first truly beautiful thing she'd worn in years. Half-mourning, but hopeful.

Would James think she looked nice in it?

Never mind that.

Miss Rebecca Thorne, the village seamstress, stepped forward with pins tucked into her cuff, and helped her to step into the iris dress. "Up you go. I need to pin the hem."

Georgiana stepped onto the platform in front of the mirror. "It's beautiful, Miss Rebecca."

"You're beautiful, Mrs. Fairfax, and would look good in any-thing. But I'm so glad you like it."

Georgiana's fair hair was a wonderful contrast to the dark gown. And the purple brought out her light blue eyes, making them appear almost lavender. She'd not felt so lovely in a long time.

Cecily emerged from the fitting screen glowing in a primrose-yellow muslin with delicate white embroidery and puffed sleeves. "Georgie, look." She spun in a circle. "It's like sunlight."

Georgiana's chest swelled with both pride and a surprising pang of longing. Had she ever been so fresh, so untouched by life's complications? Cecily's innocent delight was everything Georgiana had hoped to preserve by giving her a Season. A chance for a good marriage. And now she would have it, thanks to James Ashford. Their guardian angel.

"Oh, Georgie, how exquisite you are." Cecily brought her hands to her mouth. "You look like a queen."

"Are we sure about the color?" Lavinia asked from the other end of the shop as she stepped out from the fitting screen. "Her skin's awfully pale next to the purple."

"I disagree, Mother," Cecily said. "She's stunning."

"'Tis a pity, really," Lavinia said. "That she refused to use it to her advantage."

The younger women ignored her, focusing next on Cecily's gowns. They were showstoppers. One in soft sea-foam green tulle, layered over satin, with a floral appliqué along the bodice. The second was rose-pink silk, simple and stunning, cut to flatter her every movement.

She would turn heads. Georgiana was sure of it and suddenly terrified of what that meant. How would she get along without her little sister by her side? Everything was about to change. For the better, of course. For Cecily anyway. But her marriage would leave Georgiana alone, other than Lavinia, whom she feared she would never get rid of.

Lavinia had ordered four gowns in total: a crimson satin with jet beads, an overly dramatic lilac trimmed in ostrich feathers, a navy with pearl-studded sleeves, and a walking suit in plaid that Georgiana couldn't look at too long without blinking.

"I shall wear the crimson to the first ball," Lavinia declared, examining herself in the mirror. "Nothing too festive, of course. Just something quietly commanding."

"Quietly," Cecily whispered to Georgiana, "like a cannon."

Georgiana bit her lip to hide a smile.

The room bustled with fittings, hem measurements, lace trims, and last-minute sleeve adjustments. But beneath it all, Georgiana felt a steady pressure building. Each stitch, each pin, was one step closer to London. She didn't feel ready to leave the safe cocoon of Ashford Manor, where she felt useful and respected.

She couldn't bear to think of ever parting from James. But she must face the truth. The restoration would be done by the end of July. Ben was to stay and supervise the rest of the restoration, with her and James coming from London every week or so to see that progress was being made. And he would have no more use for her.

At least they would have a few more months together.

Then, an awful thought occurred to her. What if James met a woman he wanted to marry? She had no doubt the mamas of the *ton* would overlook his scandalous past in exchange for his handsome fortune and face.

The two people she loved most in the world would leave her alone with her mother.

She gulped in a breath of air. The *two* she *loved* most?

Was it true? Did she love James Ashford? The answer came surprisingly swiftly. *Yes, you little fool. You have loved him from the beginning.*

Her love for him was all-consuming. Shattering and dreadfully frightening. She would have a broken heart before long, with nothing but the memories of these wonderful months she'd had with him.

THE EVENING AFTER their fittings, Georgiana sat alone in the drawing room. The fire had burned low, casting long golden shadows across the freshly painted walls. Outside, rain tapped against the windows, creating a soft melody. She would miss the quiet of the country when they were in London.

Georgiana curled her legs beneath her on the settee, her shawl draped around her shoulders. She hadn't meant to stay up, but Cecily had gone to bed hours earlier, humming like a songbird about sea-foam and rose silk, and Georgiana had found herself restless. Excited. Nervous. In two days time, they would leave for London.

The door creaked open behind her, and she looked up to see James enter, hair tousled, a book under one arm.

"Georgie, you're still up? I thought everyone had retired."

"Not quite everyone," Georgiana replied, smiling softly. "Couldn't sleep."

"May I join you?" James asked.

"Yes, please."

He crossed the room and settled into the armchair across from her. Why did he have to be so handsome? And why did her nerves seem to awaken the moment he came into view?

"Did I mention, I've got interviews in the morning? For the butler and valet."

"Oh? With Mrs. Ellsworth?"

He nodded. "She insists I need a valet who knows the difference between a Windsor knot and a simple twist. And a butler who can help keep away unwanted suitors."

Georgiana smiled. "She's not wrong. You're a gentleman and you must act accordingly."

"Are you nervous to go to London?" James asked. "Because I'm feeling very much so and like I'd just like to stay here and hide away."

"I feel the same way."

He tilted his head against the chair back, watching her. "But your gowns are ready? Are you pleased with them?"

"I'm embarrassed to admit how much. They're beautiful and

make me feel young and hopeful." She went on to gush over the gowns, telling him about their hues and cuts and details, like her mother might. "Dear me, I sound like my mother."

"There's nothing wrong with enjoying something beautiful. Or feeling beautiful in them. I can hardly wait to see you."

"Really?" Her pulse quickened. "I was wondering what you would think of them." Flushing, she looked down at her hands resting on her lap. "If you would approve."

"As the seamstress said when I stopped to pay the bill this afternoon, you would look exquisite in crude burlap, so really what you wear is of no consequence. You shine, Georgie, from the inside out. Your wit and intelligence enhance your physical beauty so that a man has trouble thinking straight when in your presence."

She lifted her gaze, head spinning with delight. "I've never had anyone say anything so kind to me. Thank you, James. And thank you for paying the bill at the shop. I didn't expect you to pay for Mother and me."

"Not long ago, the amount would have been my entire month's salary, but that is no longer the case. Therefore, it is my pleasure to give you something that makes you feel pretty. I would pay any price for that."

She grinned, warmed through and through by his kind words. "There's an amount one should pay or not pay for gowns, no matter one's fortune."

"You're no fun." He smiled back at her before sobering. "Did your husband tell you how beautiful you are? He must have thought he was the luckiest man alive to have you to wake up to every morning."

She swallowed, imagining what it would be like to wake up next to James. Suddenly, it felt very important that he know the truth. There was nothing she wanted to keep from him. She wanted to open herself up and show all the soft, vulnerable parts she kept hidden to him. "He didn't wake up to me. In fact, he didn't join me in my bed at any time." She peeked up at James, who was staring at her with a look of wonder.

"What are you saying, Georgie?"

She tucked her hands beneath her shawl. "My husband was a dear friend. But our marriage was not a great romance."

"Why not?" James asked. "You had a lot in common. And it sounds like he chose you, even though you had no dowry. Usually that means a love match, does it not?"

"Perhaps. Our situation was unique." She paused. Could she really tell him the truth about something so personal? "I didn't know this until our wedding night, but Robert preferred men to women."

James continued to stare at her, clearly shocked. "Did you suspect? Before you married, that is?"

"Not at all. I was an innocent back then. I'd not even known that there were others like him, living in secrecy. But we came to an understanding. I would allow him to have freedom to do as he wished, with whomever he desired, in exchange for his mentorship. If I couldn't have love, I would have work that mattered to me. Perhaps I even thought, in the back of my mind, that something could happen to him and I'd be left without anything but an ability to earn my own way."

"I cannot believe what you have endured." James shook his head. "You deserved so much better."

"The night we were married, I thought things would go as they usually do on wedding nights." She blushed, remembering how embarrassed she'd been to stand in front of Robert in her lace nightgown, shivering from cold and nerves, only to have him sit her down in front of the fireplace to tell her who he truly was.

"But he told me the truth, right then and there. I'm grateful he didn't try to bed me, to be honest. Had he done so and I'd found out the truth later, I would have been even more humiliated."

"What did you do when he told you?" James asked, sitting forward slightly, clearly absorbed in her story.

"I cried." She chuckled. "Which I mostly never do. I'm not a crier like some women. I can stuff a feeling down just as well as a man."

James laughed. "Is that what men do?"

"A lot of them."

"Anyway, continue with your story."

She'd run out of his bedchamber to her own, where she climbed under the covers and cried herself to sleep like the little idiot she'd once been. "I woke up the next morning with swollen eyes and a broken heart. I've always been a romantic and I truly thought we were in love. Clearly, I didn't know as much about the world as I thought I did."

"It's not your fault. How were you to know?"

"The signs were there. He'd never done more than touch my hand. I thought it was noble of him. A true gentleman. But in hindsight, of course, I realized that wasn't at all true."

She watched James closely, as he absorbed all this information.

"Regardless of how crushed I was, I'd thought of a plan. I told him what I wanted and he agreed to teach me the craft of architecture. In that way, it was a successful union for me. From that day forward, a close friendship developed between us. There was no one like him. Funny and witty. He made me laugh every day. I loved him very much, albeit platonically. He had several men he spent time with on a regular basis but he always came home for supper, even if he went out again. We had a small staff and I'm sure they knew the truth but no one said a word inside or outside of the house as far as I could tell. He was the kind of man who instilled fierce loyalty and affection from everyone he came in contact with. But he was not a rich man." Her chest tightened, remembering the reading of his will, discovering that he'd left her only a small amount. He'd not discussed their finances with her. She'd assumed they were doing well enough that she needn't worry over money ever again. And that may have been true. Had he lived.

James tilted his head to the side, watching her. "Did you do as he did, take lovers?"

She shook her head, chuckling without mirth. "I wouldn't even know how to go about finding a lover. All of it felt too messy for my taste. Getting involved has always seemed too risky. I had no intention of having my heart broken by some scoundrel."

"That way no one could betray you as your father did. As Robert, in the end, did as well."

"How so?" She felt defensive of her late husband. He'd told her the truth. Yes, it had been after the marriage. However, she had been the one in desperate need of a spouse.

"He left you without enough to live on, for one."

"For two?"

"He didn't tell you about his true nature until you'd already married him. To me, this reeks of betrayal."

"If you'd known him, you'd see it differently."

She could see by the glint in his eyes that he disagreed.

"As I said, you deserved better. But how brave you were. Still are." James shifted slightly, his tone soft. "I don't know that I've ever admired someone as I admire you."

"But why?"

"We don't have enough time in the world for me to tell you all the ways, nor I the poetic tongue to do so."

"Oh, James, you do say the nicest things."

"Don't give up on love, Georgie. Someday, I expect you'll meet someone who was made to love you and only you."

"How can you say that when you don't believe in love for yourself?"

He met her gaze. "I actually don't know. I simply know that you are a gift to whoever is lucky enough to be in your life. Including mine."

They sat in the quiet, the fire crackling low, the ache in her to touch him, to confess how much she loved him, nearly overwhelming her.

Tomorrow, everything would change. London awaited.

But tonight, for one quiet hour, it was enough just to sit with him and be seen.

CHAPTER THIRTEEN

James

JAMES WAS STILL reeling over Georgie's revelation about her husband the night before. James was no innocent. He knew there were men who enjoyed the company of other men, but it was always in secret. They lived under the constant threat of social ruin, imprisonment, or even execution if discovered. Homosexuality between men was not only stigmatized, it was illegal, punishable under sodomy laws in Britain. Many gay men, especially those of the gentry or professional class, married women to fulfill societal and familial expectations. From what he knew, these marriages often involved little to no physical intimacy, and may have only been platonic partnerships.

Discretion was everything. Codes, body language, and phrases in Latin or French were used to test safety. London had known meeting areas called Molly Houses, which were essentially secret pubs or lodging houses where they could find others seeking similar companionship. These places were constantly surveilled and raided. He'd always felt a deep sorrow for the men who were forced to live lives of deception.

However, he'd never met anyone, man or woman, who was in a marriage of that variety.

It made his heart hurt, thinking of sweet Georgie in her dressing gown, hearing the news that her marriage would not be at all what she expected. Like he'd said to her last night, she deserved better.

Now, he stood near the fireplace in the drawing room, absently adjusting the cuffs of his shirt as the morning light filtered through the tall windows. February had brought the crocuses and soon to bloom daffodils and early blooming cherry trees but the chill in the air remained.

Mrs. Ellsworth was seated near the hearth, her hands folded neatly in her lap, watching him with the mild patience of someone who had already accepted she'd be needed to steer this process.

"Are you certain I really need a valet?" James asked. "I've gotten along without one for months now."

Mrs. Ellsworth didn't look up from her notes. "Lord Ashford, it's not a question. You must have one."

He glanced at her. "It seems like a waste of money."

Her mouth softened into something close to a smile. "You and your brother wanted to be returned to the life you were meant to have. That is happening. Now."

"All right, fine."

"The first interview is for the butler position," Mrs. Ellsworth explained.

A knock came, and Mrs. Ellsworth rose to admit the first candidate. A tall, silver-haired man entered, posture straight and expression calm. He moved with quiet assurance and nodded once in greeting.

"Mr. Isherwood," Mrs. Ellsworth said. "Formerly in service to the Earl of Stanhope."

"Lord Ashford." He bowed. "Thank you for receiving me."

"Thank you for coming." James gestured to the chair opposite. "Please."

Mr. Isherwood sat, folding his hands over his lap.

They spoke for several minutes. He explained his experience overseeing large households, his preference for quiet efficiency over spectacle, and his ability to handle unexpected challenges with composure.

James asked few questions but listened closely. There was a steadying quality about the man. His voice was even, his gaze direct, his answers free of flattery.

"Are you aware of the history of my family?" James asked. "My father?"

"I am, my lord."

"And it doesn't bother you?"

"It bothered me that they hung an innocent man. We all knew it at the time."

James sat forward. "Who do you mean by we?"

"Those of us who have worked for the noble houses in this area. His reputation was such that it was impossible for any of us to believe differently. Although tragic and irreparable, I am pleased to see that justice has returned."

"Very good," James said. "I must warn you, though. I have not been raised a gentleman. There is much for me to learn. I hope you'll be patient with me."

"Whatever you need, Lord Ashford, I shall do and be honored to serve."

Mrs. Ellsworth offered a small nod behind Mr. Isherwood's back. James followed it.

"I believe you'll suit us well," James said. "Welcome to Ashford."

The man bowed again. "Thank you, my lord."

He departed, and a few minutes later, the second candidate entered. He was a much younger man, dressed in a clean but unassuming coat. His hair was neatly combed, and his gloves were tucked respectfully under one arm.

"Mr. Digby," Mrs. Ellsworth said. "He comes with a reference from the Marquess of Leland's household."

The young man stepped forward. "My lord."

James studied him. He had expected someone stiffer. This man seemed quietly confident, but not ingratiating.

"I understand you've served as both footman and valet?"

"Yes, my lord. Most recently for Lord Leland's eldest son. I was his valet until he married last year."

"What do you consider the most important part of your role?" James asked.

Digby took a moment before answering. "To make your day run more smoothly than it otherwise would. To anticipate what you need, not just respond when asked."

James nodded slowly. "And what if I don't always know what I need?"

"Then we'll learn it together, my lord."

"I don't know how to dance," James said. "What would you tell me to do about that?"

"I know the perfect instructor for you, my lord," Digby said. "If you hire me, I shall put it all together for you."

"You're hired, Mr. Digby," he said.

"Thank you, my lord."

Once Digby had gone, Mrs. Ellsworth returned to her chair. "I'm pleased, my lord. I hope you are as well."

"He seems more than adequate. And he's willing to work for a man like me, which won't be easy."

"Nonsense."

"I'm not learned in the ways of Society," James said. "Part of his work will be helping me to appear a gentleman, when really I am a working man."

"But, my lord, you are a gentleman. It was stolen from you for a time but that has changed."

James sat as well, the warmth of the fire easing into his shoulders. "What do you think people will see when I arrive in London? A man in a fine coat pretending to be something other than a soldier or tavern owner. Or a clever card player."

Mrs. Ellsworth's voice was gentle. "What they see or think of you is not your concern. You must see yourself as worthy. Whether they see you as a gentleman or a tavern owner matters little compared to how you see yourself."

James didn't respond right away. He stared into the flames, thinking through what she'd said. It was true. If he felt like an imposter, others' impressions had no bearing on, well, anything. He would be miserable, regardless.

"If I may suggest, my lord, that you simply take it one day at a time. Everything will fall into a rhythm of familiarity soon enough."

"Thank you, Mrs. Ellsworth. As always, your counsel is wise."

"It is my honor, Lord Ashford."

THE FIRE HAD burned low in the grate when Digby knocked once on the bedchamber door. "Your bath is ready, my lord." Digby bowed slightly while his free hand automatically straightened a candlestick on the side table. "If it pleases you."

James blinked from where he sat in his shirtsleeves, thumbing through estate papers. "You've prepared a bath? Is this something I should expect every night?"

"Yes, my lord." Digby moved to the mantel, straightening another candle before lighting a fresh taper. "I notice how stiff you are in the morning and a bath will do you good."

"War injuries," James said. "They've made me less limber than I should be."

"I understand, my lord, having served myself. Tomorrow will bring rain and the dampness will settle in your bones. A warm bath tonight will help."

James glanced toward the window but it was too dark to see the nature of the weather. However, this time of year in England was almost always chilly and damp. "Can you sense the rain?"

"The air has that particular weight to it," Digby said. "Your body knows it too, I'd wager. Old injuries often do."

"Very well. You've convinced me." James followed Digby into the adjoining chamber, where a hip bath had been positioned before the fire. Steam rose from the water's surface like incense, and towels rested in neat arrangements. Mrs. Ellsworth had recently purchased new linens and towels for the household. Memories of living in his cramped apartment above the tavern were beginning to fade with each decadent day.

Digby withdrew a small vial from his waistcoat, adding several drops to the water with the reverence of a man mixing medicine.

"Lavender?" James asked, catching the familiar scent from his childhood bath. A memory surfaced of a time not long before they took his father away. His father had visited the nursery after traveling for a few days on business. Sebastian had already bathed and was in his pajamas, but James was still in the water, getting a thorough scrubbing from the governess, who complained about the dirt under his fingernails and behind his ears.

Papa had dismissed the governess, saying he would finish getting his boys ready for bed and she could retire early. James understood now, as an adult, how unusual it was for a man with the title of duke to spend such intimate time with his children. But perhaps he'd sensed how the loss of their mother had left a void that only he could fill.

James could not remember what they talked about, if anything, but the scent of lavender oil had remained fresh in his memory. From then on, he'd associated that smell with the gentle love of his father. His gut twisted with grief. If only he could see him one more time. Ask him questions about himself. Stories he could keep and pull out when he was especially missing him.

"Lavender reminds me of my childhood," James said to Digby. "But I smell something else too. What is it?"

Digby corked the vial, looking pleased with himself. "Aye. This is my own blend. Lavender for the nerves, bergamot for clarity, and mint to sharpen the senses. I was taught to blend oils by a housekeeper in my first household. She said a man's bath should restore more than just his body."

James studied him, curious about Digby's past. "How old were you then?"

"Eleven, my lord." Digby began working the buttons of James's waistcoat, his fingers sure despite their calloused tips. "Boot boy, initially. Then scullery. I learned that staying useful meant staying fed. My mother depended on my wages. Like yours, my father passed away when I was young, leaving just me to care for my mother." His voice carried the quiet matter-of-factness of someone who'd never had the luxury of childhood.

"Is she still alive?" James asked.

"Yes, my lord. She lives in the village with her sister. They are my only family."

James's stomach clenched as those careful hands moved to his shirt. His fists closed automatically, an old defense. He did not want anyone to see his back, the scars that told part of the story of his life. "I can manage the rest."

Digby paused, meeting his eyes. "Of course, my lord. Though I should mention—I've seen much in my years of service. Nothing troubles me."

James forced his hands to unclench and slowed his breathing. Digby would not judge him. He understood how it was to grow up hard. And anyway, a gentleman was expected to use his valet in this way, even though it felt odd to James. "Very well. Continue."

The shirt came away with gentle efficiency. He waited for a reaction from his new valet but none came, even though the scars across his back were impossible to hide.

"Courtesy of my cousin's husband." James kept his voice carefully light. "He didn't much care for me or my brother."

Digby's hands stilled as he folded the shirt—always in thirds, James had noticed, a habit that spoke of order imposed on chaos. When he spoke, his voice was quiet but firm. "It pains me to see what was done to a child. To any child."

"He was a man who found pleasure in power over the power-less." James stepped into the tub then, the hot water a shock at first but he quickly acclimated. He had to admit, it felt good to sink low into the water and let it soothe his tired muscles. Despite his new title, he had worked as hard as any of the men they'd hired to restore his home. Just today, he'd helped to clear a pile of bricks from one of the upstairs rooms.

Digby knelt beside the bath, adding another drop of oil. The mint sharpened the air, clearing James's head as he relaxed further. "Digby, I could grow accustomed to this."

"As you should, my lord." Digby offered a sea sponge. "As far as your cousin and her husband. They'll answer for it someday. Whether in this life or whatever comes after."

James took the sponge, smiling at the memory of the frequent scoldings he'd gotten from the governess. "When I was a boy—before we were sent away—I was always getting a tongue lashing for being dirty. They couldn't keep me from playing outside in the mud and dirt."

"A boy should have that freedom."

James chuckled. "Our governess did not agree. But Papa did. He didn't mind that I would rather be outside than inside sitting quietly with a book."

"Do you have many memories of him?"

"Yes, quite a few. Which is surprising given how young I was when they took him from us. He was an unusual man for his time and station in life. He spent a lot of time with his children. We were quite attached to him."

"I hope soon this house will be filled with the sounds of children playing, both inside and out."

He glanced up at Digby as a strange sensation came to his belly. Children. Laughter. Love.

Suddenly, he knew with certainty that he wanted that. He had been mistaken when he told Georgie he could not imagine a scenario in which he would marry and have a family.

There was one sole reason for that. Georgie. He could imagine it with her. He wasn't sure when it had happened, but his desires for the future and his belief that good things would come to him had shifted.

He wanted it with her. But would she ever consider such a

prospect? He would do his best to win her heart. Yes, just like that, he understood his purpose going forward. It was to win Georgina Fairfax's heart and hand.

TWENTY MINUTES LATER, James sat in his robe before the hearth while Digby moved through the bedchamber.

"Tell me, Digby, do you find it tedious?" James asked. "Dressing a man? Taking care of his boots?"

Digby's hands stilled for a moment. When he looked up, his gaze was steady, loyal. "My lord, I consider myself a lucky man to have acquired such a position. There is no such thing as tedious work if one approaches it as both important and artful."

"Important and artful. I like that idea very much."

"I understand this is a period of adjustment for you." Digby's voice held no judgment, only understanding. "It's my privilege to serve you however you need."

Moved by his words, James fought against the sting behind his eyes. "It does not bother you that I'm a little rough?"

Digby folded a pressed cravat with deliberate care. "Not at all. In fact, it makes me feel proud to help you. Even if you do not yet feel a gentleman, you will very soon."

"You have a momentous task ahead of you," James said, chuckling. "To make me appear a gentleman will take more than a new wardrobe."

"I'll not let you stumble, my lord."

"Digby, may I share a concern with you?"

Digby glanced up from brushing James's coat. "Indeed, my lord."

James ran a hand through his still damp hair. "The Season will soon be upon us and I find myself woefully unprepared. I do not know the rules of Society. I've not been trained to be a gentleman. I am sure there are whispers still about my family.

Everyone will be watching me, out of curiosity and perhaps malice too. People love to see a man fail."

"And why does their opinion matter? You have wealth and power now."

"Normally, I would not care. I'm still a rogue, under all the finery. But it's not just me at stake." James's voice grew tight. "Cecily needs to make a good match. She's beautiful and clever, but if I embarrass her, it would lead to trouble. I'm sponsoring her, so I must present well." He halted, then forced himself to continue. "And there's someone else I care about. Someone whose reputation could be damaged by association with me."

Digby set down the brush, giving James his full attention. "Mrs. Fairfax?"

Heat crept up James's neck. "Is it so obvious?"

"Not to all, but I pay particular notice to everything you do and say." Digby's mouth quirked slightly. "She seems a woman of considerable sense."

"She is. Which is exactly why I can't afford to make a fool of myself. One wrong step, one moment where I look like the uncouth devil I am, and I'll have ruined everything for them." James's hands clenched on the arms of his chair. "Most concerning? I don't know how to dance properly. I'll be expected to lead ladies through the quadrille, the waltz—God help me—and I'll likely step on their feet or miss the timing entirely." James dropped his head into his hands. "Can you imagine? The gossips will have a field day. 'Lord Ashford, returned from exile, still can't manage a simple country dance.' They'll tear me apart, and by extension, they'll destroy Cecily's prospects." And possibly drive Georgie away.

Digby was quiet for a long moment, folding a cravat. "My lord, these are all problems we can solve."

"How can I possibly learn to dance in time?" James asked.

"Monsieur Lefevre. He will help."

James blinked. "Who?"

"A dancing master of considerable skill. French, naturally—

they have the best sense of these things. He's discreet, efficient, and has transformed gentlemen with far less natural grace than yourself." Digby's tone grew practical. "I took the liberty of making inquiries after our conversation about the Season yesterday. He is available, if you're willing."

James stared at him. "You already arranged this? But how did you know?"

"I made preliminary inquiries only. The decision remains yours, my lord. But I've found that practical solutions tend to ease abstract worries."

"You think he can teach me? Truly? In time for the Season?"

"Monsieur Lefevre has prepared gentlemen for their first Season in less time with remarkable results. You have natural coordination and, more importantly, strong motivation. Those are his favorite pupils. Although he'll never let on. He's known for his vigor and insistence on excellence, not compliments. Or coddling, as he puts it."

"You make it sound so simple."

"My lord, if I may be so bold, learning to play the part of a gentleman is considerably easier than the other challenges you've faced. Your childhood. The war." Digby smiled. "You will flourish. I've no doubt."

"And if I stumble? Step on Mrs. Fairfax's toes in front of half the *ton*?"

Digby straightened another book as he passed. "Then we shall ensure you recover with such grace that they remember your composure, not your misstep. But you won't stumble, my lord. Certainly not after Monsieur Lefevre is finished with you."

James studied his new valet. Digby was a man who excelled at his job. If Digby could do it, so could he.

"What about the rest of it? All the rules and such?" James asked.

"There are many, but we'll take them one at a time."

Digby began ticking them off calmly, as if reciting a familiar prayer. "When attending a ball, you must bow when entering the room, and again to the hostess. Only once you've done so may you begin requesting dances. Never ask a lady for more than two in one evening, lest it appear you are courting her."

James muttered, "What if I am?"

Digby's brow lifted slightly. "Then be prepared to explain your intentions to her brother or father by morning."

And what if she had neither of those? He kept that question to himself.

Digby continued. "During the meal, you'll speak first to the lady on your right, then the lady on your left, never across the table unless addressed. Napkin in your lap, not tucked under your chin, and you must wait for the hostess to lift her fork before beginning."

James frowned. "Seems a lot of rules for a simple supper."

"Indeed. And then there's conversation. Stick to safe topics—music, books, the weather, perhaps horses. Never politics. Never scandal. Never religion."

"Even if I'm dying to speak my mind?"

"Especially then."

James shook his head, half in admiration, half in despair. "Anything else?"

"A few small items. Never remove your gloves unless eating or shaking hands. Don't dance the same set with the same lady twice. Never, under any circumstance, speak ill of another gentleman or lady in mixed company. If a lady drops her fan, you may retrieve it, but do not comment on the fact unless she thanks you."

James gave him a long look. "This is certain to be a disaster."

Digby's eyes twinkled. "My lord, I disagree. You must try not to worry overly much."

James swallowed hard against the sudden tightness in his throat. "I will do my best, especially if it helps Mrs. Fairfax and Cecily. I shall do my best to learn. And yes—please arrange for Monsieur Lefevre to come."

Dance lessons? A new wardrobe? Learning all of these rules?

Who had he become and was he ready for it?

Whether or not he was capable, change was coming. He vowed to hold steady, regardless of what was to come his way in the days ahead.

THE CHAIRS HAD been pushed to the edges of the drawing room, the rug rolled up, and the polished floor left bare and gleaming in the late afternoon light. Sun streamed in through the tall windows, catching flecks of dust as they floated through the air like dancers themselves.

James stood stiffly in the center of the room, boots planted too wide, hands awkward at his sides. His cravat felt too tight, though he'd tied it the same as always. In a frighteningly short amount of time, he'd be in London ballrooms, holding strangers in his arms, making small talk with women whose names he'd forget by morning.

The thought made his chest tighten.

Across from him, Monsieur Lefevre clapped twice. "Non, non, non! You are not squaring off for battle, Lord Ashford. You are asking a lady to dance. There is finesse, not force. Grace, not… whatever this is." He gestured broadly at James's stance.

James exhaled slowly, jaw tight. "This is ridiculous."

"Mais non," Lefevre said, stepping lightly across the floor as if carried by invisible strings. "This is courtship in motion. It is poetry of the feet. Think of all the beautiful ladies in London, waiting to be swept across the floor!"

James's stomach turned. Beautiful ladies. Waiting. Expecting.

At that moment, the door creaked open.

"I'm not interrupting, am I?" Georgiana's voice was warm with amusement.

James turned, heat prickling the back of his neck. "Only my humiliation."

She stepped fully into the room, and the tightness in his chest loosened. How pretty she looked in her simple day dress, with a pink flush to her cheeks.

"Monsieur Lefevre, I presume?" Georgiana asked.

"But of course, madame!" Lefevre bowed with a theatrical sweep. "A pleasure to meet the lady of such grace. Perhaps you have come to rescue your poor Lord Ashford from footwork catastrophe, oui?"

James shot her a look. "I am hopeless."

"Surely not?" Georgiana smiled kindly at him. "You're naturally athletic. You will improve in no time at all."

Lefevre clapped again. "This is divine providence! You will partner him. We cannot waltz alone, n'est-ce pas? And see how his shoulders drop already, just from your presence? Magnifique!"

James felt his face burn. Lefevre wasn't wrong—he had relaxed the moment she'd entered.

"Are you sure?" James asked.

Georgiana stepped toward him, her hand already extended. "I cannot let you suffer alone."

Her fingers slid into his. Bare skin against bare skin. Cool and soft where his palm had gone warm. Her thumb settled against his, just the lightest pressure. He had to remind himself to breathe. This was practice. Just practice for London. For dancing with women who weren't known to him. Who would judge him for every misstep.

"Très bien!" Lefevre called. "We begin with the quadrille. A dance of approach and retreat, perfect for the London ballrooms where you will charm so many ladies, Lord Ashford."

James's hand tightened involuntarily around Georgiana's. She glanced up at him, something unreadable in her eyes.

Lefevre snapped his fingers impatiently. "Lord Ashford, you just take her hand gently. Not like you are claiming property."

Georgiana's smile curved. "Lord Ashford would never be so presumptuous."

The music began, Lefevre humming and tapping his foot in

rhythm. The quadrille required them to step apart, to circle, to return. Every separation felt like loss. Every return felt like coming home.

James focused on her. The way her skirts brushed his legs when they passed, how her fingers found his without hesitation each time the dance demanded it, how she guided him with the smallest pressure when he faltered. Her hair smelled sweet. Her hand grew warm in his.

The next movement should have taken them apart again, but somehow they'd drifted closer. Close enough that he could see the delicate curve of her eyelashes, feel her breath against his chin.

Georgiana's lips parted slightly, and for one dangerous moment, James imagined closing the distance entirely, discovering if her mouth was as soft as her hands. He did not think it was his imagination that she trembled slightly in his arms. Did she feel it too? This overwhelming longing to stay this way forever?

"No, no." Lefevre's voice shattered the moment. "This is not the quadrille anymore. You have invented your own dance, I see. Very romantic, but the London mothers will gossip, non?"

They stepped apart quickly, but not quickly enough. James's skin felt too tight, his pulse too loud. Georgiana's cheeks had turned even pinker.

"Again," Lefevre commanded, clapping sharply. "And this time, remember, you are practicing for all those London beauties, Lord Ashford. All the eligible, accomplished ladies who will want their turn in your arms."

James caught Georgiana's gaze. This was supposed to make London bearable. Assure himself that he would not make a fool of himself. Instead, it was making the thought of dancing with anyone else unbearable. He did not want accomplished ladies and their matchmaking mothers. He wanted only Georgie.

"Shall we?" Georgiana extended her hand again, gazing into his eyes. "You mustn't despair. It will grow easier."

"If we must." He took her hand again. How perfectly it fit in his.

But when the dance brought them together again, when her fingers tightened just slightly around his, he felt almost certain she shared his yearning. Could it be possible that Georgiana Fairfax was his perfect match? His love match?

Please, he prayed silently. Make it so.

CHAPTER FOURTEEN
Georgiana

RAIN LASHED AGAINST the tall windows of the drawing room, turning the late afternoon into a watercolor wash of gray and silver. Georgiana sat at the long oak table, fabric swatches and wallpaper samples fanned out before her like a deck of oversized playing cards. The storm had crept in with little warning, a moody spring tempest that rattled the panes and hissed along the eaves. But she found she didn't mind. Not in the haven of the drawing room.

She reached for a swatch of velvet in a soft blush shade, running her fingertips over its nap. Not right for the library, but perhaps one of the bedrooms? Her mind wandered to James's chambers. He'd told her how good it felt to sleep in what felt like his first real bed since he and his siblings were sent away. The thought of him in any bed at all sent an unwelcome flutter through her stomach.

Stop it, she chided herself. *He's your employer. Nothing more.*

But the way he'd held her in his arms? It had felt like more. A great deal more.

The fire behind her crackled softly, offering warmth against the chill. Mrs. Ellsworth had brought her a fortifying pot of tea, which had sat untouched. Now, though, as the thunder rumbled in the distance, she abandoned her samples, poured a cup of tea and wandered over to a chair by the fire. She'd chosen *Much Ado*

About Nothing to read in preparation for James's ball. She'd forgotten how much she enjoyed this particular play. Beatrice and Benedick, forever sparring, forever denying what everyone else could see, intrigued her in a way it hadn't before now. She didn't want to examine that too carefully but she knew why. Even if she would never admit it to anyone but herself.

She'd just settled in, opening the play to the first page, when the door creaked open.

"Georgie, good afternoon," James said, his voice like warm honey.

Her pulse jumped. She looked up to find him leaning against the doorframe, rain-damp hair curling at his collar. He'd changed into a dark waistcoat and open shirt, no cravat in sight. The casual disarray made him look younger. Dangerous.

"Have you been out in this weather?" She aimed for lightness.

He pushed off the doorframe and approached. "I had to go into the village to meet with a few of the local businessmen. Rain was coming down hard by the time I left."

"Would you like a cup of tea?" Georgiana asked. "I'm having one and reading an old friend." She held up the play to show him.

"Actually, I could use a brandy to ward off the chill." He poured himself a drink from the decanter on one of the side tables and then dropped into the chair across from her, long legs stretched toward the fire. His eyes fell to the book in her lap. "I think that is my favorite of his comedies."

"I share your opinion. I'd forgotten how much I enjoyed this one."

"One of the best couples ever written, in my humble opinion," James said. "I once spent time with an actress who played Beatrice."

"Time?" She laughed, knowing exactly what he meant.

He chuckled. "My reputation as a rogue is not without merit."

"I shall put all thoughts of that part of your life aside," Georgiana said.

"She used to use me to help her memorize her lines. I fancied myself quite the actor."

"No, really? I must hear you."

His eyebrow quirked. "It's been a while but I'll try. However, only if you read Beatrice's part."

"I'm no actress," Georgiana said, allowing herself a turn at flirtation. "In more ways than one. I'm afraid I cannot perform as your actress friend did, on stage or off."

A flash of heat sparked in his eyes but was quickly masked. "Go on then so that I might judge your talent."

She opened to Act IV, the scene where Benedick confesses his love for Beatrice. James leaned forward, elbows on knees, to see the text. Their heads bent together over the book.

"'Lady Beatrice, have you wept all this while?'" James began, as Benedick.

"'Yea, and I will weep a while longer,'" Georgiana answered as Beatrice.

They continued trading barbs, James's delivery growing more animated. When he reached Benedick's admission of love, his voice dropped lower. "'I do love nothing in the world so well as you. Is not that strange?'"

For a moment, their eyes met. She could barely breathe. Oh, how she wished it was James speaking to Georgiana instead of merely playing a part. She could almost believe he loved her but no, she mustn't allow herself to be lulled into a fantasy that would leave her bereft when it proved false.

Thunder crashed outside, causing the windows to shake.

Georgiana broke contact, looking back down at the page. James leaned closer, placing his finger on a line farther down the scene. "This is the line that stirs my soul. 'I love you with so much of my heart that none is left to protest.'"

Her breath caught. She stole a glance at him. The firelight played across his features. Surely there was no finer man in the world than the one next to her.

"What a gift it would be to love someone that much." His

voice was barely above a whisper. "And have it returned."

"Yes." The word escaped before she could stop it.

He shifted forward in his chair. The book slipped to the floor, forgotten between them. "Georgie, how beautiful you are in this light. Any light."

She should stop this. Should make some joke, change the subject, remember her place. Instead, she lifted her chin, meeting his gaze directly. "They spend so much of the play running from each other. And themselves, I suppose."

"Out of fear." His hand moved to the arm of her chair, fingers inches from hers. "But what if they'd confessed their feelings to themselves and each other sooner?"

Lightning illuminated the room. In that split second, she saw raw hunger in his expression that matched the ache building in her chest.

"There wouldn't be much of a play then," Georgiana said softly. "If Shakespeare hadn't kept them apart until the end."

He moved, one hand sliding to cup her cheek. His thumb traced her bottom lip, and her breath shuddered out.

"Tell me to stop," he said roughly.

She leaned into his touch instead, eyes fluttering closed. She felt him shift closer, felt the warmth of his breath across her lips—

The door burst open with a bang.

They sprang apart like guilty children.

"Oh dear me." Mrs. Ellsworth stood frozen in the doorway, eyes wide. "I do beg pardon. I was just—supper is—ready. Mrs. Honeycutt said you've asked to eat downstairs tonight?"

"Thank you, Mrs. Ellsworth." James's voice was remarkably steady, though Georgiana noticed his hands clenched the arms of his chair. "We'll be along shortly."

The housekeeper bobbed a curtsy and fled.

Georgiana stared down at her lap, afraid to meet his gaze.

"Georgie." His voice was gentle now. Careful.

She forced herself to look up. He was watching her with an expression she couldn't read.

He stood, holding out his hand to assist her to her feet. For a moment, they were chest to chest, her head tilted back to meet his eyes.

"There's much to say between us," he said quietly. "Isn't there? Yet, I cannot find the right words to say exactly how I feel."

Thunder rolled across the sky, and she shivered despite the fire's warmth. "Nor I. Only that I'm frightened."

"Of what?"

"Of caring too much. Of having my heart broken by a man who says he will never marry."

"If the right person comes along, a man might discover there are… other ways to secure happiness."

Georgiana felt the blood drain from her face. Other ways. The phrase echoed in her mind, each repetition making his meaning clearer. He wasn't speaking of marriage at all. He was speaking of… arrangements. The kind respectable women didn't discuss, but whispered about in scandalized tones.

"I see." Her voice came out barely above a whisper.

"Georgie?" He frowned, clearly puzzled by the change in her expression. "What's wrong?"

She stepped back, her chest tight with humiliation. How foolish she'd been, standing here like some lovesick girl, imagining he might actually—that a man of his station—would ever consider her worthy of his name.

"I must go." She turned toward the door, desperate to escape before the tears burning behind her eyes could fall.

"Wait—" He reached for her arm, but she pulled away.

"Please don't." Her voice cracked despite her efforts to control it. "I understand perfectly what you are suggesting, and I—I cannot. I will not."

She fled before he could respond, leaving him standing by the dying fire, his hand still outstretched and complete bewilderment written across his features.

DOWNSTAIRS, IN THE kitchen, golden lamplight pooled on copper pots and the worn wooden table, but Georgiana felt the atmosphere shift the moment she entered. Mrs. Honeycutt bent over her stew pot with unusual concentration, while Mrs. Ellsworth busied herself with plates, avoiding everyone's eyes.

They knew. Of course they knew.

"Please sit," Mrs. Honeycutt said without turning. "Storm's made everyone restless tonight, but I have something to warm our bellies."

James pulled out Georgiana's chair, his fingers brushing her shoulder as she sat. The simple touch made her stomach clench with equal parts longing and shame. She couldn't bear to look at him—not after what he'd suggested, not when her traitorous body still responded to his nearness.

Cecily watched them both with barely concealed curiosity, chin propped on her hand, eyes wide. "Quite the tempest. Thunder rattled the windows something fierce. I do hope nothing was… interrupted."

Heat flooded Georgiana's cheeks. "What could possibly have been interrupted?" she asked, her voice pitched too high.

"Other than our discussion of Shakespeare," James said. "We were discussing the upcoming ball."

"Yes," Georgiana seized on the excuse. "Discussing the performance. Nothing more."

Mrs. Ellsworth dropped her spoon. The clatter rang through the kitchen like a gunshot.

"Butterfingers tonight," the housekeeper muttered, her cheeks flaming.

Cecily, bless her, began chattering about her latest ideas for the gardens. Georgiana pushed food around her plate, ridiculously aware of James across from her. When their feet accidentally brushed under the table, she jerked back as if scalded, nearly knocking over her water glass.

The meal stretched endlessly. Finally, she pleaded a headache and escaped to her room. Once safely in the space she shared with Cecily, she collapsed onto the bed, pulled her knees to her chest, and let the tears fall at last.

AN HOUR LATER, Cecily found her still curled on the bed, fully clothed.

Her sister came to perch on the side of the bed, smoothing locks of hair away from her forehead. "What has happened? And don't tell me nothing because I know you. Something's happened between you and James. You were as jumpy as startled birds during supper."

"What did Mrs. Ellsworth say?" Georgiana asked. "About what she saw upstairs?"

"She said nothing at all but I could tell something had agitated her. What *did* she see upstairs?"

Georgiana sat up, her hands clenched in her lap. The memory of his thumb on her lip made her stomach flip. "It doesn't matter. It can't matter."

"Why?" Cecily's brush stilled. "Because he's our employer? Because of what people might say?"

"Because he's convinced he's too damaged for love. Because I'm someone he hired to restore his family's legacy, not fall in love with him." Her voice cracked. "I cannot love another man and have him refuse to marry me. It was bad enough with Robert rejecting me as he did. But to be James's mistress? My heart cannot do it. I want more, Cecily. I want to be his wife. Bear his children. Be in a marriage where we actually share a bed."

Cecily took Georgiana's hands, her expression one of bewilderment. "He asked you to be his mistress? Are you sure?"

"He didn't say it directly but the implication was there."

Tears pricked her eyes. "What am I doing? What am I supposed to do? I am in too deep already."

"Oh, Georgie." Cecily squeezed her fingers. "You left everything behind to protect me. You've stood up to creditors and gossips and Father's ruin. You even manage Mother, which we both know is no small feat. You're the bravest person I know. You will simply tell him the truth. It is either marriage or nothing."

Georgiana stared at their joined hands. "He told me before— he cannot marry. Or won't. I cannot participate in something untoward. If he wants a mistress, I am not that woman. No matter how badly I wanted him to kiss me."

"He tried to kiss you?"

"Mrs. Ellsworth came in and interrupted, but yes, I believe that was what would have happened."

"Lord Ashford is an honorable man who respects you. If he was about to kiss you, it's because he cares deeply for you."

"What if he's happy we were interrupted? Relieved. Just the thought of that is too much to bear, which tells me how far I've let myself fall. I'm playing a dangerous game. One that will hurt me if I continue."

"What if he isn't happy you were interrupted?" Cecily countered. "What if he's lying awake right now, wondering the same things?"

The thought of James sleepless, perhaps pacing his room, perhaps thinking of her was too much.

"I don't know what to do," Georgiana said.

"Perhaps, just this once, you don't have to do anything. Simply let this wonderful thing between you unfold as it should. You've never learned the art of letting go, my dear sister. But it might be time to leave it up to destiny. If I'm correct, a great love story is unfolding before our very eyes. Please, don't push him away out of fear. Let something good happen. You deserve all the happiness in the world."

"What if he will not marry me?"

"Then you will walk away and you will be all right. You do not need him."

"But I want him," Georgiana said. "I want all of him."

"Have a little faith, Georgie. Look at all you've done with your life despite all the blows and hardships. You will see soon that a reward is coming your way. In the form of one large, rugged, dangerously handsome man."

They stared at each other in the lamplight. Thunder rumbled distantly, the storm moving on.

"Let him come to you, Georgie. And he will. Please don't run away before you even know what he truly wants." Cecily stood, pressing a kiss to her sister's head.

They both prepared for bed. When she finally slipped under the sheets and warm blankets, she closed her eyes and let the scene from earlier replay over and over in her mind until she fell asleep.

CHAPTER FIFTEEN

James

THE STORM HAD passed by morning, leaving the grounds soaked and steaming under a brittle crust of early sunlight. James stood at the window in his bedchamber, sipping coffee and watching the mist rise from the distant fields. The manor had the hushed stillness of a household not yet fully awake, but the quiet did nothing to settle his restless thoughts.

He hadn't slept well.

The previous evening's scene in the drawing room kept looping through his mind, but not the parts he'd expected to dwell on. Not her laughter or the way her eyes shone in the firelight, but that final, terrible moment when everything had gone wrong. The way her face had drained of color. The crack in her voice when she'd said she understood what he was suggesting.

But what in blazes had he suggested?

He'd replayed their conversation a dozen times, examining every word. He'd been speaking of marriage—hinting at it as delicately as he could manage. When he'd said a man might discover other ways to secure happiness, he'd meant other than remaining a bachelor forever. Other than his previous resolution never to wed.

So why had she looked at him as if he'd insulted her?

James exhaled slowly, rubbing a hand down his jaw. The confusion gnawed at him worse than the sleeplessness. He'd thought they understood each other. Thought she might welcome his tentative overtures toward something more permanent between them.

Instead, she'd fled as if he were some sort of predator.

A knock at the door interrupted his brooding.

"Enter," he called.

Digby stepped inside, impeccably dressed despite the hour, carrying a silver tray with fresh linens.

"Good morning, my lord. Shall I assist you with your toilette?"

James set his cup aside. "Yes, thank you, Digby."

As the valet moved efficiently about his duties, James found himself grateful for the man's steady presence. If anyone might have insight into the mysterious workings of the feminine mind, it would be Digby.

"Digby," he said as the man laid out his fresh shirt. "May I ask you something?"

"Certainly, my lord."

James hesitated, uncertain how to frame his question without impropriety. "When a gentleman believes he's made his honorable intentions clear to a lady, yet she reacts as if he's offered her some form of insult instead…"

Digby's hands stilled on the waistcoat. "Ah."

"Have I said something wrong without realizing it? Something that could be misinterpreted?"

The valet's expression remained perfectly neutral, though James caught the slightest hint of understanding in his eyes. "In my experience, my lord, the most well-intentioned words can sometimes be heard quite differently than they were meant. Particularly when delicate matters are discussed with excessive subtlety."

"You think I was too subtle?"

"I think, my lord, that a lady of refinement might require rather more explicit assurance of a gentleman's honorable intentions than he realizes. Especially if there are social considerations at play."

James frowned as Digby helped him into his shirt. "Social considerations?"

"A lady of modest circumstances might be more sensitive to implications of impropriety, my lord. More likely to assume the worst rather than the best of a gentleman's suggestions."

The pieces began falling into place with sickening clarity. Of course. He'd been thinking of their class difference as an obstacle to overcome, but she might see it as proof that marriage was impossible. That he could only be offering something far less honorable.

"Good God," he breathed. "She thinks I was propositioning her."

"It would explain the lady's distress, my lord."

James closed his eyes, mortification washing over him. No wonder she'd run. No wonder she could barely look at him over dinner.

"How do I fix this, Digby?"

The valet fastened his waistcoat with practiced hands. "I believe, my lord, that this particular misunderstanding calls for absolute clarity. No more subtle hints or delicate implications."

James nodded grimly. He'd spent so much time trying to be a gentleman that he'd forgotten sometimes being direct was the more honorable course.

He would have to find her today and make his true intentions unmistakably clear—before she convinced herself he was a complete scoundrel.

LATER THAT MORNING, he went out to the gardens, hoping to find Georgie. He had the feeling she'd been avoiding him since last night. She hadn't joined them for breakfast and she wasn't in her usual place in the study. Cecily had hinted that she might be out for a little fresh air.

The air outside was damp and rich with the scent of turned earth and wet grass. Mist clung to the hedgerows, and the first shoots of tulips poked up from the ground. He followed the gravel path through the orchard, past the boxwood maze, and toward the stone bench beneath the ancient hawthorn tree.

And there she was.

Georgiana stood with her back to him, her cloak wrapped tightly around her shoulders. The pale gray wool made her seem wrought from the morning mist itself. In her hand, she held a small leather-bound book. Her sketch journal.

"The garden calls to restless souls, it seems," he said softly.

She turned, and he caught the faint curve of a smile. "Indeed it does. The stillness helps me think."

"May I share your sanctuary?"

She gestured to the bench beside her. "I should welcome the company."

They settled together, and for a time neither spoke. The silence between them felt fragile, as if the wrong word might shatter whatever tentative peace they'd found. She traced idle patterns on her journal's worn leather cover, and he found himself studying the way the soft light caught her fair hair.

"When I was a child and my mother and father were at odds, which was often, I used to steal away to our garden. It was where I first started to draw. Sometimes Cecily would join me. I think she grew to love flowers and trees during those times."

He looked out across the dew-silvered hedges. "I have always found peace outside, even during the hard years at the Langstons." He paused, then found himself speaking words he'd never shared. "I spent so many years feeling utterly alone, convinced that isolation was my natural state. That perhaps some people are simply meant to walk through life without connection."

Her hands stilled on the journal. "You have never struck me as someone who belongs alone."

"No?" He turned to study her profile. "For the longest time, I believed I had nothing to offer another person. That the damage in me ran too deep." He drew a breath. "But lately, I've begun to wonder if I was wrong. If perhaps solitude isn't a virtue, but simply… fear."

Without hesitation, her gloved hand found his where it rested on the stone bench. The simple touch steadied him more than any words could have. "Fear can masquerade as many things. Wisdom. Practicality. Self-protection."

He looked at her then, truly looked, and saw understanding in her eyes. Not pity, but recognition. "You speak as one who knows something of fear disguised."

A rueful smile touched her lips. "I'm doing my best to choose courage instead. However, it must be said—you've made that choice easier."

The air itself seemed to hold its breath, weighted with what neither dared speak.

James felt the pull of her. Not merely her beauty, though that stirred him profoundly, but something deeper. The quiet strength that had carried her through loss, the gentle humor that surfaced despite her trials, the way she saw past his carefully constructed walls to whatever goodness might still remain.

"Do you want to speak about last night?" James asked.

Her eyes met his, and he saw uncertainty there, perhaps even hope. "I… yes. I think we should."

Relief flooded through him. "Georgie, I fear there may have been a misunderstanding. What I said about a man discovering other ways to secure happiness—"

"My lord?" Mrs. Ellsworth's voice carried across the garden. "Forgive the interruption, but a letter has arrived for Miss Georgiana. The messenger said it was urgent."

James bit back his frustration as the housekeeper approached, holding out a cream-colored envelope. Georgiana's face went pale the moment she saw the handwriting.

"Thank you, Mrs. Ellsworth." Her voice sounded unsteady. Perhaps even terrified.

The housekeeper departed, and James watched with growing concern as Georgiana stared at the letter as if it contained a serpent.

"Georgie? What is it?"

With trembling fingers, she broke the seal and unfolded the paper. As she read, the color drained completely from her face. Her hands began to shake.

"No," she whispered. "No, he cannot—"

"What's wrong?" James reached for her, but she jerked back, the letter fluttering to the ground.

"I must go. I must—Cecily needs to know—" She was already backing away, panic clear in her voice.

"Georgiana, wait. Tell me what's happened."

But she had already turned and fled toward the house, leaving James alone with his unfinished explanation and a growing dread about what that letter contained.

AFTER THE MIDDAY meal, James found Mrs. Ellsworth in the stillroom, her sleeves rolled to the elbows as she bound dried lavender into neat muslin sachets.

"Here you are with yet another task," James said, pausing in the doorway. "You work too hard."

She glanced up, her weathered face brightening. "Idle hands are the devil's playground, as your dear mother was fond of saying."

A genuine smile touched his lips as he entered, trailing his fingers along the worn wooden worktable. "Did she truly say that, or have you invented maternal wisdom to suit your purposes?"

"Every blessed morning as she tended the household accounts. She had such a way of making even the most tedious tasks seem purposeful." Mrs. Ellsworth's expression grew tender. "You've inherited her heart and courage. She loved so deeply, especially you and Sebastian and Lord Ashford. She delighted in your every moment. I like to think she's somewhere, watching how you've grown into an honorable man, despite what happened to you. I see your father in you, too. He was steady in a storm, as you are."

James studied his hands as if seeing them anew, but his usual ease seemed forced today. The weight of the morning's encounter in the garden pressed heavily on his shoulders.

Mrs. Ellsworth set down her work, studying him with keen eyes. "What troubles you, my lord? You've the look of a man wrestling with his demons."

He settled into the chair opposite her, suddenly feeling less like the master of the house than the boy who used to steal warm biscuits from this very room. For a long moment, he said nothing, then released a heavy sigh.

"I've made a fool of myself, I'm afraid."

"How so?"

"With Mrs. Fairfax." The name left his lips like a confession. "I've developed feelings for her. Quite strong ones, actually." He ran a hand through his hair, disturbing its careful arrangement. "This morning I attempted to speak to her about what happened between us last evening, but before I could properly explain myself, she received some sort of urgent letter that clearly distressed her. She fled before I could clarify my intentions, and now I fear she still believes I was suggesting something improper."

Mrs. Ellsworth resumed her work, fingers deft with long practice, but her expression remained thoughtful. "Did she, now?"

"I suspect she thinks my intentions are dishonorable. And perhaps she's right to be wary. What right do I have to pursue her? She deserves a man unmarked by scandal, someone who can offer her a future unclouded by the past. A man who is whole, instead of broken into a thousand pieces."

Mrs. Ellsworth's hands stilled on the sachets, and she fixed him with a look that had seen through his excuses since boyhood.

"Are you sure you're interpreting her correctly?"

"What do you mean?"

"I mean that girl looks at you the way a drowning woman looks at a lifeline—with equal parts longing and terror." Her voice carried the warmth of a lifetime spent dispensing both remedies and counsel. "Mrs. Fairfax isn't indifferent to you, my lord. She's frightened."

"Frightened? Of what?"

"Of hoping for something she believes she cannot have. Of caring for someone who might disappear from her life as others have done." Mrs. Ellsworth leaned forward slightly. "That young woman has been hurt by everyone in her life except for sweet Cecily. She is protecting herself, perhaps believing what you seem to believe."

"And what's that?"

"That you're incapable of loving anyone as she wants to be loved because of what you endured as a child."

James traced a crack in the old oak table, considering her words. "Even if that were true, what am I to do? I can hardly pursue a woman who flees every time we attempt a serious conversation."

"You tell her the truth. All of it." Her eyes found his with pointed meaning. "Not just that you desire her company or find her pleasing, but that you've fallen in love with her. That your intentions are honorable and permanent. You must let her know you're not some passing fancy or temporary amusement."

His throat constricted. "And if she still rejects me?"

"Then at least you'll know where you stand, and she'll know exactly what she's choosing to refuse." Mrs. Ellsworth reached across the table, her work-roughened hands covering his. "But I've seen the way she watches you when she thinks no one is looking. I've seen how she softens in your presence, how she fights her own inclinations. That's not indifference, my lord. That's a woman at war with herself."

The stillroom grew quiet save for the soft rustle of dried

herbs and the distant sound of voices from the kitchen yard. James watched dust motes dance in the slanted light, feeling something loosening in his chest.

"You truly believe she might… care for me?"

"I believe she already does. The question is whether she'll allow herself to act on those feelings." Her voice gentled. "Give her the choice, Lord Ashford. Tell her your heart completely, and then let her decide. But don't make that decision for her by retreating before the battle is even fought."

James nodded slowly, his spirits lifting incrementally. Rising from his chair, he moved toward the door, then paused on the threshold.

"Mrs. Ellsworth?"

"Yes, my lord?"

"Thank you. For coming back to me."

Her smile was radiant. "It's been my greatest privilege, watching you become the man your parents raised you to be. Now go win that girl's heart properly."

He stepped into the corridor, the comforting scent of lavender clinging to his coat. Please, God, let Mrs. Ellsworth be right.

JAMES WAS HEADED to the drawing room for a brandy when he spotted Mr. Isherwood hovering near the base of the stairs like a bird of prey, silver tray clutched against his chest and that hard expression he wore when the household accounts didn't balance.

"My lord." The butler's voice could have cut glass. "A word, if you please."

James wiped his palms on his already-stained waistcoat, noting how Isherwood's gaze followed the movement with barely concealed horror. "What can I help you with, Isherwood?"

"I've been made aware that you've taken your meals in the kitchen." Each word dropped like a stone. "With the staff."

"Indeed I have," James said. "They are my favorite times of the day."

Isherwood's fingers tightened on the tray's edge. "My lord, in my previous positions, I observed that the most successful households maintain clear distinctions between master and servant. It is not merely tradition—it is necessity. Now that Mrs. Ellsworth and I have hired appropriate staff, you must transition to a more formal dining experience."

"Because I'm too good to eat with people who actually work for a living?"

"Because respect flows downward from the master." Isherwood stepped closer, his voice dropping to an urgent whisper. "The moment you blur those lines, my lord, the moment you become just another man sharing a pint and a laugh, you lose the authority to lead them. And they need leading."

James felt his jaw clench. For weeks now, the kitchen had been his sanctuary—the only place in this echoing mausoleum where laughter came easily and no one expected him to have answers he didn't possess. "So I should what, exactly? Eat alone in that tomb of a dining room while perfectly good company sits twenty feet away?"

"Yes." No hesitation. "Because that's what lords do."

"No. I won't do it."

"In every great house I've served, my lord, the master who maintained proper distance was the one whose staff remained loyal, whose household ran smoothly, whose reputation remained unblemished." The butler's voice grew more insistent. "Mrs. Fairfax and her sister are guests, my lord, however helpful they've been with the restoration. But if you continue treating them as equals, the staff will begin to see them as such. And when word spreads to the village? God help us then."

James went very still. "What about the village?"

"People talk, my lord. About the pretty young ladies living under your roof. About how familiar you've all become."

The implication stung. James's hands curled into fists. "You're suggesting I'm somehow hurting their reputations? But I'm sponsoring Cecily for the Season."

"I'm suggesting that propriety exists for a reason." Isherwood met his eyes steadily. "One dinner, my lord. Tonight. In the dining room, as your position demands. Let me show you that being the master of this house doesn't have to mean being alone in it."

James stared at him for a long moment, hearing the desperation beneath the butler's formal tone. Finally, he nodded once, sharp and bitter. "But I shall be alone."

"My lord?"

"Fine. I will do as you ask. For one night. As a test."

"Very good, my lord." Isherwood's shoulders sagged slightly with relief.

On the other hand, James died a little inside at the thought of being apart from the people who had become his family. Especially Georgie.

THE DINING ROOM sprawled before him like a mausoleum dressed for company. Every surface gleamed—silver so polished it threw back distorted reflections of his face, bone china that caught the candlelight like captured moonbeams, crystal that sang when the evening breeze stirred the curtains. The mahogany table stretched endlessly in both directions, a dark sea with James marooned at its center.

Digby had trussed him up properly—forest green coat that fit like armor, linen so starched it could stand on its own, hair tamed with enough pomade to build a small sculpture. He looked like the oil paintings lining the corridor. Dead men in expensive clothes.

The first course arrived with ceremony that would have impressed visiting royalty. Footmen glided in and out like ghosts, their practiced silence more oppressive than shouting. James lifted his spoon, solid silver, heavy as a weapon, and tasted Mrs. Honeycutt's bisque.

It was perfection. Creamy, herb-kissed, with that bright citrus note she'd been perfecting for weeks. In the kitchen, he would have praised it, watched her cheeks flush with pleasure, maybe stolen a second helping directly from the pot while she scolded him for poor manners.

Here, it tasted like ash.

The claret was probably worth more than most families saw in a year. James drained half the glass in one swallow, hoping for warmth, for courage, for anything to fill the hollow ache spreading through his chest. Through the tall windows, he could see the east lawn and the blooming of the cherry trees.

A laugh echoed faintly from below where the rest of them were eating together. The sound felt like a knife between his ribs.

The lamb arrived, pink and perfect, accompanied by vegetables arranged like artwork. James cut into it with mechanical precision, each slice exactly as Digby had demonstrated. Chew. Swallow. Reach for his glass. Repeat. Like a clockwork gentleman, all moving parts and no soul.

His fork scraped against china, the sound sharp in the cavernous silence. Somewhere in this house, real people were sharing real conversation, their voices overlapping in the comfortable chaos of belonging. And here he sat, lord of nothing but empty space and echoing loneliness.

And he missed Georgiana's company so much it took his breath away.

James pushed back from the table so abruptly his chair scraped against marble. The untouched lamb grew cold, the perfect vegetables congealed in their artful arrangement. He stared down at the waste of it all—the ceremony, the isolation, the suffocating weight of propriety.

He dropped his napkin over the ruins of his meal and walked out, leaving the ghosts of dead Ashfords to finish dinner alone.

CHAPTER SIXTEEN
Georgiana

THE MANOR WAS quiet as Georgiana padded barefoot down the corridor in her dressing gown, her slippers barely making a sound on the worn rugs. She hadn't been able to sleep. The anticipation of London, the looming responsibilities, Julian's letter burning in her mind, and her growing, confusing feelings for James.

When she reached the drawing room, she paused in the doorway. James sat in one of the wingback chairs by the fire, his coat discarded and a book forgotten on his lap. His posture was relaxed, one ankle resting over the opposite knee, a half-empty glass of wine in hand. The flickering light from the hearth gilded the sharp lines of his jaw and caught in his intense, watchful eyes that seemed to see too much. He looked up at her arrival, his expression softening. Her breath caught.

"Couldn't sleep either?" James asked, sounding gruff.

She shook her head, stepping into the room. "I thought perhaps a fire would quiet my thoughts."

He gestured to the chair opposite. "Join me."

She curled into the seat, drawing her robe tighter across her chest. This was entirely inappropriate for her to be with him in her night clothes but she didn't even care. Not anymore. She just wanted to be wherever he was.

"Thank you for inviting Mother to stay here tonight. She

claims the inn was simply too loud to sleep properly and she wants to look her best." Georgiana chuckled, rolling her eyes.

"Your mother is a difficult woman, but she is not without her good qualities," James said.

"Such as?"

"She has excellent taste."

"And loves to spend other people's money," Georgiana said.

The fire snapped and whispered between them, and she was acutely aware of how the light played across his features, how his breathing seemed to deepen as he watched her settle.

"Hard to believe we leave tomorrow." His fingers tightened almost imperceptibly around his glass. "London beckons."

"Yes. I'd like to say I was looking forward to it but I'm not. I'd rather stay here and continue our work together."

His eyes sharpened slightly. "Is your reluctance about London connected to that letter you received this morning? You seemed quite distressed by it."

Heat flooded her cheeks. She could never tell him about Julian—about the assault, about how powerless and ashamed she felt. "Just some unpleasant correspondence from my past. Nothing that need concern you."

Something shifted in his expression, a subtle withdrawal that made her chest tighten. "I see."

The silence stretched between them, no longer comfortable but weighted with unspoken tension. She watched him take a longer sip of wine, his jaw working as if he were chewing on something bitter.

"It's for Cecily," he said finally, his voice cooler now. "And it's only a few months. We'll be back here before you know it."

She watched the flames dance for a long moment before speaking, desperate to recapture the warmth that had been there moments before. "I've been focused on her future and now that we have a chance to make her dreams come true, it occurs to me that I will lose her in the process. She will become a wife and a mother and I'll be left behind. Probably looking after my mother."

James's brow furrowed, but there was something more guarded in his expression now. "What do you want? For yourself? Not Cecily. Not your mother."

"I don't know." Her voice caught slightly.

"I don't believe you." But the words came out sharper than before, almost challenging.

Her mouth opened in surprise. "Why not?"

"Because a woman of your sensibilities and passions wants to live a full life. I want to know what a full life means to you. Do you want to keep working? Do you want a husband and family? A life in the city or the country?" He leaned forward suddenly, resting his forearms on his knees, but something desperate edged his voice now. "Tell me what you want."

I want you.

"No one's ever asked me that before," Georgiana said instead.

"I'm asking you," he said, his voice low, urgent, but she caught the frustration underneath. "I want to know everything about you, Georgie."

The words made her fingers tingle, but she heard the emphasis on everything and felt the familiar nervous twist in her stomach. He wanted to know everything, but would he still feel that way if he knew her better? Were there things in her past that would make him look at her differently?

She felt tears prick at her eyes ad blinked them away quickly, but not before he noticed. His jaw tightened, and she saw something close off in his expression.

She swallowed hard. "I want to be loved and to love in return."

He smiled, but it didn't quite reach his eyes. "See? That wasn't so hard."

She hesitated, feeling her hands tremble slightly around her empty palms. "I was so naive when I married Robert. I had no idea he had a secret life, one he'd hidden even from me. It was such a disappointment to realize that what I thought was between us was not at all what I wanted or needed. And it's made me bitter and afraid to let anyone in." Her voice broke on the last word, and she looked away, unable to bear the intensity of his gaze.

James's face tightened, his knuckles white around the wine glass. "Robert was wrong to use you in that way. What he did is not about you, though. I hope you know that. You're lovable, Georgie. Any man who enjoyed the company of women would give a limb to lie with you in bed."

"What if that's not true? What if I'm too ugly inside for anyone to truly love me?" The admission came out as barely a whisper.

"There's not one ugly thing about you. Inside or out," he said after a moment, his voice rougher than before, but she caught the doubt creeping in at the edges. "But I understand very well what you're saying because I've believed it about myself."

The fire crackled between them, and Georgiana found herself studying his profile, remembering the empty chair at dinner. "You didn't join us for dinner tonight."

His shoulders tensed. "No. I didn't."

"We missed you." The words came out smaller than she intended. "I missed you. I thought perhaps... after this morning's conversation was interrupted, you might not want to be around me."

Something raw flashed across his features. "Christ, Georgie, no. That's not—" He dragged a hand through his hair. "Isherwood insisted I dine in the formal dining room. Said it was proper. Said I was blurring lines that shouldn't be blurred."

"And you listened to him?"

"I sat alone in that mausoleum for an hour, listening to your laughter echoing from the kitchen below, feeling like the loneliest man in England." His voice turned bitter. "Apparently that's what lords do. Maintain distance to preserve dignity."

Relief flooded through her, followed quickly by hurt. "But you still chose to listen to him over joining us."

"Because he said." James stopped, his jaw working. "Because he suggested that my behavior might be damaging your reputation. Yours and Cecily's."

"I see." But she didn't, not really. If he truly cared for her, wouldn't he have ignored the butler's concerns? Wouldn't he have chosen her company over propriety?

The silence stretched between them again, heavier now. She watched him take another sip of wine, and when he spoke again, his voice was carefully controlled.

"I've told you how I've believed I was too broken for love. Family. A future that meant something." He paused, his throat working. "When I was ten years old, I watched them take my father away. Watched them kill him for a crime he didn't commit. And I learned that day that the world breaks things. Good things. Innocent things. That justice is a lie we tell ourselves. Yet, now, all these years later, redemption's come to our family. To me. And I find myself questioning everything I once thought I'd take with me to the grave."

Georgiana's hand moved of its own accord, reaching across the space between them before she caught herself, her fingers hovering in the air before she pulled back.

He noticed. Of course he noticed. And something in his expression shuttered completely.

"I convinced myself I was meant to be alone." His gaze found hers, but it felt distant now, as if he were looking through her rather than at her. "That perhaps some people carry too much darkness to offer anything clean to another person. That I was too damaged by what I'd seen, by what I'd lost, to ever love or be loved in return." He stopped, his hands clenching. "I thought your presence here had changed everything."

Thought. Past tense. Her chest ached with the weight of everything unspoken, everything she couldn't tell him.

"For me too," she whispered.

But even as she said it, she could feel him pulling away, retreating behind walls she didn't know how to scale. He was sharing his deepest pain with her, and she was giving him nothing in return. She could see it in his eyes—the growing certainty that she would never truly let him in.

"Sometimes I think the boy who watched his father hang never really left that courtyard. That I'm still him, still ten years old, still believing that everything good gets destroyed."

"But you don't really believe that. Not anymore."

He was quiet for so long she thought he wouldn't answer. When he finally spoke, his voice was flat, resigned. "No. But perhaps I was wrong to think otherwise." He cut himself off, shaking his head. "It doesn't matter."

"It does matter. Tell me what you were going to say."

"That I thought there was a possibility to put back together what was once broken." His eyes met hers briefly before looking away. "But maybe some things are meant to stay broken."

Her stomach hollowed, leaving nothing but emptiness. "How can you say that?"

"Because you won't let me in, Georgie." The admission came out raw, desperate. "You say you want to be loved, but you won't trust me with whatever's troubling you. You pull back every time we get close to something real."

Shame burned in her throat. He was right, but how could she explain? How could she tell him about Julian's hands on her, about how dirty and broken she felt inside? How no matter what she did, she could not rid herself of him? He had found her, no matter where she went. And she had a terrible feeling he would be in London, wreaking havoc.

"It's not that simple—"

"Isn't it?" He stood abruptly, moving to add another log to the fire with sharp, agitated movements. "Either you trust someone or you don't. Either you let them know you or you keep them at arm's length."

The fire had died lower, and the room had grown cold. She shivered, and he noticed immediately, his face softening despite his frustration.

"Here, take this." James reached for his discarded coat. He draped it over her shoulders, his hands lingering just a moment too long, his fingers brushing against the curve of her neck. She felt the warmth of his touch like a brand, and her breath stuttered.

A charged silence filled the space between them, but it felt different now—weighted with all the things she couldn't say.

"I'm glad you'll be in London with us." Her voice broke slightly on the words, betraying everything she wasn't saying.

"So am I," he said, but the words came out mechanical, distant.

"And maybe someone wouldn't care if you were broken. Maybe they'd want you exactly as you are."

He covered her hand with his, and she felt the calluses on his palm, the steady warmth of him. His thumb swept across her knuckles, but when he looked at her, his expression was guarded. "You make me want to try. To choose courage instead of fear."

She held her breath, waiting for more, but he seemed to catch himself, pulling back emotionally even as his hand remained on hers.

The fire threw shadows across the room as the dark night pressed against the windows.

"It is growing late," James said finally, his voice once again carefully neutral. "And we'll be up before the sun."

She fought against the disappointment pooling in her stomach and managed a benign smile. "An early start will be best if we're to reach London before evening."

He stood, offering his hand. When he lifted her to her feet, she stumbled slightly, drawing too close. His jacket slid from her shoulders and onto the floor. They remained, inches apart, looking into each other's eyes, and for a moment she thought she saw the James from before—warm, open, wanting.

His gaze moved to her mouth. "It seems unfair to all the others that a woman should be as beautiful as you." He brushed his thumb against her bottom lip as he'd done before, and it had the same effect. Stars burst in her stomach and sent sparks through her entire body.

But then something shifted in his expression, shutters falling across his eyes. He backed away, gesturing toward the door with painful politeness.

"You should precede me out of the room, or I cannot promise to behave as a gentleman."

She wasn't sure exactly what that meant, but she heard the dismissal in it. The careful distance. She nodded and moved toward the door. However, she paused just outside the drawing room, turning back to face him as he followed her out. In the dim corridor, lit only by a single sconce, the space between them felt even more intimate and too stimulating.

"Georgiana." He spoke softly, stepping closer.

They stood inches apart, looking into each other's eyes. Despite everything that had gone unsaid, despite the barriers he'd erected between them, she could see the longing in his gaze.

"You are everything a man could want. I do hope you know that to be true." James reached up, brushing his thumb against her bottom lip as he'd done before, and it had the same effect. Stars burst in her stomach and sent sparks through her entire body.

The sensation faded as that familiar barrier in his eyes slammed back into place.

"Goodnight, Georgiana."

Georgiana. Not Georgie.

She hurried toward her room, heart pounding against her ribs, trying not to cry and praying no one had seen them in such an intimate exchange.

WHEN SHE RETURNED to her room, she discovered her sister had not yet retired either.

Cecily sat cross-legged on her bed, her copper hair loose

around her shoulders, brushing out the last tangles of the day. A small candle burned on the bedside table, casting flickering golden light that made everything feel softer, younger—like they were girls again, whispering secrets in the dark.

"I thought you were asleep," Georgiana said.

"I was trying, but I can't seem to relax. I'm terrified of what is to come," Cecily said.

"What in particular frightens you?"

"Of London. Of everything. What if I fail? What if no one wants to dance with me at the balls? What if everyone notices this terrible hair?" Cecily pulled on a stray curl.

Georgiana crossed the room and perched beside her sister. "You will not fail. And your hair is lovely because it's unusual. Thanks to James, I mean, Lord Ashford, you'll have a dowry. I wouldn't be surprised if you're engaged by the time the Season ends."

"Oh, how I hope you're correct. But I'm not clever like you. I'm shy when I first meet people and can never think of anything witty to say."

Georgiana took her sister's hand gently. "You must simply be yourself. Don't try too hard to be what you think the world wants. Because, honestly, they'll be fools not to see your worth. You're kind, and clever, and open-hearted. You have something most people don't—genuine goodness. You don't need to pretend to be anyone else but you."

"But I'll be alone without you." Cecily's voice cracked. "You've always been the brave one. The steady one. What if I can't manage on my own?"

"You won't be alone," Georgiana said. "I'll be right there, every step of the way."

Cecily blinked fast, trying not to cry. "Do you think Mother will behave herself?"

Georgiana laughed under her breath. "That is an entirely different question."

Just then, as if summoned by the mention of her name, the

door opened and Lavinia stepped inside, her wrapper tied hastily and her eyes bright with barely contained excitement.

"My dear girl." Lavinia closed the door behind her with exaggerated care. "I do hope you won't think me terribly improper, but I couldn't help but notice… that is to say, when I went down for a bit of sherry just now…"

Georgiana felt the blood drain from her face. "What are you talking about, Mother?"

"I saw you with Lord Ashford in the corridor." Lavinia's voice carried that particular tone of triumph she got when she'd discovered a particularly choice bit of gossip. "In your dressing gown, no less. The way he looked at you, the way he touched your face." She pressed a hand to her chest. "Oh, my dear, I do believe his intentions are becoming quite clear."

Each word felt like a stone dropped onto Georgiana's chest. She watched her mother's face, flushed with satisfaction, and felt a deep shame. The moment had been private, precious—not meant for anyone else's eyes.

Cecily made a small sound of distress. "Mama, perhaps you shouldn't—"

"What were you doing lurking about the corridors anyway?" Georgiana asked, her voice sharper than intended.

"I told you, I was seeking a glass of sherry to help me sleep." Lavinia settled herself on the edge of Cecily's bed uninvited. "And I couldn't help but observe that his lordship seems quite attached to you. The way a gentleman becomes when his feelings are engaged."

"Mother, listen to me carefully." Georgiana spoke with as much sternness as she could muster, given the nervous thumping of her heart. "You are not to say a word about any of this to anyone. Do you understand? Not to Lord Ashford, not to the staff, not to anyone we meet in London."

Lavinia waved a dismissive hand. "Of course, dear. I'm not a fool. These things must be handled delicately." She leaned forward conspiratorially. "But you must encourage his attentions.

Be charming, be agreeable. A man like Lord Ashford doesn't come along every day."

"You mustn't interfere," Cecily said quietly from the bed. "If Lord Ashford has feelings for Georgie, then he'll act on them in his own time and his own way. Any pushing from you will only drive him away."

Lavinia's expression tightened slightly. "I have managed to keep this family afloat for years, Cecily. I think I know a thing or two about securing advantageous connections."

"Mother, it's late." Georgiana took hold of her mother's arm and guided her toward the door. "We all need our rest before the journey tomorrow."

"Yes, of course. We must all look our best." Lavinia paused at the threshold, her eyes gleaming. "This could change everything for our family, Georgiana. Don't let the opportunity slip away."

Georgiana walked her mother back to her room, murmuring soothing words until Lavinia finally settled. When she returned to her own room, Cecily was standing by the window, arms wrapped around herself.

Georgiana let out a breath and dropped onto her bed, suddenly exhausted.

"She's going to meddle, isn't she?" Cecily murmured.

"Almost certainly," Georgiana said with a grim smile. "And I expect she'll only get worse once we arrive in London."

"I'll keep close watch on her," Cecily said. "We can ask Mrs. Ellsworth to help too."

Georgiana nodded, but her mind was still on James's words. *You make me want to try. To choose courage instead of fear.*

She would need that courage now. All of it.

Chapter Seventeen

Georgiana

THE CARRIAGE ROCKED gently as it pulled away from Ashford Manor at first light, wheels crunching against frost-hardened earth. A pale blush colored the horizon, bathing the countryside in ghostly gold. Inside the carriage, warmth clung to wool cloaks and lap rugs, though Georgiana still found herself rubbing her hands together, more from nerves than chill.

James sat beside her, close enough that she could feel the heat radiating from his body in the confined space. When the carriage swayed, his thigh pressed against hers through layers of fabric, and she found herself hyperaware of his solid presence, the way his shoulders filled his coat, the clean scent of sandalwood that clung to his skin.

Cecily sat opposite her, positively alight with excitement, her cheeks already pink despite the early hour. She leaned toward the window, her breath fogging the glass. "Do you think there will be violets in bloom in Hyde Park?" She twisted to face Georgiana before her sister could answer. "Do you suppose the modiste on Bond Street still displays gowns in the window? I remember seeing one with a bodice embroidered entirely in gold thread."

Georgiana gave her a small smile, though her stomach clenched at the mention of Bond Street. Julian would know all her old haunts, all the places she might go. "You were young. It's possible the gown grew more elaborate in your memory."

"Perhaps," Cecily said dreamily, "but I remember how it shimmered in the gaslight. I can still see it." She looked out the window again, fingers drumming against her lap. "I can't believe we're really going. And that I'm going to have my debut. Lord Ashford, you've been too good to me."

"Nonsense," James said, his voice rumbling in the small space. "We will all enjoy ourselves immensely. Your sister and I will enjoy shopping for new pieces for the manor. You'll attend parties and balls and shine like the star you are."

Parties and balls. Georgiana's breath caught. Julian would be at every one of them. Watching. Waiting. Her hands began to tremble in her lap, and she clasped them tightly together.

Georgiana's eyes pricked with grateful tears, though fear twisted in her chest. It was true what Cecily said. He was too good to them. And she was about to lead them all into danger.

The carriage hit a particularly deep rut, and she was thrown against James's shoulder. For a moment, she felt the solid strength of him, the way his arm instinctively came up to steady her. She wanted to stay there, to let him shield her from everything that waited in London.

"Sorry," she murmured, pulling back, though her skin burned where they'd touched.

"Think nothing of it," he said quietly, but she caught the way his eyes lingered on her face, as if he could sense her distress.

Across from them, their mother groaned into her gloved hand. "This seat is unbearably stiff." Lavinia squirmed against the velvet cushions. "And the dust. I've never known country roads to be so treacherous. I shall certainly arrive with one side of my face more wrinkled than the other."

"I asked you to wear a traveling hat with a veil," Georgiana said.

Lavinia sniffed. "A veil would only make me look like I'm in mourning. Which I am not. And now I'm worried this green silk does not suit me."

"You selected it yourself," Cecily reminded her gently.

"I was rushed," Lavinia huffed. "And now I do not look my best."

"We are going straight to our rented townhome, Mother," Georgiana said. "You may change when we arrive."

"You'll be the belle of every drawing room, Mother," Cecily said with forced cheer. "Think of all the eligible older gentlemen who will be enchanted by you."

Georgiana's stomach lurched violently. Eligible gentlemen. Julian would be among them—wealthy, titled, charming when he chose to be. And he would see Cecily as leverage, a way to get closer to Georgiana herself. He might try to ingratiate himself with her family, play the perfect suitor while using Cecily's innocence to manipulate the situation. The thought made her feel sick.

"Cecily," she said, her voice sharper than intended. "You really must be careful in London. These people of the *ton* are ruthless. You're just the kind of young woman they prey on."

James glanced at her with concern. "Georgiana's right. There are men who would take advantage of your innocence."

Men like Julian. But Julian wouldn't want Cecily for herself— he'd use her to get to Georgiana. She could still feel his hands on her, still hear his whispered threats about what he knew, what he could reveal. Her breathing grew shallow.

"I'll be careful," Cecily said, looking puzzled by Georgiana's intensity. "Anyway, we have James to protect us. Surely no one would dare mistreat us, knowing he's looking after all of us."

But James couldn't protect them from Julian's secrets, from the hold he had over her. If he told anyone the truth about Robert and his brother, the scandal would have repercussions for Cecily. And all her hard work and James's money would be for naught. Georgiana's hands were shaking now, and she pressed them against her skirts, trying to still them.

"It is true, dear one," James said in an indulgent tone he often used with Cecily. He clearly adored her. "But you still must choose caution. I'm a stranger to the ways of Society, and thus less useful to you than I would wish to be."

"Regardless, we're grateful to have you with us," Georgiana said.

James's gaze found hers, and she saw understanding there—not of the specifics of her fear, but of its depth. In the swaying carriage, with his warmth beside her and London growing closer with every mile, Georgiana felt caught between longing and terror, safety and exposure.

London awaited. And with it, Julian Fane.

THE CARRIAGE CRESTED the final hill just as the morning fog began to burn away, revealing the sprawling metropolis stretched below, a vast quilt sewn from smoke and stone, stitched together with winding streets and threaded with the silver ribbon of the Thames.

London.

Even from this distance, the skyline trembled with motion. Hundreds of chimneys puffed their morning breath into the air, carriages trundling over cobbled streets, windowpanes catching and fracturing the pale March sunlight. The hum of it, even muted by distance and glass, vibrated through Georgiana's chest. She prayed silently that this was the right thing for her sister.

She pressed a gloved hand to the window as they rolled into Mayfair proper. The leather of her glove made a soft squeak against the glass, leaving a faint imprint that quickly faded. The air around them transformed, growing thicker not with the countryside scents of loam and wildflowers, but with coal smoke, expensive perfume and horse dung.

Cecily gasped beside her, the sound childlike in its wonder. Her sister's cheeks flushed pink with excitement, eyes wide beneath the brim of her bonnet. "I'd forgotten the hustle of it all. Isn't it exciting?"

"It is." Georgiana nodded, watching the parade of fashionable ladies drifting in and out of shops like exotic butterflies, their gowns a riot of colors against the sooty gray buildings. She smoothed her travel-wrinkled skirts, suddenly conscious of her provincial appearance. "We're not in Sussex anymore."

"Indeed we are not," Lavinia said, sounding fully recovered from her previous bout of nausea.

The carriage slowed, wheels crunching over freshly swept cobblestones as they approached the townhouse James had leased for the Season. Georgiana's stomach tightened with anticipation but also nerves. Again, she hoped she had made the right choice for her innocent and sweet sister.

Their temporary home was a three story, tawny brick building that stood between two statelier homes on a quiet crescent near Grosvenor Square. Not the most fashionable address, but respectable enough to open doors. It was the best James could do on such short notice and she was grateful. Iron railings wrapped around the front garden where crocuses and yet to bloom daffodils pushed through the soil, and a line of slim white columns framed the glossy black door. The brass knocker gleamed like liquid gold in the strengthening sunlight. The fanlight above the door was etched with an intricate floral motif that cast dappled shadows on the marble step below. Cream silk curtains with a subtle damask pattern, had been drawn back from tall windows, indicating Mrs. Ellsworth's arrival the day before.

It wasn't grand like the Mayfair palaces where dukes and earls entertained, but it would suit them just fine.

James stepped out first, his tall frame unfolding from the carriage with the easy grace that always made Georgiana's pulse quicken. He extended a hand to help them down, his eyes crinkling at the corners as he smiled. "Will it be all right for you?" James asked, his voice low enough that only she could hear.

"It's perfect." She allowed herself a moment of unguarded honesty as her fingers lingered in his. "Just right. I cannot thank you enough."

He smiled, sending something fluttering low in her stomach, like moths' wings against her stays.

"Very good." James released Georgiana's hand after a fraction too long. "Let's go in, shall we? I believe Mrs. Ellsworth will have tea waiting."

"Thank the good lord." Lavinia held up her skirts as she eyed the muddy street. "I will perish if I don't have a hot cup of tea very soon."

"I must confess to being a little hungry." Cecily turned in a full circle. "But look at this. We're really here."

James offered his arm and Georgiana took it, gathering her skirts to ascend the shallow steps. Before they could do so, a voice rang out behind her, cultured, languid, and utterly unmistakable.

"Well, well. If it isn't the indomitable Mrs. Fairfax in London."

She froze, the blood draining from her face as though a stopper had been pulled. Nausea rose in her throat, and for a moment she thought she might be sick right there on the pavement. The world narrowed to the sound of her own heartbeat thundering in her ears, so loud she was certain everyone could hear it. Her hands began to tremble where they rested on James's arm. It was him. Julian Fane.

Turning slowly, her half-boots scraping against the stone steps, she found herself face to face with a man she hadn't seen in over a year. The man who had scared her so badly the last time she saw him that she fled to Brighton to avoid him. Julian Fane, the younger brother of Robert's lover, stood on the pavement in a dark green coat that emphasized the breadth of his shoulders. His gloves were an immaculate white, his boots polished to a mirror shine, and his smile as predatory as any she'd ever seen. She could barely breathe, remembering the smell of his hot breath on her neck when he'd cornered her in the drawing room of the home she'd shared with Robert, the way his hands had grabbed at her.

"What a glorious surprise to see you in London." He tilted his head slightly as his gaze traveled over her with insulting thoroughness. His voice dropped to a murmur that wouldn't carry to the others. "You're radiant."

James stepped forward protectively, and she felt him tense beside her, clearly sensing her distress even if he didn't understand its source. He held out his hand, his jaw set. "Lord James Ashford. Who might you be?"

Julian's eyes flicked briefly to James's outstretched hand, then took a fraction too long to shake it. "Mr. Julian Fane," he said with a slight incline of his head. "You must be the recently restored Lord Ashford. Congratulations on your reemergence."

She shivered, her breath coming in shallow gasps. On the outside he was as charming as anyone she'd met. But his good manners hid a sinister side. A man who had never been denied anything he'd ever demanded. Except for her.

James's expression remained unreadable, though Georgiana noticed the subtle way his shoulders squared, as if preparing for impact. She could feel his concern radiating from him, could see him taking note of her pallor, her trembling. "You have me at a disadvantage, Mr. Fane. How do you know my name?"

Julian's smile didn't reach his eyes. "Oh, news travels quickly in Town. You and your brother are the only thing anyone's gossiped about in months. You know how it is here."

"I don't actually," James said stiffly. "But I intend to find out."

Julian shifted his gaze back to Georgiana, his smile turning pointed. "I simply happened to be passing by. Though what luck to encounter such a charming tableau." He turned toward Cecily and Lavinia. "Miss Linley. Lady Linley. How nice to meet you."

Cecily, still standing on the bottom step, tilted her head, obviously trying to figure out who he was. "A pleasure to meet you, Mr. Fane."

Julian offered a gallant bow. "Your sister spoke of you often during our friendship."

Cecily's brow furrowed slightly, but she curtsied politely. "Then you have the advantage of me, Mr. Fane."

Georgiana's chest tightened. They had hardly been friends. The word felt like a violation.

"Darling, how do you know each other?" Lavinia asked, apparently forgetting her desperate need for tea now that a handsome young man had arrived.

"My brother Thomas was Robert's dearest mate," Julian said smoothly. "Which meant that the lovely Mrs. Fairfax and I were shuffled off to spend time together while they did…whatever it is they did together."

Black dots floated in front of Georgiana's eyes, and she gripped James's arm tighter to keep from swaying. This was Julian's way of threatening her. He knew as well as she did the true nature of Robert and Thomas's relationship. It was true that they had often been sent off to occupy themselves while the men spent time together. She shuddered to think about exactly what had transpired. None of it mattered now, anyway.

"It's a pleasure to make your acquaintance, Mr. Fane," James said, his tone cool and final. She could hear the protective edge in his voice, could feel how carefully he was watching her reaction. "But you must excuse us. We've had a long journey."

Julian's gaze flicked between them, lingering a heartbeat too long on Georgiana's hand resting on James's arm. Something in his posture shifted, just slightly. A tightening. A quiet spike of possessiveness masked behind perfect posture.

"Of course. Far be it from me to intrude." He swept another shallow bow. "Do enjoy settling in. I daresay this Season will be unforgettable."

Georgiana didn't breathe until he'd turned and disappeared into the afternoon foot traffic. His boots clicked with the kind of casual arrogance that came from being the second son of a noble family. A man who moved through the world certain it would part for him.

Only when he was gone did James speak, his voice low and urgent. "Friend or foe?"

"Foe," she whispered, barely able to get the word out. "I'll tell you about him later." She would have to now. There was no way around it.

But even as she said it, she knew she wouldn't. Couldn't. The shame was too deep, the secrets too dangerous.

Lavinia had remained curiously silent through the entire exchange, but now cleared her throat delicately. "Well, he's handsome, I'll grant him that. And hopefully well-connected."

Cecily still looked faintly puzzled. "What an odd man. He smiled so much, but it didn't seem right."

"No," Georgiana said softly, stepping up to the door on unsteady legs. "It wasn't. And you best pay attention to your instincts here, my love. There are foxes and snakes at every turn."

THE TOWNHOUSE WELCOMED them with the warm glow of gas lamps already lit, their flickering reflections dancing across polished marble floors. A wide hall stretched from the entry, lined with soft gray wainscoting and faded gilt-framed paintings of mostly landscapes, softened by time. A graceful staircase rose from the far end, its banister worn smooth by generations of hands.

The parlor off the front hall was cheerful, if a bit under-furnished. Mrs. Ellsworth's influence was evident already. There were fresh flowers on the table, a coal fire laid and burning low in the hearth, the faint scent of lavender lingering in the air.

"It's charming," Cecily said, twirling once in the open space between the sofa and hearth. "Not grand, but… welcoming."

Lavinia made a sound like she was suppressing a sigh. "It'll do, I suppose."

Georgiana let her gaze drift upward to the crown molding, then to the dark wood architrave above the door. There was beauty in this house. Quiet beauty. A place to hide in plain sight.

After a light supper of cold chicken, warm rolls, and tea,

Cecily excused herself, claiming she was too excited and too tired to manage conversation. Lavinia retired shortly after, complaining of "carriage head" and the scandalous lack of footmen.

Georgiana remained by the hearth in the drawing room, one slippered foot curled beneath her on the settee. James stood near the window, the long drape pushed aside slightly as he looked out over the gaslit street. Even from across the room, she could sense the tension in his shoulders, the careful stillness that meant his mind was working.

"Is something troubling you?" she asked softly.

His shoulders rose and fell. "That man on the street today. Julian Fane. There's something between you, isn't there? I could feel your terror."

She nodded, then stared into the fire for a moment, her hands twisting in her lap. Her pulse had finally begun to slow, but her throat still felt tight. "I should've told you about him sooner."

James turned. "Tell me now."

She looked up, and his expression held none of the teasing warmth she had come to know. It was still and serious, a man bracing for whatever truth she had to give. The firelight caught the sharp line of his jaw, and something low in her stomach fluttered despite everything.

So she gave it.

"Julian Fane is the younger brother of Thomas Fane. He was Robert's closest friend. They were companions, in the way Society doesn't name aloud." She paused, watching for James's reaction. There was none. No flinch, no raised brow. Only stillness. "Julian knew about his brother and Robert and looked the other way. However, he was resentful that his older brother was the heir and not him, since he couldn't see Thomas marrying anytime soon. From the first time I met Julian, I sensed hostility toward Robert. I thought it was because of the relationship Thomas and Robert shared. But I came to realize later that it was really about me."

"Go on," he said, his voice deadly quiet.

"Julian and I were forced together more often than I liked. He grew fond of me, I suppose you could say. However, I didn't return the feeling. He always made me feel as if I wanted to wash my hands." She shifted her gaze to the fire, her hands trembling now. "One evening, Julian came to the house uninvited. Robert was away. Julian was let in by our housekeeper—he was the brother of Robert's best friend, so no one saw any need for concern. But I was caught unawares. Julian cornered me in the drawing room."

James's hands slowly curled into fists at his sides.

"He grabbed me and tried to kiss me, saying that we might as well act on our feelings since Thomas and Robert clearly did. I pushed him away but he laughed and said I'd only resisted because I didn't yet know I wanted him. He said he understood the coldness of my marriage and that he could provide what Robert could not." Her voice broke. "He frightened me. And disgusted me."

The muscle in James's jaw jumped. "Did he—"

"No. Not that night. I managed to get away. I told Robert the next day, and he told Julian never to return. This was only a month before Robert was killed." She took a shuddering breath. "Julian came to the funeral, pushing himself on me once again. I begged Thomas to keep him away from me, which he did. I left for Brighton after that, hoping Julian wouldn't know where I was, but he found out. Somehow, he always knows where I am."

James began to pace, his movements sharp and controlled, like a predator in a cage.

"Julian's never fully left my life. He's written to me, asking for an opportunity to court me now that Robert's gone. Countless letters. I never answer. I've stopped reading them and now just toss them into the fire. I was hopeful that he would not know where I went after I left Brighton. Yet, once again he found me. He has written to me twice since I've been at Ashford Manor."

"Twice?" James's voice was lethal. "You burned those letters in front of me. Why didn't you tell me?"

"I was ashamed. And afraid."

"Afraid of what?"

"That if I'm too unkind to him, he'll tell everyone about his brother and Robert. If he exposed his brother's secret life, he would become the heir. And I wouldn't care if it was just me that would be exposed, but it's Cecily. If this gets out, it could ruin her chances of a good match."

James stopped pacing and turned to face her, his eyes blazing. "Let me understand this correctly. This bastard assaulted you, has been stalking you for over a year, and you've been handling it alone because you're worried about protecting his brother's secret?"

"When you put it like that—"

"That's exactly how it is." His voice was cold as winter steel. "He's a predator, Georgiana. And he's been hunting you."

She felt tears prick her eyes. "I don't know what to do to get rid of him. I'm so tired, James. So tired of carrying all this weight."

James crossed the room in three quick strides and sat beside her on the settee, gathering her hands in his. "You're not alone anymore. I'm going to end this."

"What will you do?"

"Whatever it takes." The promise in his voice was absolute. "He'll never touch you again. Never threaten you again. I'll make sure of it."

"But how? You can't be with me every second. And he'll be at all the balls—"

"Then I'll be at all the balls too. I'll shadow you so closely he'll never get near you." His thumb traced across her knuckles. "And if he tries anything, anything at all, I'll destroy him."

The fierce protectiveness in his voice sent warmth flooding through her. "You'd do that? For me?"

"Georgiana." He lifted their joined hands and pressed his lips to her knuckles. "I'd do anything for you."

The air between them crackled with tension. She could see

the want in his eyes, could feel it in the way his thumb continued to stroke across her skin. She leaned closer, drawn by the warmth and safety he represented.

"James…"

He cupped her face with his free hand, his thumb brushing across her cheek. "You're so beautiful. So brave." His voice was rough with emotion. "I want—"

But then he stopped, pulling back slightly even as his eyes remained locked on hers.

"No." He dropped his hands and stood abruptly, putting distance between them. "Not like this."

"What?" Confusion and hurt flooded through her.

He ran a hand through his hair, his breathing unsteady. "You're upset and vulnerable. You've just told me about the worst thing that's happened to you, and I won't take advantage of that."

"You wouldn't be taking advantage—"

"Wouldn't I?" He turned to face her, and she saw the struggle in his expression. "You're seeking comfort, protection. And God knows I want to give you both. But when I…" He swallowed hard. "When we come together, it should be because you want me, not because you need someone to chase away the shadows."

Her heart clenched at the nobility in his words, even as her body ached for his touch. "And if I said I wanted you anyway?"

"Then I'd ask you to tell me again tomorrow. When Julian Fane isn't lurking in your thoughts. When you can be certain it's really me you want, and not just safety."

The restraint was clearly costing him—she could see it in the tension of his shoulders, in the way his hands clenched at his sides. But he held firm.

"You deserve better than a man who would take advantage of your fear," he said quietly. "You deserve someone who will wait until you're sure."

Tears spilled down her cheeks, but they weren't tears of sadness. They were tears of gratitude, of recognition. Here was a man who could have what he wanted but chose to protect her from her own vulnerability instead.

"Thank you," she whispered.

He nodded once, sharp and decisive. "Go to bed, Georgiana. Tomorrow we'll start planning how to keep you safe."

She stood on unsteady legs and moved toward the door, pausing on the threshold. "James?"

"Yes?"

"Tomorrow I'll still want you."

She left him standing there, and as she climbed the stairs, she heard him release a shuddering breath that told her how much his restraint had cost him.

CHAPTER EIGHTEEN

James

WHAT IN THE name of God was he doing? He hadn't meant to touch her like that. Not for so long. Not with such obvious affection. Not like she was his.

James sat in the chair before his bedroom hearth, staring at the small, flickering fire. His hands still felt the warmth of her fingers pressed between them. He'd kissed her knuckles. And then walked away like some kind of saint when every fiber of his being had screamed at him to pull her closer.

The look in her eyes when he'd stepped back—hurt, confusion, want—was burned into his memory. Christ, he wanted her. Had wanted to kiss her properly, to show her exactly how he felt about Julian Fane's threats, to promise her with his body what his words couldn't express.

Instead, he'd been noble. Honorable. It felt like hell.

The door creaked open. Digby stepped inside, impeccably dressed despite the hour.

"Shall I draw your bath, my lord?"

"No." James reached for the brandy on the side table and poured a generous measure. "Just leave me to my misery."

Digby moved to stoke the fire, the familiar scrape of iron against stone filling the silence. "Might I venture that the evening didn't go as planned?"

James let out a harsh laugh. "I had the woman I'm half-mad

for in my arms, and I walked away."

"Ah." Digby arranged tomorrow's clothes with quiet precision. "And you regret the walking away?"

"I regret everything. Walking away, not walking away sooner, letting myself care for her in the first place." James took a burning sip of brandy. "She deserves better than a man who wakes screaming from nightmares."

"And yet she chooses to sit beside you every evening. To trust you with her sister's future. To confide her darkest fears."

"Because she doesn't know what I really am."

Digby paused in his work. "What are you, my lord?"

The question caught James off guard. "A man with blood on his hands. A man who's seen too much darkness."

"I see a man who's clawed his way out of ruin with nothing but grit and honor. A man who remembers every name in the village and would throw himself in front of a carriage to save a stranger." Digby's voice was gentle but firm. "That's what Mrs. Fairfax sees too."

James stared into the fire. "What if I break her? She's been through hell already."

"What if you heal each other?" Digby stepped forward, his expression unusually serious. "Whom we love is not really in our control, my lord. But what might truly hurt her is words that are never spoken, feelings never expressed. Love that is never given a chance to bloom."

"You sound like you speak from experience."

A shadow crossed Digby's face. "I let someone special marry another because I was too afraid to show her who I really was. Love has no use for cowards, my lord. None at all."

The admission hung in the air between them. James studied his valet with new understanding.

"She said she'd still want me tomorrow," James said quietly.

"Then perhaps you should believe her."

James nodded slowly, feeling something settle in his chest. Tomorrow he would deal with Julian Fane. And tomorrow he would stop running from what he felt for Georgiana.

"Thank you, Digby."

"It is my honor to serve, my lord. In all things."

As Digby quietly left the room, James remained by the fire, planning. Julian Fane had made his first mistake by showing himself today. James would make sure it was his last.

THE NEXT MORNING, James rose to a note from his brother, informing him that he would be calling upon him later that morning. He had arrived in Town two days prior and was looking forward to seeing him.

The sisters had all gone out to look at the shops and buy a few last-minute items for the ball they were to attend that evening and Lavinia had accepted a luncheon invitation, leaving him alone to await Sebastian's visit. It was late morning by the time he arrived, announced by Mr. Isherwood. James rose as he entered, delighted to see him. He embraced his brother warmly.

"It's good to see you," James said. "I'll ring for tea. How is Rose?"

"She sends her warmest regards and deep apologies that she couldn't come herself," Sebastian said, settling into a chair near the fire. "She's keeping to her chambers these days, but she insisted I bring you this." He handed James a small wrapped package. "And she made me promise to tell her everything about Mrs. Fairfax and her sister."

James smiled as he rang for tea. "Rose is always curious about people."

"Especially when it concerns her brother-in-law's romantic entanglements."

He shot his brother a look. "Entanglement might be a strong statement."

"Whatever you say, little brother." Sebastian glanced around the townhome's modest but elegant drawing room. "This isn't bad, considering your last-minute decision to attend the Season."

"It'll do for a few months," James said. "I'd have liked it to be finer for Cecily's sake, but it was the best we could do on short notice."

A maid arrived with tea, giving James a moment to think of how exactly to describe the last few months. After the maid left, James began to tell his brother about Mrs. Fairfax, their deep friendship, her financial difficulties, and her desire to make her late husband's business a success so that Cecily might have a Season and marry well.

"I felt compelled to help," he said. "Given our past, I have a soft spot for those needing a second chance."

"It's wonderful," Sebastian said. "You'll change her life. All of their lives."

"I hope so."

"And what of Mrs. Fairfax herself?" Sebastian peered at him with eyes that knew every inch of his brother. They had no secrets. They'd clung to each other and Sophia when they'd been sent to live with the Langstons. It was no use trying to avoid the topic.

"I find myself in the unenviable position of harboring romantic feelings for her."

"I suspected as much. Why is that unenviable?" Sebastian leaned back in his chair. "Rose and I can attest that friendship is the foundation of every good marriage."

James ran a hand through his hair. "Because she's been through enough without adding my complications to her life."

"I disagree," Sebastian said firmly. "And so would Rose, if she were here. I suppose you believe you're not good enough for her."

James nodded, a lump rising in his throat. His brother knew him too well. "Her first marriage was loveless—romantically speaking, anyway. She deserves so much more than a man with my demons."

"We've heard rumors about Mr. Fairfax," Sebastian said

carefully.

"How?"

"Rose's lady's maid, Prudence. She knows everything about everyone, and Rose insisted I ask about the family's... circumstances."

James spoke quietly as he told his brother what he knew of Robert's situation, then his voice hardened as he described Julian Fane. "The blackguard was here when we arrived yesterday. He's been stalking her for over a year—writing letters, somehow always knowing where she is. He cornered her once, tried to force himself on her."

Sebastian's expression darkened. "That's more than troubling. What are you doing about it?"

"I told her I'd handle it, but I need help. He'll be at tonight's ball, probably every social event this Season. I can't be with her every moment."

"You won't have to be alone in this," Sebastian said. "I'll help keep watch. We'll arrange for others we trust to do the same."

"Rose will be furious she's missing all the excitement," Sebastian continued with a slight smile. "She's already declared that Mrs. Fairfax is family, by the way. I'm to tell you that you're a fool if you don't pursue her properly."

James felt heat creep up his neck. "Rose said that? How did she know?"

"In far more colorful language, actually. She also said, and I quote, 'Tell James that any woman willing to restore Ashford Manor clearly has excellent judgment and the patience of a saint—exactly what he needs.' As far as how she knew? You did speak of her quite fondly and very often in your letters over the last few months."

Despite everything, James found himself smiling. "Yes, perhaps I was a bit effusive."

"Speaking of tonight, are you prepared for the ball?"

"My new valet, Digby, has been drilling me relentlessly. He even hired a dancing master—a rather horrible little Frenchman who beat me into submission. Georgie helped by partnering with me for practice."

Sebastian's eyebrows rose. "You call her Georgie?"

"It suits her," James said defensively.

"I'm sure it does." Sebastian's knowing smile was infuriating.

Before James could respond, the front door opened down the hall. A flurry of voices followed—Cecily's bright with excitement, Georgiana's lower and more measured, the swish of packages and the clink of hatboxes.

Their footsteps approached and then Georgiana entered first, cheeks pink from the cold, arms laden with parcels. She paused mid-step when she saw Sebastian. "Oh! I didn't realize we had company."

James stood, far too quickly. "We do."

She wore a deep violet pelisse trimmed in black, the fur collar brushing against the soft skin of her neck. Her hair was slightly windblown, her lips still parted in surprise. His stomach fluttered. After last night's restraint, seeing her again felt like a physical blow.

Cecily stepped in behind her, carrying an enormous hatbox, beaming with delight. "The modiste said I have excellent shoulders," she announced to the room, before realizing a stranger was present. She covered her mouth, flushing. "Oh, I'm sorry. I didn't realize we had company."

James introduced the women to his brother.

Georgiana offered a graceful curtsy. "I've heard so much about you, Lord Ashford."

"And I you, Mrs. Fairfax." He turned to Cecily. "And you as well, Miss Linley."

Cecily curtsied, smiling widely. "Your brother has saved us. We are so grateful."

"From what I hear, you and your sister do very well taking care of yourselves," Sebastian said. "But thank you."

"I am sorry Lady Ashford couldn't join you," Georgiana said.

"She sends her regrets and this." Sebastian gestured to the wrapped package. "She's eager to meet you when she's able, but for now she's keeping to her chambers."

Understanding flickered in Georgiana's eyes, and she nodded with a gentle smile. "Please give her my regards."

James watched the exchange, noting how naturally Georgiana handled the delicate situation, how Sebastian's eyes lit up with immediate approval. His brother was studying them both with barely concealed amusement.

"We're grateful to you for giving Ashford Manor life again," Sebastian said. "I cannot express adequately how much it means to our family."

"It has been my pleasure," Georgiana said. "In fact, the project has been a great gift in more ways than one. Your family home is extraordinary."

"We should let you visit," Cecily said, still clutching her hatbox. "We have much to prepare for tonight's ball. I am nervous as a cat facing a den of wolves."

"You will do splendidly," Sebastian said. "I look forward to seeing you both there."

After the sisters had excused themselves and their footsteps faded up the stairs, Sebastian turned to James with obvious amusement.

"Well, this explains why you were so eager to sponsor a Season."

"It's not—" James began.

"Of course it's not," Sebastian said mildly, though his expression suggested he believed otherwise entirely. "And I'm sure calling her 'Georgie' is perfectly innocent as well."

James ran a hand through his hair, heat creeping up his neck. "You are a terrible brother."

"And you are clearly smitten," Sebastian replied cheerfully. "Rose is going to be absolutely delighted when I tell her."

James looked away, knowing any protest would only make things worse.

He was well and truly doomed—and his brother was enjoying every minute of it.

Chapter Nineteen

Georgiana

GEORGIANA'S BREATH CAUGHT as she looked around the ballroom, taking in the vaulted ceiling painted with cherubs and trailing vines in soft pastels. Marble columns wrapped in gold leaf rose from the edges of the room, their capitals carved with delicate acanthus leaves that seemed to flutter in the flickering light. Between them, tall windows draped in midnight blue velvet were pulled back to reveal moonlit gardens beyond, the glass reflecting the warm amber glow within.

Tables draped in cream silk lined the perimeter, their surfaces scattered with white roses and baby's breath, the petals still dewy from the conservatory. Crystal goblets caught the light at every angle, throwing tiny rainbows across the pristine tablecloths. The air itself seemed to shimmer with the heat of so many bodies in motion, perfumed with jasmine and the faint sweetness of champagne.

At the room's heart, the dance floor gleamed like a mirror-dark lake, its parquet pattern of mahogany and cherry wood polished to such perfection that the dancers seemed to float above their own reflections. The musicians, half-hidden in their alcove behind a screen of carved rosewood, drew their bows across strings that sang of longing and possibility.

Above it all, three magnificent chandeliers cast light about the room.

She turned to her sister, who looked luminous, her gown of pale sage green tulle catching the candlelight. The color made her hair gleam like polished copper and lent her an ethereal softness that made Georgiana's chest swell with pride. Her baby sister was a beauty. A single pearl nestled in the hollow of her throat, and her gloves were embroidered at the wrists with tiny ivy leaves, a subtle nod to youth and new beginnings. Cecily practically sparkled as she was led to the floor by a smiling young viscount introduced earlier that evening.

Georgiana stood near the perimeter of the room, gloved hands clasped at her waist. Her soft lavender silk gown felt good against her skin. The bodice was modestly cut, the sleeves edged with pale silver embroidery that shimmered only when she moved. A small cluster of violets had been pinned at her shoulder, fitting for a widow still navigating Society's unspoken rules. Despite the color, she did not feel like a widow tonight, only a woman.

In fact, she'd been pleased at her reflection in the mirror. She'd felt beautiful and young, with her hair pinned just so by Mrs. Ellsworth and her eyes sparkling with excitement. For so many months now, the weight of caring for her sister and mother and the worry about all of their futures had made her feel tired and used up. Tonight, however, she almost felt the hope of new possibilities.

She turned, catching James watching her from across the room. Lord help her, he looked devastatingly handsome in a deep charcoal coat with a crisp white cravat, the fine cut of his waistcoat hinting at the strength beneath it. His dark hair was freshly trimmed, his boots polished to a military gleam. But it wasn't his clothes that made her pulse flutter. It was the way he looked at her. Not with heat or possessiveness. More respect and admiration if she were to name it.

Their eyes met. Held.

And then, of course, Lavinia arrived, appearing at Georgiana's elbow in a storm of violet plumes and lime-green satin.

"Don't you think I did well? Dressing our Lord Ashford?" Lavinia asked.

"I have to agree, Mother. He looks as fine as any gentleman here."

Her mother smiled, a hint of triumph gleaming in her eyes. "Thank you, darling. That's lovely to hear. And look at Cecily, dancing as if she'd been to dozens of balls."

Georgiana's gaze tracked Cecily's movements across the floor. "It's true. She's graceful and so pretty. And from her full dance card, I would say we're not the only ones who think so."

"You're looking beautiful too," Lavinia said. "Lord Ashford can't keep his eyes off of you."

"Don't be silly." She glanced back to see if he remained in the same spot, but he was gone. She tried to ignore the little knot of disappointment that he hadn't come her way.

"This is going to be a marvelous evening," Lavinia said. "I'm going to sneak off to play cards with a few of my friends. Do you mind?"

Lavinia was being suspiciously agreeable. What was she up to?

Georgiana smiled tightly. "No, by all means, go and enjoy yourself. You deserve a fun night."

"Darling, how sweet of you to say." Lavinia gave her hand a quick squeeze before she turned to head out of the ballroom to the art room, just off the main hall.

But instead of going, Lavinia's face lit up at the sight of someone approaching from behind Georgiana.

"Oh, Mr. Fane. How delightful to see you again," Lavinia said.

No. No. No.

Georgiana's fingers tightened on her dance card, the delicate ivory threatening to snap. She turned slowly, stomach lurching.

Julian drew close, his midnight coat immaculate, his smile sharp as broken glass beneath its polish. "Lady Linley, good evening." He offered Lavinia a bow before turning to Georgiana.

His gaze traveled down her form with deliberate slowness. "Mrs. Fairfax. You are exquisite this evening."

A droplet of sweat made its way down her spine. She wanted desperately to excuse herself and find James but she knew it was impossible. Not with her mother there and people around to notice.

Lavinia beamed, oblivious. "Mr. Fane, how nice you look this evening."

"How kind of you, Lady Linley. I'm feeling rather festive." Julian stepped closer. Too close. The scent of his cologne made her stomach turn.

Lavinia tittered. "I do hope you have time to dance with at least one of my daughters this evening."

"I shall do my very best," Julian said.

Lavinia spotted someone she knew and was off before Georgiana could stop her.

"Alone at last," Julian said, leaning slightly to whisper in her ear.

"I believe Cecily's about to finish her dance." Georgiana kept her voice steady despite the tremor in her hands. "I must go."

But Julian shifted, blocking her path with practiced ease. "Why must you always run from me?" His voice dropped, meant only for her. "I hoped to find you here tonight. And beg for a dance."

"I don't think so," Georgiana whispered, aware of others around them. "You know how I feel about you. I've no interest in you whatsoever. The sooner you understand that, the better. There are plenty of single women here tonight who would love the pleasure of your company. However, I am most certainly not one of them."

"You wound me, Mrs. Fairfax." Julian placed his hand over his heart.

To his credit, he did seem hurt. What was wrong with this man? Was he truly this delusional? And why her anyway? There were plenty of other women with much fewer complications.

Julian's eyes glittered with something ugly. "Though I can't help but wonder if you're merely playing hard to get. It's what you did before, after all. Leading me on with those pretty blushes, those stolen moments in the garden. We both know how close we came to—"

"Stop." The word came out sharp enough to draw glances. Georgiana forced her voice lower, though fury made her hands shake. "Whatever fantasy you've constructed in your head, it bears no resemblance to reality. You assaulted me and then refused to leave me alone. Let me make it perfectly clear. I do not want your company. Ever. In fact, I do not want you anywhere near me."

"Temper, temper." He smiled, reaching as if to touch her arm.

She stepped back, but her heel caught her hem. For one horrifying moment, she thought she might stumble but then, like a miracle, James appeared by her side, solid as a shield, his hand steadying her elbow with perfect propriety.

"There you are." James's voice cut through the noise like a cavalry charge. "Mrs. Fairfax, you promised me this waltz."

Julian straightened, irritation flashing across his features. "I wasn't aware men kept dance cards, Ashford."

James's expression remained pleasant, but his eyes were as cold as a winter morning in February. "I keep one. For her and her only." He shifted slightly, his broad shoulders blocking her view of Julian entirely. "If you'll excuse us."

"I'll find you later," Julian said to her.

James drew closer to Julian, his right fist clenched. "No, you will not find her. You will not harass her this evening. Or any other one, for that matter."

"And what gives you the right to say such a thing?" Julian asked, eyes flashing with contempt. "You have no hold on her."

"Neither do you," James said. "Good night, Mr. Fane."

Georgiana took his arm, fingers gripping perhaps tighter than necessary. As they walked away, her legs started to shake.

James led her onto the floor. The opening notes of a waltz filled the air, and he drew her into position with infinite care. Through her gloves, she felt the warmth of his hand, steady and sure.

"You're trembling," he murmured, beginning to move them in slow circles.

"I'll be fine." But her voice cracked slightly.

"Look at me." When she did, his eyes held hers with fierce protectiveness. "He won't touch you. Not while I draw breath."

The silk of her skirts whispered against his legs as they turned. His thumb brushed against her palm through the delicate kid leather. Such a small gesture, but it anchored her.

"I don't know what I'm going to do," she whispered. "He's going to be everywhere this Season."

"And so will I." He spun her gently, the room blurring into watercolor around them. "I'm not afraid to hurt him if I have to."

She pressed her lips together, fighting the burn behind her eyes.

"I'm here and I'm not going anywhere." He drew her perhaps an inch closer than strict propriety allowed.

Around them, the ballroom continued its glittering dance, but in James's arms, Georgiana finally felt the world steady. When they turned again, she caught sight of Cecily, still laughing with her partner, blissfully unaware.

Safe. They were both safe.

For now, that was enough.

THE FINAL NOTES of the waltz dissolved into a ripple of polite applause, but Georgiana hardly heard them. Her hand remained in James's, their fingers still linked as if the music hadn't stopped, as if the world beyond this moment had simply ceased to exist.

"Come." His thumb brushed across her knuckles. "Let's get

you some air."

She didn't protest. Her pulse still raced, her breath shallow from more than just the exertion of dancing. James led her through the throng with the confidence of a man on a mission, his hand warm and steady at the small of her back. The crowd parted for him instinctively—some out of respect, others of curiosity—but he barely seemed to notice.

They stepped through a set of tall glass doors and onto the terrace. Cool night air swept over them, fragrant with lilacs and the green scent of dew-heavy grass. Beyond the balustrade, the garden flickered with lanterns and moonlight. A few guests strolled the gravel paths or stood in murmuring pairs beneath sculpted hedges, but out here, under the open sky, the world felt blessedly quiet.

Georgiana wrapped her arms around herself, the silk of her gown no match for the evening chill.

Without a word, James shrugged out of his coat. When he draped it around her shoulders, his hands lingered for just a heartbeat, his fingers grazing the curve of her neck. The coat carried his warmth, his scent. She wanted to bury her face in the fabric. Forever.

"Thank you." She pulled the glorious jacket tighter.

He moved to stand beside her at the railing, close enough that she could feel the heat radiating from his body. His hands gripped the stone balustrade, knuckles white in the moonlight.

"I'm sorry he frightened you."

"He always frightens me." She stared into the garden, her own hands finding the cool stone. Their fingers were inches apart now, so close she could feel the tension humming between them. "Even when he's smiling. Especially when he's smiling. He has this way of making threats sound like compliments. But I know better." She stopped, jaw clenching. "Last time, he told me how easy it would be to ruin us completely. How a few well-placed rumors about my Mother, about our finances, and about Robert's past could destroy any hope Cecily has for a decent match."

A muscle ticked in James's jaw. The sounds of distant strains of a quadrille and the rustling of leaves filled the silence between them.

"I wanted to—" James's voice came out rough. He stopped, drew a breath. "I wanted to drag him outside and make him answer for every word."

She turned to look at him then, startled by the violence threading through his tone.

His eyes were hard, his voice low and fierce. "I know it would have caused a scene. I knew I couldn't do it. But God help me, Georgie, I wanted to."

Her throat tightened. Part of her was thrilled at his protective fury, even as the practical part of her recoiled. "I don't want you drawn into his web. Julian doesn't fight fair. He'd find a way to twist it, make it your scandal instead of his."

"I don't care about scandal. We've weathered enough of it, haven't we?" He stopped, turning toward her fully. "I care about you much more than I care about gossip."

She stared up at him. "James, I feel as if all I do is cause you trouble." Her voice came out breathless. "I cannot have you or your family hurt over my mistakes."

"I'm not trying to make this harder." He closed the gap between them until they were merely an inch apart, close enough now that she had to tilt her head back to meet his eyes. "But none of this is your fault. Regardless, I can't pretend it doesn't make me want to tear him apart."

"I understand. If I had your strength I may have done so already." She pressed her palms flat against the stone railing, grounding herself even as every instinct screamed at her to close the distance between them. "I don't want anything to get in the way of Cecily's success. He makes me very uneasy in that regard. He's treacherous. And this is our only chance. Because of your generosity."

"You don't have to shoulder this alone." His hand moved on the railing, his pinky finger brushing against hers. Such a small touch, yet it sent fire racing up her arm. "Not any longer."

The gentle words nearly undid her. "I've always had to. And I've felt so alone." The admission slipped out raw and unguarded. She started to turn away, mortified.

"I know, Georgie girl. I know." His voice was infinitely gentle. "You've been carrying everyone for so long. Your mother, Cecily, the business. No one's ever carried you."

Her eyes burned. She bit her lip hard enough to taste copper, fighting the sob that wanted to escape. Here, in the moonlight with his coat around her shoulders and his warmth so close she could lean into it, she felt dangerously close to crumbling.

A beat passed. Two.

"You don't have to be strong every moment," James said. "If you ever do fall apart, I'll be there to catch you."

The ache in her chest was so sudden, so sharp, she nearly gasped. For one wild moment, she imagined what it would feel like to let go and step into his arms and let him take care of her. The longing was so fierce it frightened her.

His hand found hers then, fingers intertwining, warm and solid and real.

They stood like that, hands linked, bodies so close she could feel his breath stirring her hair. Her pulse thundered. If he leaned down—if she rose up on her toes—their lips would meet.

The thought made her tremble.

But he didn't move. And neither did she.

Because they both knew that people watched for moments just like this between a man and woman, opening her up to ruin.

Even if every fiber of her being ached to let him take her in his arms and kiss her senseless.

Out of the corner of her eye, she saw several men walking onto the terrace. She stiffened. "I should go back inside. We cannot risk being alone like this." The words scraped her throat raw.

He nodded, but his fingers tightened on hers for just a moment before releasing her. "I'll join you in a few minutes."

She stepped away on unsteady legs, shrugging out of his coat and holding it out to him. When he took it, their fingers brushed again, and she nearly lost her resolve entirely.

At the glass doors, she couldn't help but glance back.

James stood alone at the railing, his white shirt gleaming in the moonlight, staring out at the garden as though trying to make sense of forces beyond his control.

Walking away from him felt like tearing something vital from her chest. And the terrifying truth was, she wasn't sure how many more times she'd be strong enough to do it. She must remember her reason for everything. Cecily.

With that in mind, she walked back inside.

THE SUPPER ROOM shimmered with candlelight and gossip. Long tables gleamed beneath white linen and silver, laden with lobster patties nestled in pastry shells, champagne jellies quivering like her own unsteady nerves, and syllabub so frothy it seemed barely tethered to its dish. The cloying sweetness in the air made her stomach turn. Towers of sugared fruits gleamed beneath cloches of etched glass, while footmen moved like clockwork among the crowd, offering delicacies and replenishing wine.

Georgiana pressed her back against the cool marble column, a glass of chilled punch trembling slightly in her gloved hand. She was still catching her breath after the waltz, but the coolness of the drink did nothing for the heat pulsing in her cheeks or the hammering of her pulse against her too-tight corset.

The scent of jasmine and sherry announced her mother's approach before Lavinia materialized at her side.

"Darling," Lavinia said, settling beside her with a concerned frown. "You look flushed. Are you feeling quite well?"

"I needed some air earlier." Georgiana's voice came out steadier than she felt.

"Ah." Lavinia nodded knowingly. "Lady Pemberton was just telling me about poor Mrs. Hartwell. Do you remember her? The colonel's widow? She's forty-three now and living on her sister's charity. Such a difficult position for a woman alone."

Georgiana's grip tightened on her glass. "What does that have to do with anything?"

"Oh, nothing specific, dearest. Only that Lady Standish mentioned—in the kindest way, you understand—that you and Lord Ashford stepped outside together." Lavinia selected a candied violet from a passing tray, her tone carefully casual. "I do hope you're being careful about appearances."

The marble column felt suddenly inadequate against Georgiana's back. "We spoke for perhaps five minutes."

"I'm sure it was perfectly innocent." Lavinia's voice carried just a hint of worry. "But people do talk, and your reputation is so important. Especially now that Cecily needs every advantage."

The words stung because they were true. Georgiana forced herself to breathe. "I'm well aware of what's at stake."

"Of course you are. You're such a thoughtful girl." Lavinia paused, studying her daughter's face with apparent maternal concern. "I must confess, I'm rather puzzled. After what I witnessed that night before we left Ashford Manor—the way he looked at you, touched your face—I rather expected he would have declared himself by now."

Georgiana's cheeks burned. She couldn't very well explain the intimacy of their conversations, the way he'd restrained himself out of honor, the promises hanging unspoken between them.

"There's nothing to tell. We are friends."

Lavinia's expression softened with what looked like genuine bewilderment. "Oh, my dear. The way that man looks at you. What on earth is he waiting for?" She shook her head gently. "I only worry that you might be waiting for something that may not come. You're still young enough to attract a good man's attention, but not indefinitely."

Each word felt like a small weight settling on Georgiana's chest. The glittering room suddenly felt suffocating.

"I need to return to Cecily," she managed.

"Of course, darling." Lavinia touched her arm lightly. "I only want what's best for you. For both my girls. But perhaps... perhaps you might encourage him along? Men can be so slow to act without a little guidance."

Before Georgiana could respond, Cecily came hurrying up to them, cheeks bright with excitement.

"I've met the most wonderful man. And his mother's invited us all to dinner the day after tomorrow."

"How lovely," Lavinia said, her earlier concerns immediately forgotten. "Tell us everything."

"It's Viscount Alderidge's son, Nathaniel," Cecily bubbled.

Lavinia's eyes lit up with genuine pleasure. "What excellent news. I must introduce myself to his mother properly."

As her mother moved away, Georgiana felt the familiar weight of expectation settling around her shoulders. Lavinia's words had been loving, even reasonable—which somehow made them cut all the deeper.

CHAPTER TWENTY

James

TWO NIGHTS AFTER the ball, James escorted Lady Linley, Georgiana, and Cecily to dinner hosted by the charming Lady Alderidge. Two nights, and he still hadn't managed a single private moment with Georgiana since their encounter on the terrace.

Not for lack of trying. The past two days had been a whirlwind of social obligations—morning calls that required his presence as Cecily's sponsor, afternoon visits where Lavinia hovered like a protective hawk, and evening engagements where propriety demanded they maintain careful distance. Every time he'd caught Georgiana's eye across a drawing room, every time their fingers had brushed during an introduction, the memory of her trembling in his coat had threatened to undo his composure entirely.

He had been delighted to learn that Sebastian would also be in attendance tonight. He was not delighted to learn that somehow Julian Fane had managed to score an invitation as well.

The Alderidge estate was grand in a way that whispered, rather than shouted, its wealth. Wainscoting gleamed in the candlelight, polished so fine it mirrored the flame. A massive chandelier presided over the entrance hall like a benevolent monarch, scattering gold and crystal rainbows across every marble surface.

James adjusted his cravat as they entered the drawing room, flanked by Georgiana, Cecily, and Lavinia—each dressed to charm in their own very different ways. The drawing room itself was a masterpiece of understated elegance: deep burgundy walls lined with portraits of distinguished ancestors, their painted eyes seeming to follow the guests with benevolent curiosity. Persian rugs in rich jewel tones warmed the polished oak floors, while crystal decanters caught the firelight from their perch on a mahogany sideboard that had likely graced this room for generations.

Georgiana had chosen deep plum silk, elegant and understated, with a delicate silver pin at her collarbone. The color made her skin luminous, though James noticed the slight tension in her shoulders, the way her gloved fingers worried at her reticule's silk cord. Cecily sparkled beside her in pale blue satin, her copper hair swept up like a flame, but her usual animated chatter had given way to an endearing breathlessness that spoke of nerves and hope in equal measure. Lavinia was a confection of feathers, lime green taffeta, and barely veiled ambition—practically vibrating with satisfaction at having secured an invitation to such an exclusive gathering.

The pre-dinner ritual unfolded with the precision of a well-rehearsed dance. Footmen moved silently between the guests, offering crystal glasses of sherry and port from silver trays that reflected the warm glow of beeswax candles. The scent of bergamot and lavender wafted from strategically placed arrangements of hothouse flowers, mingling with the masculine notes of tobacco and leather from the gentlemen's clothing.

The Viscount and Viscountess of Alderidge greeted them with warm smiles and practiced poise. Lady Alderidge was a striking woman in her fifties, her dark hair threaded with silver and her intelligent brown eyes missing nothing as she assessed each guest. She wore deep emerald silk that complemented her husband's more subdued burgundy velvet jacket. The Viscount himself was tall and distinguished, with graying temples and the kind of quiet authority that came from generations of responsibility.

Their son—Nathaniel—stepped forward to greet Cecily with a soft-spoken compliment and an easy smile that sent the girl glowing. "Miss Linley, you look absolutely radiant this evening. That shade of blue is quite perfect on you." He was tall, refined, with golden-brown hair that caught the candlelight and intelligent gray eyes that seemed genuinely delighted by Cecily's presence. There was an innate confidence about him that required neither arrogance nor flourish—the kind of man who listened more than he spoke and made others feel heard.

James approved of him instantly. The young man's attention to Cecily was respectful but unmistakably interested, and when she stammered a thank you, color rising prettily in her cheeks, Nathaniel's smile only grew warmer. And that only made James's gut twist tighter.

Because it wasn't Cecily he was watching tonight.

It was Georgiana. He wished he could be alone with her and tell her once and for all his intentions. He wanted her hand in marriage. He wanted her all to himself. Forever.

From his strategic position near the marble fireplace, James had a clear view of the entire room. He accepted a glass of port from a passing footman and settled into observation, noting how the other guests—a carefully curated selection of Society's finest—moved through their social choreography. Lord Pemberton held court near the French doors that led to the terrace, regaling a small group with tales of his recent hunting expedition. The Honorable Mrs. Whitmore examined a collection of miniatures displayed on an étagère, her lorgnette glinting as she made appreciative murmurs. Two younger gentlemen engaged in animated discussion about the merits of their respective hunters, while their wives compared the latest fashions from Bond Street.

But James's attention kept drifting to Georgiana. All evening, his eyes tracked her. The gentle way she leaned toward her sister during conversation, offering quiet encouragement when Cecily's nerves threatened to overwhelm her social graces. The subtle grace with which she navigated the drawing room, moving from group to group with an ease that belied the tension he could read in the set of her spine. How she smiled when she thought no one was watching—a soft, genuine expression so different from her public composure that it made his chest tighten with longing.

He watched her accept Lady Alderidge's compliments on her gown with modest gratitude, saw her deflect questions about her own marriage prospects with practiced skill, turning the conversation back to Cecily's accomplishments with the deftness of a seasoned diplomat. When Mrs. Whitmore made a pointed remark about the challenges facing families of "uncertain fortune," Georgiana's response was so perfectly pitched— acknowledging the truth while maintaining dignity—that even James felt a surge of admiration.

James was acutely aware of Julian's presence throughout the evening—the way the man circled like a predator, always positioning himself to catch Georgiana alone. But James had played this game before, in different circumstances with higher stakes. Every time Julian moved closer to Georgiana, James was there: offering his arm when she needed to cross the room, engaging her in conversation when Julian approached, ensuring she was never without protection. It was a delicate dance, one that required him to appear casual while remaining constantly vigilant. But he also knew tonight wasn't about him. It was about Cecily. About preserving the future they were all working so hard to build. Young Nathaniel was clearly smitten, and the Alderidges seemed genuinely pleased with the match developing between their heir and the copper-haired beauty who hung on his every word. This was the culmination of months of careful planning, the moment when Cecily's debut would either secure her future or leave her vulnerable to Society's fickleness.

So he kept his distance, playing his role as the protective guardian, engaging in conversations about business and politics while his heart remained wholly focused on the woman in plum silk who moved through the room like poetry made flesh.

Until the footman announced dinner and guests began filtering toward the dining room in order of precedence, James realized with a start that cut through his contentment like a blade: Georgiana had been seated by Julian Fane. And James was on the opposite end of the table.

JAMES HAD BEEN talking politely to Lord Alderidge when movement in his peripheral vision made him glance toward the drawing room's far end. The guests had begun to drift between the drawing room and the adjacent music room, where Lady Alderidge's youngest daughter was demonstrating her skill at the pianoforte. Conversations flowed smoothly, punctuated by the soft clink of crystal and the rustle of silk.

Then he saw Julian Fane slip past the farthest marble column and out through a side door that led to the conservatory, only moments after Georgiana had risen from her seat near the windows, presumably to find the ladies' retiring room.

But what if she'd gone out to the terrace for a breath of fresh air? She'd mentioned how warm the room was when they'd first arrived. What if Julian had seen her exit and was following her?

An instinct, immediate and sickening, to find her—to protect her at all costs—overwhelmed any other concern. He excused himself, not even waiting for a response before setting down his glass and following. His footsteps were muffled by the thick Persian runners that lined the corridor, but his pulse thundered in his ears loud enough to drown out the distant sound of polite laughter from the drawing room.

The hallway beyond the main entertaining rooms was quieter, lit only by a few wall sconces that cast dancing shadows on the papered walls. Portraits of long-dead Alderidges watched him pass with oil-painted eyes. The terrace doors stood ajar at the corridor's end, spilling moonlight across the polished floor.

The scent of blooming lilac and something sweeter—perhaps the honey fragrance of hawthorn blossoms, or the heady perfume of early wisteria—met him as he stepped outside. But there was something else underneath it, something that made his skin crawl. The metallic taste of fear, sharp and wrong in the crisp spring air.

The terrace was a marvel of stone and wrought iron, filled with hardy plants that thrived in London's unpredictable climate. Moonlight streamed across the flagstone, painting everything in shades of silver and shadow. Bare branches of climbing roses rustled softly against their supports, and somewhere water trickled from a small fountain designed to look like a natural spring.

But all James could see was Julian.

He had her backed against a marble pedestal that held a particularly prized orchid, its white blooms seeming to glow in the darkness. One hand was braced near her shoulder, his body angled to trap her against the cold stone. He was leaning in too close, his voice a silken threat that carried easily in the humid air.

"I've been patient long enough," Julian whispered, his breath stirring the delicate curls that had escaped her coiffure. "You can't keep running from what we both know is inevitable. I've already sacrificed everything for you—do you think I care about Thomas's reputation? About the title? I'd burn it all down to have you. You're mine, Georgiana. You always have been."

Georgiana's face was pale as porcelain, her eyes wide with terror that made James's hands clench into fists. She was pressed as far back against the pedestal as she could manage, her entire body rigid with revulsion.

"Please," she whispered, so quietly James almost missed it. "Someone will see us. Let me go."

"No one is coming." Julian's free hand reached toward her face. She turned her head sharply to avoid his touch. "They're all too busy with your sister's little performance. We finally have time to settle this properly."

James didn't think. He moved.

The sound of his footsteps on the terrace's stone floor made them both turn. Relief flooded Georgiana's features. Julian's expression shifted to cold calculation, as if James were nothing more than an inconvenient interruption.

"Step away from her." James's voice cut through the night air like a blade.

Julian turned with deliberate slowness, his hand remaining braced against the pedestal, still caging Georgiana. "Lord Ashford. How tediously predictable." His smile was razor-sharp. "This is a private conversation. You're not needed here."

James stepped forward, using his height and breadth to force Julian back. "She said no. That's all I need to hear."

"Did she?" Julian's mask slipped, revealing something predatory underneath. "You don't know her like I do. She's always wanted me—the way she used to look at me when Robert wasn't watching. She's trembling with need right now."

Rage coursed through his veins, not because he believed his revolting words, but because he could see Georgiana flinch as if she'd been struck. She was indeed trembling—but with disgust and fear.

James's fist connected with Julian's jaw before conscious thought could intervene. The crack echoed across the terrace as Julian staggered backward, crashing into the stone wall. A delicate orchid teetered on its stand before toppling, shattering against the flagstones in a shower of soil and ceramic.

For a moment, the only sounds were Georgiana's sharp intake of breath and the distant tinkle of the fountain. James stood over Julian, every muscle coiled for further violence, while Julian slowly straightened, dabbing at the blood on his lip with a silk handkerchief.

"You think you've won something here?" Julian said softly, his voice deadly calm. "I have nothing left to lose now. My brother's secrets, her husband's secrets—I'll destroy them all if I can't have her. At least then we'll be ruined together."

"Try it." James reached for Georgiana's hand. She took it immediately, her fingers ice-cold and trembling.

Julian's eyes glittered with malicious satisfaction. "Actually, I think I'll start with her reputation. Did you know about her husband's little proclivities? How easily a few whispers could destroy what's left of her standing in Society?"

The threat hung in the air like a poison cloud. James felt Georgiana's grip tighten on his hand, saw the terror that flashed across her features. Footsteps echoed from the corridor—voices, drawn by the crash. This was a disaster. If the guests found Georgiana in a compromising position, it would destroy everything. Her reputation, Cecily's prospects, all of it.

Lady Alderidge appeared first, her face a mask of controlled fury at having her perfect evening disrupted. Behind her came a handful of other guests, their eyes bright with curiosity and scandal-hunger.

In that split second, James made a choice that would change everything.

"There's no cause for concern." He managed to speak with absolute authority. "Mrs. Fairfax is my fiancée. I was defending her honor from an unwelcome advance."

The words hung in the sudden silence. James felt his heart hammering against his ribs as gasps rippled through the small crowd. Beside him, Georgiana went very still.

Julian laughed, the sound harsh as breaking glass. "Lies. If that were true, why wouldn't it be known? She belongs to—"

"She agreed to marry me just tonight," James interrupted, his voice gentling as he looked at Georgiana. This was the greatest gamble of his life, but seeing her cornered, terrified, had made the choice for him. "Making me the happiest man alive."

The silence stretched taut as a bowstring. Georgiana stared up at him, her eyes searching his face as if trying to read his soul. He willed her to see the truth there—that this wasn't just a lie to save her reputation. That he meant every word.

"Yes," she said finally, her voice steady despite the tremor in her hands. "It is I who am made happy. Happier than I ever thought possible."

The murmur that rose from the crowd was like the buzzing of disturbed bees. James heard Lady Alderidge's sharp intake of breath, saw other guests exchanging meaningful looks that would fuel gossip for weeks.

A blur of pale blue silk burst through the doors as Cecily appeared, her face white with panic. "Georgiana! What happened?" Her gaze took in Julian's bloodied lip, James's protective stance, her sister's pale complexion.

"Everything's all right now." Georgiana's voice shook slightly. "James was… defending my honor."

"As we have become engaged just this evening," James said, hoping Cecily would quickly understand.

Cecily's eyes sharpened with just that. She looked between her sister and James, then smiled with surprising composure. "Of course he was. Though I suppose the secret's out now." She turned to address the curious crowd. "As Lord Ashford said, they've only just become engaged. We hadn't planned to announce it so dramatically."

Lavinia materialized behind Cecily like an avenging angel, resplendent in violet feathers and barely contained excitement. "Engaged? Did I hear you correctly?" She pressed a hand to her chest. "Is it true?"

Lady Alderidge nodded approvingly. "Lord Ashford was defending his fiancée's honor from that dreadful man." She gestured toward Julian like he was something meant for the rubbish bin.

Lavinia paused, then drew herself up with sudden dignity, as if remembering her role. "Well, of course. I knew this would happen eventually. A mother always knows these things. Lord Ashford is a true gentleman. Worthy of my eldest daughter, just as I have foreseen all along." Lavinia spoke with a growing confidence, smoothing her skirt. "I told Georgiana from the very beginning that Lord Ashford was clearly smitten."

"As you say, mothers always know," Lady Alderidge said, sharing a smile with Lavinia.

Before the situation could spiral further into further theatrics, Lady Alderidge gestured to her butler, who had appeared as if summoned. "Please escort Mr. Fane to his carriage. He is no longer welcome in this house."

Julian straightened his cravat with deliberate care, his eyes never leaving Georgiana's face. "This isn't over. Enjoy your little charade. But we both know the truth."

As the butler firmly guided Julian away, his parting look promised retribution that made Georgiana shrink closer to James's side.

Once Julian disappeared into the corridor, an awkward silence fell. The other guests stood uncertainly, clearly torn between returning to the party and lingering for more drama.

"Perhaps we should return to the drawing room," Lady Alderidge suggested with pointed diplomacy. "I believe congratulations are in order, but this evening has been quite eventful enough."

As the small crowd began to disperse, murmuring excitedly among themselves, James found himself alone with Georgiana, Cecily, and Lavinia on the moonlit terrace.

Lavinia's voice was trembling with emotion, "Well, this is certainly not how I imagined the evening would unfold. But I could not be more thrilled to welcome Lord Ashford into our family. I should open a matchmaking business. I have such a keen eye for these things."

Georgiana shot her mother a look that could have frozen flame, but Lavinia was too overcome with joy to notice.

"We should go back inside," Georgiana said quietly, her composure beginning to crack. "People will talk if we linger."

"Let them talk," Cecily said fiercely, linking arms with her sister. "Let them talk about how Lord Ashford protected you and how happy you'll be together."

As they walked back toward the house, James caught Georgiana's eye. The question he couldn't ask aloud hung between them: *Was any of it real? Do you want this? Or have I just trapped us both in an elaborate lie?*

Her answering look was unreadable, a mixture of gratitude, confusion, and something that might have been hope.

God help him, he prayed it was hope.

CHAPTER TWENTY-ONE
Georgiana

THEY LEFT THE party soon thereafter, but it felt like walking through a dream. She couldn't remember if she'd said anything further to her sister or mother or if Lady Alderidge was furious over the interruption to her dignified dinner party. All she knew is that Julian was finished. He could not hurt her again.

James's hand at her elbow guided her through the crush of guests, past curious stares and barely concealed whispers. Georgiana smiled and nodded at appropriate moments, but her mind reeled with a single, thundering question: *Did he mean it?*

Or had he simply been saving her from ruin? It was like him to do so, putting her needs above his own. He'd done so much for her and Cecily. Now, this. Would he feel trapped? Forced to make good on his public promise? She couldn't bear to think she'd wrecked his life simply because she had felt a panic taking over her and had stumbled outside for fresh air. She'd not seen Julian until it was too late. If James had not come when he did, she would have been forced to marry Julian or risk Cecily's reputation. That she could not have abided, thus she would have had to accept that Julian Fane had won.

The carriage waited in the torchlit courtyard, blessedly dim and private. James handed her up, his touch careful, almost hesitant, as if he could not be sure she wanted to leave with him. If he only knew her true feelings. She would go anywhere with him. Just for one more moment with him. What would become of them now?

She settled against the leather seat, keenly aware of every sound: the creak of springs as he climbed in beside her, the driver's call to the horses, the first rumble of wheels against cobblestone. The space felt impossibly small. His thigh was inches from hers, close enough that she caught the warmth radiating from his body.

Neither of them spoke.

Street lamps cast fleeting pools of golden light through the window, illuminating the strong line of James's jaw, the way his hands rested tense against his knees, the careful distance he maintained between them despite the intimate confines.

Georgiana pulled off her evening gloves with trembling fingers, needing something to do with her hands. The soft kid leather seemed suddenly suffocating. James's gaze dropped to watch her fumble with the tiny pearl buttons.

"Georgie, look at me," James said quietly, her name barely audible above the carriage wheels.

She did so, and the concern in his dark eyes nearly undid her. Was it possible that he didn't regret his declaration? His false marriage proposal? She thought he might be angry with her but it did not seem so. In fact, he seemed worried, not mad. Unsure even.

"Are you all right?" James asked.

The simple question shattered something inside her chest. *All right?* How could she be all right when her entire world had shifted on its axis in the space of a heartbeat?

"I don't know," she whispered, the honesty escaping before she could stop it. "I don't know what to think, other than I'm sorry I've dragged you into my mess."

The carriage hit a rut in the road, jolting them closer together. His shoulder brushed hers, and the contact sent electricity singing through her nerves. She didn't pull away. Couldn't.

James stroked her cheek with the knuckles of his right hand.

"I told you before. You are not alone. Not when I'm here."

"Did you mean it?" The words tumbled out, raw and desperate. "When you said… what you said. Was it real, or were you simply saving me?"

"Real." His voice was hoarse with emotion. "How could you not know my heart? Why else would I have done something so reckless? I would do anything for you, Georgie. It's you I want. You I dream of. Since the first, it's been you. I was simply too cowardly to tell you how I felt. Because if you do not share my feelings, I might, quite simply, die of heartbreak."

"How is it possible? Me? Of all the women in the world?" She turned to face him fully, her heart hammering against her ribs. In the shifting lamplight, his expression was naked, vulnerable in a way she'd never seen before.

"I'm consumed with you. You've become my whole world. The person I want to see first thing in the morning and the last thing at night. I've tortured myself, trying to convince myself that you would never want a man like me. Or any man at all. You're so strong and independent and all I want is to take care of you. Yet, you don't need me. Not really."

"I do, though. Isn't that clear after what's happened?"

"Do you mean because of Fane?"

"Yes. If you'd not come out when you did, I would be ruined. I'd have had to marry him."

"Over my dead body. Or his. One way or the other, I would not have allowed that to happen. It just so happens that I love you to distraction. Even if you don't love me now, perhaps you could at some point? I will be good to you. Give you anything you want, including your work. You may live freely as my wife. I won't dictate your life, only ask that you will be part of mine."

Her breath caught. "James. I'm overwhelmed."

"I am too. Overwhelmed by you. Every time you walk into a room, all I can think is how I long to take you in my arms and kiss you. Or talk to you all night long, asking you every detail of your thoughts and dreams. I want to give you everything the world has to offer. When I saw you there, trapped by him, I thought this night might end in a death. Either his or mine. But I hope instead that you'll see how pure my heart is when it comes to you. I'm mad for you, Georgie. Utterly, completely in love with you."

The carriage turned a corner, and suddenly they were pressed together, her silk skirts pooling against his dark trousers. She could feel his breath against her temple, could smell the spice and salt of his skin.

"Please, say something," James said. "Or I might perish right here in this carriage."

"There's so much I want to say. Words upon words that have gathered in the back of my throat for weeks now. I was so afraid you were being noble. That you felt obligated to rescue me. Again. But it's not that, is it? You love me? Just as I love you."

His hand found hers in the darkness, fingers interlacing with desperate tenderness. "Never obligation. Never rescue." His thumb traced across her knuckles, and she shivered at the touch. "You rescued me. From loneliness. From a bleak existence, fueled by revenge instead of love. You've changed me from the bitter little boy who missed his father to a man who wants to be a good husband and father. A family man. Me. Isn't it funny when you really think about it?"

"Not funny. More like a miracle." Tears spilled down her cheeks, and she didn't care. "I didn't think it was possible you shared my feelings. I have so little experience when it comes to matters of the heart. I only know my work, not love."

"But you love me?"

"I do. From the first moment you came storming out of your house, I think I fell for you."

"How is it possible? I've longed for this moment but never thought it would really happen." He lifted their joined hands to press her knuckles against his lips. "I want you to be my wife, Georgie. You're my heart."

"And you're mine."

The carriage began to slow, the familiar streets of Grosvenor

Crescent coming into view. Their private moment was ending, but somehow that made it more precious, more urgent.

"James, does this mean you'll kiss me? Finally?" She turned toward him fully. In the confined space, their faces were mere inches apart.

"Are you sure?"

"We're engaged, after all. No harm can come to us now." Georgiana's voice trembled with anticipation but also desire. If he didn't kiss her right then and there, she might never recover. "Please, don't make me beg."

James let out a quiet laugh as his hand lifted to cradle her cheek. His thumb brushed away a tear that had yet to fall. "Then God help me, I will kiss you now."

He leaned in slowly, giving her every chance to pull away. But she didn't. She moved toward him with equal urgency, as if she'd been waiting her whole life for this moment. Because she had.

Their lips met in a kiss that was at once tender and consuming. It was not the tentative brush of a man uncertain of his welcome, nor the desperate claiming of one driven by possession. It was love in motion.

Georgiana's hand slid up to his shoulder, anchoring herself as the world tilted. His other arm wrapped around her waist, drawing her closer until the layers of fabric between them felt irrelevant. She felt everything—his warmth, his strength, his love as he deepened the kiss by slow, aching degrees.

When they finally parted, breathless and flushed, she smiled up at him. "Well, I finally understand what all the fuss is about. The subject of poets and playwrights? It all makes sense now."

Chuckling, he kissed her once more, softer this time, with a kind of wonder that made her chest ache. "And to think—I get to kiss you whenever I want. How could a man deserve such a blessing?"

"When can we marry? I don't want to wait."

"We'll do it as soon as possible. I don't want to wait a moment longer to take you into my bed."

Outside, the carriage had come to a stop. But inside, their journey had only just begun.

THE NEXT MORNING, still feeling as if she were in a happy dream, Georgiana was reviewing the invitations when Isherwood appeared in the doorway, his expression carefully neutral in that way that always preceded unwelcome news.

"Lady Alderidge has called, madam. She requests an audience with you and Miss Linley."

The card slipped from Georgiana's fingers. Nathaniel's mother. Here. Now. Without warning.

"Show her to the drawing room," she said. "And ask Mrs. Ellsworth to prepare tea immediately."

She found Cecily in the morning room, embroidering by the window, and delivered the news in hushed, urgent tones.

"She's here?" Cecily's needle stilled, her face paling. "Oh, dear me."

"Breathe." Georgiana smoothed her sister's hair with hands that trembled only slightly. "We knew this moment would come. We're ready."

But neither of them felt ready as they entered the drawing room to find Lady Alderidge already seated, her posture regal as a queen holding court. She was a handsome woman in her fifties, with dark brown eyes and an air of authority that could freeze boiling water.

"Lady Alderidge." Georgiana curtsied perfectly, Cecily following suit. "What an unexpected pleasure."

"Mrs. Fairfax. Miss Linley." The countess inclined her head a precise degree. "I do hope you'll forgive the impropriety of calling unannounced, but given recent developments, I felt we should become acquainted without delay."

They arranged themselves carefully—Georgiana and Cecily on the settee, Lady Alderidge in the wingback chair that seemed to transform into a throne beneath her. Mrs. Ellsworth arrived with tea service, her timing impeccable as always.

Lavinia appeared moments later, somewhat breathless and dressed in sky blue. "I apologize for my tardiness. We were out late last night, as you know."

"Not at all," Lady Alderidge said. "I thought it only right to pay my respects, especially considering the friendship blossoming between our children."

Georgiana poured tea with steady hands, though her pulse hammered. "We're grateful for your visit. And for Nathaniel's kindness to Cecily."

Lady Alderidge studied them each in turn. "My son has not been interested in anyone until now. He's taken with you, Miss Linley." Her gaze shifted to Georgiana. "However, I must be certain he is not being led by infatuation into a family of uncertain standing. Last night was quite eventful—not in a way I would wish repeated. And your sudden engagement to Lord Ashford naturally raises questions."

Georgiana felt Cecily tense beside her. "Any mother would wish to protect her son's future. But our family, while not always fortunate, has been raised with care and integrity."

"It's rumored you've been restoring Lord Ashford's home and calling yourself an architect," Lady Alderidge continued. "Some may wonder if your engagement was fabricated to cover scandal, or perhaps to elevate your sister's prospects."

"My late husband trained me in his profession," Georgiana said firmly. "After his death, I had to support my family as I could. As for my engagement—Lord Ashford agreed to sponsor Cecily before any understanding between us. Our feelings developed naturally."

Lady Alderidge turned to Cecily. "Tell me, child, what makes you suitable for my son?"

Cecily straightened, and something shifted in her bearing.

Gone was the nervous girl who'd been surprised by the visit. "I offer myself, Lady Alderidge. My heart, my loyalty, my determination to be worthy of the love I've been given. I hope to be judged not by my father's mistakes but by the life I intend to build with your son—founded on genuine affection and mutual respect."

Lady Alderidge's teacup paused halfway to her lips. For a moment, approval flickered in her eyes.

The drawing room door opened and James appeared, as if summoned by the tension. "Lady Alderidge, what an unexpected pleasure. I apologize for not being here to greet you—I was meeting with my solicitor about my upcoming nuptials."

Moving to stand beside Georgiana's chair, he placed a gentle, possessive hand on her shoulder.

"Lady Alderidge has expressed concerns about our engagement," Georgiana said.

"Then let me address them directly." James's voice carried quiet conviction. "I love Georgiana. Our engagement is not a stratagem but the culmination of months of growing affection. And if you have concerns about Cecily's future, know that I intend to settle ten thousand pounds upon her as a dowry, plus a trust for her future children. Both sisters are family to me now."

Lady Alderidge's expression softened almost imperceptibly. "I can see that you love her. Rare these days to see a love match."

She rose gracefully, gathering her reticule. "I feel I understand the situation better now. I shall convey my thoughts to my husband and son."

"I do hope to entertain a call from Nathaniel regarding his intentions," James said. "Cecily is very dear to me."

"There is no better man than my son," Lady Alderidge replied, then smiled—just a small lift at the corners of her mouth, but enough to transform her countenance entirely. "Good day to you all."

After the door closed behind her, the room seemed to exhale collectively.

"Well," Lavinia said brightly, reaching for a leftover biscuit, "that could have gone worse."

"She was terrifying," Cecily admitted. "But I think I held my own."

"You were magnificent," Georgiana said, beaming at her sister.

James squeezed Georgiana's shoulder gently. "We all were. And now," he said, his eyes twinkling, "I believe we have some happy news to share with the rest of our household."

They had survived their first test as an engaged couple. Georgiana had the feeling there would be many more to come—but with James beside her, she found she was no longer afraid.

CHAPTER TWENTY-TWO

James

ON A WARM June afternoon, the gravel drive crunched beneath the carriage wheels as it pulled to a stop before the grand front steps of Ashford Manor. James stood at the top, the late afternoon sun behind him, hands tucked behind his back, feeling like a boy. His brother and sister were there for his wedding but also to see the restoration. He could hardly wait to show them all the work he and Georgiana had done together.

The carriage door opened, and Sophia was the first to emerge, a blur of pale blue muslin and graceful energy. "James, there you are."

He was halfway down the steps before she reached him, pulling her into a tight embrace. His baby sister. Here at last.

"You look well, James," she said, stepping back to study him with narrowed eyes. "Positively glowing with happiness."

"Women glow. I'm simply ruggedly handsome," James said.

"The rugged seems to have been loved out of you," Sophia said.

He took in his sister, marveling at her beauty. She was fair and delicate, with a graceful way of moving and speaking. No one would believe, looking at her now, that she'd been forced into servitude at the young age of eight.

"You're beautiful, little sister. And I'm so glad you're here."

"I wouldn't be anywhere else in the world. Although, I will

miss Amelia. I've not often been away from her."

"I've no doubt she'll survive until your return to work," James said. "Speaking of which, Sebastian and I would like to have a talk about your future."

Sophia groaned. "I know." She turned as Sebastian descended from the carriage with his usual soldier's bearing, his expression unreadable.

"Sebastian," James said, extending a hand. "Welcome home."

"Thank you." Sebastian clasped his hand, then pulled him into a quick, rough hug. "Rose sends her deepest regrets that she couldn't make the journey. She's expecting the baby any day now and couldn't risk traveling, even the short distance."

"Of course," James said. "I'd hoped she could meet Georgiana before the wedding, but there will be time enough after her confinement."

"She's beside herself that she's missing it, but she made me promise to tell you how happy she is for you both. And she's already planning to spoil your future children terribly."

James grinned. "I look forward to that. Now come inside. Let me show you what we've accomplished."

They followed him through the great doors and into the main hall, where sunlight filtered through the newly restored leaded glass windows, casting golden patterns across the polished floors. Fresh plaster, soft hues of cream and blue, and woodwork gleamed like it had thirteen years ago. But it wasn't just the grandeur that made it seem like home. It was as if the memories of the happy times they'd shared together had lingered just below the surface, waiting to come out of hiding.

"I feared you would not be able to get the scent of mildew out but it smells like it once did." Sebastian gazed up at the chandelier now glowing with dozens of fresh beeswax tapers.

Sophia ran her fingers along the curve of the banister. "I didn't think we'd ever see this place again." Her voice softened. "I can remember the day they came for us."

James nodded slowly. "I do as well. But perhaps it's time to make new memories. Happy ones. All of us here together."

He led them through the rooms, beginning with the library, the dining room, and then onto the drawing room. Finally, he showed them the ballroom. "We have a ball planned for later in the summer," James said. "My soon to be mother-in-law has driven me nearly mad with the planning but it's kept her occupied, which is an important feat, believe me."

"It's all spectacular," Sebastian said.

"You can see Georgiana's imprint on every inch of the place, but the past is here too. She found a way to honor our dear Papa with every choice."

There was a moment of silence before Sophia crossed to him and wrapped her arms around his waist. "You both have done very well."

"I hope you'll consider moving in with us," James said to his sister. "And that you and Georgie will become best friends."

"We'll speak of it later," Sophia said dismissively.

Sebastian cleared his throat. "We will be discussing it later, Sophia."

Sophia's blue eyes glittered rebelliously. James had his doubts that he or Sebastian would get their way. She seemed strangely attached to her employer and the child when she should be focusing on finding a husband.

He led them to the back terrace, where the view of the orchards spread wide and golden in the late-day sun. Chairs and ribbons were already being arranged for the upcoming wedding. Flowers bloomed in tidy rows, and the scent of lilac and honeysuckle drifted on the breeze.

"This is where Cecily put her focus and I think they turned out beautifully. She loves the gardens and spent a lot of time planning their return."

Sophia's eyes glistened. "It's perfect."

Sebastian nodded once, his expression softened by something rare and quiet. "You did well, brother. Rose will be so sorry she missed seeing it, but perhaps you and Georgiana could visit once she's recovered. It's only an hour's drive, after all."

"I'd like that very much," James said, warmth spreading through his chest at the thought of introducing his wife to his sister-in-law. "For now, I'm just grateful you're both here."

They stood together in silence for a long while, the three of them watching the wind dance through the gardens.

IN THE DINING room that night, candlelight danced across freshly polished silver and crystal. Each place had been carefully arranged by Mrs. Ellsworth, love in every detail. Downstairs, Mrs. Honeycutt had spent the day preparing a feast for their pre-nuptials supper.

What an evening it would be. Being here with his siblings felt like a triumph all over again. From the time they'd learned of their family's redemption, he'd been slowly healing and coming to terms with what had happened to three innocent children. And here they were, enjoying a meal as if those hard days were only a nightmare instead of truly lived. The nature of human resilience never ceased to amaze him. The strength the three of them had shown during those frightening, painful years, were proof of what the human spirit could endure.

His brother's courage and commitment to finding the truth and then exposing it had at first seemed impossible to James. But he'd done it. Not only that, but he'd not turned away from the love between him and Rose, despite its complications. Despite the gossip that followed.

James settled into his chair at the head of the long mahogany table, the worn wood smooth beneath his palms as he surveyed his family. The table stretched nearly the full length of the dining room, dressed in white linen and trimmed with blue and cream ribbons in honor of the wedding festivities. A simple garland of fresh greenery and white roses ran down the center, interspersed with small silver candlesticks whose flames flickered in the warm June breeze drifting in through the open windows.

To his right sat Georgiana, resplendent in soft rose silk, her fingers loosely curled around a crystal wineglass. Beyond her was Cecily, laughing at something Lavinia had said from across the table. Lavinia, looking delighted with herself in a new emerald hued gown, was seated to James's left. Sebastian seemed relaxed and so unlike the fighting mad man he'd been before exposing Wentworth for the murdering liar he was. Sophia had taken the place beside Georgiana, wearing a soft blue gown.

After everyone was seated and wine had been poured by a competent footman, closely watched by Isherwood, James clinked his glass. "I'd like to propose a toast. Three years ago, when I won a tavern in a card game, it had seemed our fortune had changed. But my older brother could not accept that as our fate. Despite the odds of failure, perhaps even disaster, he changed our lives, brought us back to the legacy left to us by our dear Papa. Our reputations and fortunes restored, we are now living the lives we should have been all along. Thanks to my Georgie, our family's home shines once more. In a way, the restoration of our childhood home has mirrored that of my heart and spirit. Both were brought back to life by this beautiful woman who tomorrow will become my wife."

Georgiana looked over at him, tears shimmering in her eyes. How he loved her. He'd not thought that possible either, but he had been mistaken. Love had come for him and he had opened his heart and arms to the exquisite woman next to him. Each day that passed, he loved her more fervently.

James continued. "It might be our instinct to feel bitter for the father they took from us and the abuse we endured at the Langstons but I do not believe that serves us. Instead, we must approach the past and the future as Papa would have. With faith and hope and love. It is not with anger that we embark on this next season of our life, but one of gratitude for all that's been restored to us." His voice thickened with emotion. "When I look around this table and see the faces of all I hold most dear, it seems almost too good to be true. Thank you, Sebastian, for never giving up on our family. Thank you, Georgie, for loving me regardless of my flaws. And to the rest of you, I'm thankful you're here to celebrate the union of our two families. May God continue to bless each and every one of us."

Everyone raised their glasses, tears and laughter coming in equal measure.

The first course arrived, a white asparagus soup with cream and a touch of nutmeg, garnished with a sprig of fresh thyme from the garden, light puff pastry shells filled with tender pigeon in a white wine and tarragon sauce and a small plate of pickled vegetables and radishes in herb vinegar. Lastly, barley bread still warm from the oven, served with honeyed butter and wild strawberry preserves.

Lavinia beamed as she looked down at her soup bowl. "This is delightful. If only those who rejected me from Society could see me now, in this fine home, with my daughter about to marry Lord Ashford. When I think of the sacrifices I've made for my girls, it's all been worth it."

James noticed Georgiana and Cecily exchange a glance that held annoyance and humor. Lavinia had become much more docile and cooperative since his engagement to Georgie. He had assumed their good fortune would have made her more obnoxious but it had seemed to calm her. It hadn't taken away her vanity or self-absorption, but one could not expect a miracle.

They'd asked her to stay with them, even though Georgie was afraid the woman might drive her to madness. But in the end, Lavinia was Georgie's mother. It was their duty to take care of her. Lavinia had accepted their offer with her usual martyr act, saying how much she would enjoy London but she knew her dear daughter needed her so what could she do but say yes?

His gaze landed on his sister, who seemed distracted and even a little sad. She'd been delighted to hear of his upcoming marriage and seemed to be excited to visit their old home. However, since her arrival, he'd sensed a melancholy. Even a restlessness that made him think she'd rather be elsewhere. Surely not with the child she cared for?

"Sophia, we must speak about the upcoming Season and your participation," Sebastian said firmly, in his big brother voice. "It's important you have a chance to secure an excellent marriage. We have the dowry for you now. There's no reason to delay it any longer."

"You are getting older," James said softly. "It would behoove us to present you next Season."

Sophia looked down at her plate. "I don't want a Season. I've told you before. I am committed to staying with Amelia. I am all she has ever known. I can't betray her now."

"What of Lord Montrose? Isn't he her guardian?" Sebastian gestured with his fork. "He can hire another governess. You, dear sister, are a lady now, not staff."

"What if I don't want to be a lady?" Sophia asked.

Lavinia gasped. "Oh dear me, you mustn't say such things." She leaned forward slightly. "Think of the balls and the parties and all the men swooning over you."

"It is fun," Cecily said, shyly. "And you might find a love match, as I've done."

James hid a smile behind his hand. His soon to be sister-in-law was as starry-eyed as one could be, glowing and sailing about the manor with a slight smile displayed on her pretty face. Their families had announced her engagement to Nathaniel just last week. They would be married in the fall and move to his family's estate. Georgiana would miss her terribly. Hopefully, they would be able to visit often.

The crystal clinked softly as Sophia set down her glass with deliberate care. "Amelia is only just two years old. Lord Montrose is gone from dawn until dusk with estate business. I am the closest thing she has to a mother and I will not abandon her."

James studied his sister. There was something fierce about the way she spoke about the little girl. A quality that sounded very much like a mother. But what of this Montrose? From what he understood, the man was a good sort—a gentleman who had taken responsibility for his orphaned niece when tragedy struck his family. James had heard he was a man of deep integrity, despite the obvious grief he must have felt about the death of his sister and brother-in-law and the shock of learning he was to care for an infant. Was there more to this than just the baby? Had his sister fallen in love with her employer?

Georgiana reached under the table to squeeze his knee. She was thinking the same thing.

"We don't have to decide anything tonight," Georgiana said gently. "This is the evening before James's and my wedding. A night of celebration."

"Here, here," Sebastian said, looking slightly abashed.

The second course arrived—delicate trout glistening with lemon balm butter, roast capon carved with care and arranged beside spring carrots and young onions, and tureens of new potatoes steeped in mint and salt. As they enjoyed the food, conversation flowed easily, with Sebastian describing the changes he'd made to his estate's business practices. Taking them from illegal brandy smuggling to legitimate and lawful enterprises had not been easy, but Sebastian was so clever that they were past the worst. And now there would be a baby. James could hardly wait to meet his niece or nephew.

The third course arrived. Tender lamb cutlets glazed in red-currant, spinach and mushroom tart with its flaky golden crust, roasted marrow squash drizzled with creamy béchamel, and wine had warmed everyone's cheeks and spirits.

"I do feel terrible for the lambs," Cecily said mournfully. "But they're delicious."

"Dearest, perhaps you should acquire a dog when you marry," Georgiana said to her sister.

Cecily brightened. "That's a splendid idea. Someone to keep me company when Nathaniel is taking care of business. He's also said I am to have free rein of the gardens. I've already started working on my design."

"What about you, Georgiana?" Sebastian asked. "Will you continue to pursue business opportunities now that you'll be married?"

This had been a topic of much debate between them. James had encouraged Georgie to do as she pleased. If she wanted to continue her work, he had no intention of stopping her. However, she'd come to the conclusion that helping to run the estate and continuing their work bringing life back to the village would be enough to keep her busy. He had convinced her to take one of the rooms for an art studio, where she could draw and paint whatever she wished.

James secretly hoped that motherhood would soon be yet another focus for his smart wife but he did not say the words out loud, afraid he might hurt her if there were no children in their future. One could not take these things for granted.

Dessert was a procession of lemon syllabub, elderflower and gooseberry tart, and jewel-toned fruits nestled beside wheels of Wensleydale and Stilton.

They enjoyed the delicacies, still chattering away. To think, tomorrow he would be able to take Georgie into his bed. He was counting the hours until he could take her in his arms and show her just exactly how much he loved her.

THE LITTLE STONE church nestled just outside the village gleamed in the morning light, its weathered arches softened by garlands of spring blossoms. Sunlight streamed through the high windows, casting golden patterns over the polished pews and flickering across the stone floor like blessings. The air was sweet with the scent of apple blossoms and old stone, touched by the lingering fragrance of beeswax candles.

James stood at the front of the nave, hands clasped behind his back, his heart thudding like a drum in his chest. The cool morning air from the open doors raised gooseflesh along his arms, but he barely noticed. *This is real*, he told himself, the words a prayer and a promise. *She's coming. She chose me.* The vicar arranged the prayer book on the lectern with quiet precision. All around him, the pews were filled with friends, neighbors, and family. Faces familiar and beloved. Sophia sat near the front, Lavinia and Cecily beside them, all four looking emotional but joyful.

The doors creaked open.

A hush fell.

And then, Georgiana.

She appeared in a wash of light, her gown of soft ivory and palest gold glowing like candlelight against her skin. The silk rustled softly with each step, and her veil shimmered, pinned in place by a single rosebud. Her gaze found his immediately, steady and serene, but he caught the slight tremor in her breath, the way her fingers tightened just once on her bouquet.

And at her side, solemn and proud, walked Sebastian.

James couldn't breathe.

The sight of his brother, leading the woman he loved down the aisle, moved him profoundly. For a moment, the years fell away—grief, loss, the long climb back from ruin. All of it dissolved in the sunlight, and in her smile. *This is what redemption looks like. Sebastian bringing her to me. Me, finally worthy to receive her.*

They reached the front, and Sebastian pressed Georgiana's hand into James's, his eyes glinting with quiet emotion. He leaned close, his voice rough with feeling. "Be happy, James."

"Thank you," James whispered, the words carrying the weight of everything unsaid between them. "For everything."

Sebastian stepped back, and James turned to face Georgiana fully. She reached up with her free hand to straighten his cravat, a tender, wifely gesture that made his throat close.

The vicar began the service, his voice echoing gently through the ancient stone. James heard very little beyond the words he'd been waiting a lifetime to say.

"I, James, take thee Georgiana, to my wedded Wife, to have and to hold from this day forward, for better for worse, for richer for poorer, in sickness and in health, to love and to cherish, till death us do part, according to God's holy ordinance; and thereto I give thee my troth."

Her voice, clear but trembling slightly, followed. "I, Georgiana, take thee James, to my wedded Husband, to have and to hold from this day forward, for better for worse, for richer for poorer, in sickness and in health, to love, cherish, and to obey, till death us do part, according to God's holy ordinance; and thereto I give thee my troth."

And then, it was done. After months of yearning and longing, she was his wife.

When the vicar pronounced them husband and wife, James did not hesitate. He reached for her veil with shaking fingers, lifted it, and kissed her gently. He would save passion for later that night. For now, he wanted his friends and family, as well as the lady before him, to know how he worshiped her.

James and Georgiana turned to face the congregation. Married at long last.

He bent his head and whispered, "Shall we go home, Lady Ashford, and celebrate?"

"Yes," she whispered back, smiling through her tears.

They stepped out into the waiting spring, the air sweet with blossoms and possibility, the bells ringing their promise through the hills.

THE RECEPTION SPILLED from the gardens into the orchards, where long trestle tables groaned beneath platters of roast beef and lamb, glazed ham studded with cloves, and golden capons that had been turning on spits since dawn. Bowls of creamed turnips and buttered parsnips sat alongside trenchers of fresh bread, wheels of aged cheese, and jellies that caught the light like amber. The wedding cake—a towering confection of almond paste and candied fruits soaked in brandy—held court at the center table, surrounded by smaller sweet treats: syllabubs, marchpane, and delicate biscuits dusted with sugar.

Bunting and paper lanterns swayed overhead, casting gentle light as dusk settled over the celebration. The air was sweet with the scent of roasting meat, fresh herbs, and lavender from the nearby hedgerows, all mingling with the warm laughter of guests and the lively strains of a small country ensemble. Two violins, a flute, and a cello played beneath a rose-draped awning, their music weaving through conversations and the gentle clink of pewter cups filled with ale and wine.

Villagers sat alongside manor staff at the long tables, social distinctions softened by the joy of the occasion. The baker's wife shared stories with one of the parlor maids, while old Tom from the stables raised his cup in yet another toast to the newlyweds. Children darted between the tables, their faces sticky with honey cakes, while their mothers called gentle warnings that went largely unheeded.

Cecily and Nathaniel had claimed a spot near the musicians, tapping their feet to the rhythm as they shared a plate of syllabub. Lavinia held court with a cluster of village women, all of them debating the merits of various hat feathers with the serious consideration usually reserved for matters of state. Mrs. Ellsworth sat with the vicar's wife and several townspeople, her cup of tea in hand, offering gentle smiles to everyone who passed. Mrs. Honeycutt was not shy, flitting about, taking compliments about her food as if she expected nothing less. Even Isherwood looked marginally relaxed, though he still supervised the servers with the careful eye of a man who believed celebration was no excuse for slovenly service.

As the evening deepened, couples began to gather before the

makeshift dance area that had been cleared near the musicians. The fiddlers struck up a country dance, and soon the space filled with whirling skirts and stomping feet as villagers and gentry alike joined hands in the familiar steps.

James stood at the edge of it all, his glass forgotten in his hand.

Ashford had risen again, not merely restored, but revived. And in the heart of it all stood Georgiana—laughing with Sophia beneath a flowering pear tree, her cheeks flushed, her hair falling loose from the intricate twist she'd started the day with. The golden light from the lanterns caught the silk of her gown, making her glow like candlelight.

She caught his gaze, and without a word, began to move toward him.

He met her halfway, took her hand, and together they stepped away from the revelry. Beyond the lanterns and the tables and the joyous din of celebration, the orchard grew quiet. The music softened, shifting to a gentle air—something old and wistful, meant for waltzing beneath the stars.

They found each other's arms easily.

Georgiana rested her cheek against his shoulder, and James closed his eyes for a moment, breathing her in. She smelled of the rosewater he had come to know so well.

"You look very pleased, Lord Ashford," she murmured.

"I married you, which makes me very pleased indeed."

Her laugh was soft, secret. "I still can't quite believe it."

He tilted his head and considered. "Yes, it feels like a very good dream. But it's all real. And I am the luckiest man alive."

She leaned back just far enough to meet his gaze. "I am the lucky one."

They swayed together as the notes drifted through the orchard. Behind them, the murmur and music of celebration continued—the scrape of chairs, bursts of laughter, the calling of the country dance. But here in the hush beneath the trees, it was just the two of them, no longer haunted by ruins or regrets.

He kissed her softly and whispered, "Shall we go inside?"

"Soon," she said. "One more dance. I want to savor this moment."

So they stayed, wrapped in twilight and music, as the stars came out and the trees rustled gently overhead. In the distance, the celebration continued, their friends and neighbors and staff united in joy, dancing and feasting under the lanterns until the candles burned low.

Tomorrow would bring responsibilities and letters and tenants and plans.

But tonight, there was only joy.

THE DOOR CLOSED softly behind them, and suddenly they were alone in James's chambers—now, truly, their chambers. At least as far as the night was concerned.

Candles flickered softly across the room, casting dancing shadows on the oak-paneled walls. The bed had been turned down, revealing crisp white linens scattered with rose petals. A small fire crackled in the hearth, warming the space and filling it with the scent of applewood. On the side table sat a bottle of champagne and two crystal glasses, alongside a single white rose in a silver vase.

Georgiana stepped farther into the room, a smile spreading across her face. "James, how lovely."

He moved behind her, his hands settling gently on her upper arms. "I wanted everything to be perfect for you. For us."

"It's beautiful," she said, turning in his arms with bright eyes. Her hands came up to rest against his chest, and he could feel the excitement thrumming through her. "But you know what would make it perfect?"

"What?" His voice was already roughening.

"If you stopped being quite so much of a gentleman." She

rose up on her toes, her lips brushing his ear. "I've been wanting you for months, James Ashford. Burning for you. And now you're finally mine."

The bold declaration sent heat racing through his veins. "Georgie, my God. You may give me a heart attack."

"I know what I want. And it is you." Her hands moved to his cravat with sure fingers. "All of you. Desperately." She pulled back to meet his gaze, her eyes sparkling with determination and desire.

He caught her hands, bringing them to his lips. "Here I am. All of me. And I am fairly desperate myself."

She smiled with newfound mischief. "Though I confess, I have no idea how to get out of this gown without Mrs. Ellsworth's help."

He laughed, the sound rich and warm. "Allow me."

Her boldness seemed to free something in both of them. She helped him with his waistcoat, her touch growing more confident with each button, each layer, removed. When his hands found the fastenings of her gown, she didn't shy away but watched his face with fascination.

Silk pulled at her feet. "I used to wonder what it would be like to have someone look at me the way you're looking at me now."

"How am I looking at you?" James asked.

"Like I'm everything you've ever wanted."

"Because you are." He lifted her in his arms, marveling at the trust and desire shining in her eyes. "God, Georgie, you are everything."

She kissed him as he carried her to the bed, bold and sweet and utterly without reservation. When rose petals scattered beneath them, she laughed—a sound of pure joy that made his heart soar.

"I love you," she whispered against his lips. "Show me how to love you."

With gentle hands and whispered endearments, he did exactly that, and she met him with an enthusiasm and courage that was purely, wonderfully Georgiana.

The fire settled to glowing embers. Outside, the moon climbed over Ashford Estate, silvering the orchard and the lawn below, blessing the beginning of their new life together.

CHAPTER TWENTY-THREE
Georgiana

THE FIRE CRACKLED gently in Georgiana's bedchamber, its warmth spreading across the Aubusson carpet and reflecting off the polished mahogany of her dressing table. Georgiana stood by the tall windows, one hand resting on the windowsill, watching the early evening sky deepen to violet above the frost-touched gardens.

Behind her, Molly, her lady's maid, carefully arranged the pearl combs in Lavinia's auburn hair while Cecily observed from her perch on the window seat.

"Do hold still, my lady," Molly murmured. "These combs are determined to have their own way this evening."

"I cannot help it," Lavinia replied, adjusting her emerald silk gloves for the third time. "What if no one comes? What if they all think to snub us after everything? I have spent months—months—planning every detail of this ball. The humiliation would be complete if we find ourselves dancing alone in an empty ballroom."

"Mother," Georgiana said without turning from the window, "you know perfectly well that everyone has sent their acceptances. We have had more responses than we can comfortably accommodate."

"Acceptances mean nothing," Lavinia insisted. "People can change their minds. They can decide at the last moment that the

Ashford family is still not quite respectable enough for their company."

"Half the county has been angling for an invitation since we sent them out," Cecily added gently. "Your ball will be the event of the season."

"How I wish Rose and Sebastian could be here," Georgiana said. "But it was impossible with the baby so young. She wrote to me just today that little Edward has James's stubborn chin and Sebastian's unfortunate tendency to wake at all hours."

They had named their first born, a son, after Sebastian and James's father, the first Edward. From all accounts both mother and father were overjoyed and smitten with their baby boy.

Lavinia's expression softened slightly. "I'm sure he's adorable."

"We'll see him soon enough," Cecily said.

"There now, my lady," Molly said, stepping back to admire her handiwork.

Georgiana smiled at her maid. "Thank you, Molly, for doing Mother's hair. You may go."

The maid bobbed a curtsy and withdrew, leaving the three women alone.

"Speaking of babies," Georgiana said, drawing closer. "I have something to tell you both."

Cecily's hands stilled where she had been smoothing her skirts. "I think I know. You have a certain look."

"What look?" Lavinia demanded, rising from her chair to study her eldest daughter's face. "What have you two been keeping from me?"

"I've kept nothing from you. In fact, you're the first to know." Georgiana touched her hand to her middle, unable to suppress her smile. "I am with child."

The silence stretched for exactly three heartbeats before Cecily let out a delighted gasp and Lavinia clapped her hands together.

"Oh, my darling girl!" Lavinia rushed forward to embrace

her. "When? How long have you known?"

"Only a few days, though I have suspected for a fortnight. I have not yet told James."

"He will be beside himself with joy," Cecily said warmly, joining their embrace. "Though I confess, I wondered if you might have news when you seemed so ill when the fish course came out."

Georgiana pulled back to look at her sister. "You are remarkably observant. I thought I hid my revulsion well."

A becoming flush rose in Cecily's cheeks. "There's a reason for that." She bit her lower lip. "I was rather hoping to speak with you both privately before the evening began. You see, I also have news."

Lavinia's eyes widened. "Cecily really?"

"I, too, am expecting a baby." Cecily's smile was radiant. "The doctor said we conceived on our wedding night, if he were to venture a guess. Is it not romantic?"

"It is, dearest," Georgiana said. Her sister and Nathaniel had married just a month after her wedding to James.

"And the fish smelled heinous to me too," Cecily said.

From their calculations, the sisters would give birth within weeks of each other. The squealing that followed could likely be heard in the servants' hall, but none of the three women cared a whit for propriety in that moment.

"Sisters, expecting together," Lavinia said, dabbing at her eyes with her handkerchief. "Oh, how jealous everyone will be of me. Two grandbabies at once. I shall tell everyone tonight."

"No, not yet, Mother," Georgiana said. "It is too early to share. Promise me?"

"All right, fine. I shall keep it to myself." Lavinia sniffed in protest but it lacked any real luster. Despite their mother's maddening ways, she had become less so now that she felt safe about her and her daughters' futures. It was remarkable what security could do for one's peace of mind. Even Lavinia Linley's.

"There is something else," Georgiana said once they had

composed themselves somewhat. "I have been corresponding with Sophia, and she remains absolutely steadfast in her refusal to consider a Season. She refuses to leave Amelia. James is appalled but they cannot make her do something she doesn't want to do."

Lavinia clicked her tongue. "Such a shame. She will be a spinster before long if she remains steadfast. Think of all the fun she will miss.'

A soft knock interrupted them, and Molly appeared in the doorway. "Forgive the intrusion, my lady, but our first guests have begun to arrive."

"Already?" Lavinia flew to the mirror to check her appearance one final time.

"And Mother," Cecily said with studied casualness, "I believe Mr. Whitaker wished to speak with James before the dancing began? Do you have any idea why?"

Georgiana and Cecily had discussed it at length and felt certain Mr. Whitaker, who appeared to be a very wealthy capitalist from America, was going to ask for Lavinia's hand. They had met him while in London and he had seemed immediately besotted with Lavinia. The sisters were delighted, but not only because they were happy for their mother. Rather, they were feeling rather giddy that their mother would be an ocean away.

At the mention of the American gentleman's name, Lavinia's cheeks pinked most becomingly. "Oh. Yes. He wishes for James's blessing. He does indeed want to marry me. And best of all? He has agreed that we will live here with you for part of the year. Now that I know babies are coming, I am even more delighted."

Georgiana exchanged a meaningful look with her sister. What was to be done? Their mother was their mother, for better or worse.

"Shall we go then?" Georgiana asked. "To greet our guests and see what the evening holds for each of us?"

"Indeed." Lavinia beamed and practically ran from the room.

THE BALLROOM HAD been transformed.

Garlands of ivy and late-blooming roses wound around the pillars, while hundreds of beeswax candles cast everything in warm, golden light. The musicians, positioned on a small dais decorated with autumn leaves and ribbon, had begun with gentle airs to welcome the arriving guests. Ladies in their finest silks and gentlemen in elegant evening dress filled the space with animated conversation and laughter.

Georgiana moved through the crowd on James's arm, marveling at how many had come. The local gentry, certainly, but also neighbors from farther afield who had not set foot in Ashford Manor since before Lord Ashford was hanged. She recognized familiar faces and caught snatches of conversation, but the evening felt delightfully new and hopeful.

Ashford Manor was alive with joy.

"Lady Ashford." Lady Alderidge approached with a warm smile, resplendent in navy blue and diamonds. "What a magnificent evening you have arranged. The house looks absolutely splendid."

"Thank you, Lady Alderidge. Though I confess the credit belongs largely to my mother and sister. They have worked tirelessly these past weeks to ensure everything was just so."

"Cecily has such an eye for these things," her mother-in-law replied fondly. It warmed Georgiana's heart to see the affection Lady Alderidge obviously felt toward Cecily. Whatever misgivings she'd once had were no longer. In fact, Cecily and her mother-in-law had grown as close as mother and daughter. Georgiana felt envious of the new mother figure in her sister's life, but also relief that everything had worked out so well for her sister. It was easy to lose sight at this point in time that securing Cecily's future had been her reason for everything not so long ago. She'd accomplished not only that but, by a miracle, had found love of her own.

"It must run in the family. And where is our colorful Lavinia this evening? I have heard the most interesting rumors about a certain American gentleman. Are they true?"

"Yes, they are true. She met him at a party in London a few months back and they've been spending time together ever since. I believe we may have a marriage proposal very soon. Mr. Whitaker's asked to speak to James."

"Does that mean she'll move to America?"

"One hopes but it sounds as if they will spend time here as well as the states," Georgiana said.

"You're terrible." But Lady Alderidge laughed just the same.

At the far end of the ballroom, Lavinia glided across the floor in the arms of a tall, distinguished gentleman with silver hair and an unmistakably expensive coat. Mr. Whitaker gazed at Lavinia as though she were the only woman in the room—perhaps the only woman in the world.

"He does seem quite taken with your mother," Lady Alderidge observed. "I'm glad for her."

Georgiana nodded, smiling. "Completely conquered, I should say. And she appears to return the sentiment."

It was true. Lavinia positively glowed as she danced, her laughter carrying above the music. When the set ended, Mr. Whitaker led her to the refreshment table, hovering attentively as she selected a glass of ratafia.

Lady Alderidge placed her hand gently on Georgiana's arm. "I attended a ball here as a young woman, before Lady Ashford passed. It was a magical evening, as I'm sure this one will be. It gives me great pleasure to see her home restored and such a fine event taking place."

"Thank you for your kind words. They mean a lot to me, truly."

"Oh, how interesting." Lady Alderidge gestured subtly with a lift of her chin in the direction of a striking figure in black evening wear. "That's the Honorable Henry Montrose. He is rumored to be rather introverted, so I'm surprised to see him. From what I hear, he's content to stay at his home on the southern coast, away from Society. I do wonder why he's here?"

Henry Montrose. Sophia's employer. Georgiana's mother had sent the invitation to him, not realizing the connection between Sophia and Montrose. Georgiana discreetly observed Montrose. He was handsome, with dark hair neatly combed and expressive, sensitive eyes. Yet, he seemed tense, his expression one of controlled courtesy. She watched as Montrose's gaze swept the room systematically, taking careful inventory of the assembled ladies with what could only be described as grim determination. He did indeed seem like a man on a mission.

Georgiana merely nodded, keeping her worries to herself.

Lady Alderidge continued. "Such a tragic story, the poor man. Taking in a baby as he did after his dear sister and her husband were killed. It's quite something. Do you think he's here to find a wife and mother for his niece?"

"It could very well be." Georgiana's stomach tightened, thinking of Sophia's resolve to stay as his governess. What would she think of a new mistress? A stepmother for Amelia. It would break her. While Henry Montrose searched this ballroom for a suitable bride, Sophia was tucked away in his nursery, playing governess to his ward when she should be here, dancing and laughing as befitted a lady of her birth. The situation grew more troubling by the day.

If only she would listen to reason and come to stay with them, have a Season, and find a suitable match.

Lady Alderidge was called over to greet another friend, just as James came to stand beside her.

"Do you see Montrose?" James asked, barely moving his lips.

"Mother invited him," Georgiana said. "I didn't realize until it was too late."

"Meanwhile Sophia's at his home, caring for his child," James bit out. "I'm not pleased."

"Neither am I."

"What is Sophia thinking?" James asked. "Giving up the life she was born into. Not a servant, but a lady."

"I don't know, but you mustn't interfere. Please."

"I gave you and Sophia my word, and will not break my promise. However, I should like to speak with him." James tucked her arm against his side and headed toward Montrose.

"Mr. Montrose, are you enjoying yourself?" Georgiana asked when they reached him.

Henry turned, his face showing polite pleasure. "Lady Ashford, Lord Ashford. I'm having a nice time, thank you. I haven't attended many functions since I took custody of my niece."

James bristled beside her.

Montrose straightened his shoulders as though preparing for battle rather than pleasant conversation. "I'm told it's time for me to choose a wife. For Amelia's sake. According to my mother and father."

"You do not want a wife?" Georgiana asked.

"Not particularly, no. I like my life the way it is."

"How so?" James asked.

"I have been lucky to acquire the most loving and wonderful governess. She and Amelia adore each other. In fact, Amelia would be lost without her. She's done such a fine job that I see no need for another mother figure. Anyway, I do not think it is fair to choose a woman only because I need a mother for Amelia. But I'm afraid I'm facing pressure to do otherwise by my father and mother. Financially speaking."

"They've threatened to cut you off?" James asked. "If you do not marry."

"That is correct. My mother's been bereft since the death of my sister. She is not always reasonable these days."

"Grief does that to a person," Georgiana said.

"I plan to choose a woman to be my wife before the month's end," Montrose said. "And marry her in the new year."

"You make it sound like a business transaction," James said.

"Isn't it?" Montrose asked. "For those of us without the luck of a love match?"

"Unfortunately, it is so much of the time," Georgiana said.

Lady Alderidge returned, introducing herself to Montrose and offering to make introductions to several young ladies. "You must allow me to introduce you to some of the eligible women here.

"That would be most kind." Henry straightened his shoulders as though preparing for battle rather than pleasant conversation.

Henry's gaze followed Lady Alderidge's to take in two women standing near the punch bowl.

"Miss Catherine Wood—such an accomplished young woman. And Lady Margaret Thornfield is next to her. She has a substantial dowry, although her disposition may be in question."

Georgiana knew the women a little, although not well enough to form an intelligent opinion of either of them.

Miss Catherine Wood was a cheerful brunette with a lilting laugh and a talent for the pianoforte, though she had a habit of nervously smoothing her gloves and seldom looked anyone in the eye for long. Georgiana suspected she suffered from shyness.

Beside her stood Lady Margaret Thornfield. A striking beauty with golden hair pinned in elaborate curls and eyes the cool gray of winter mist. Her posture was perfect, her smile practiced to the edge of sincerity. Dressed in pale sea foam silk with pearl embellishments, she radiated exactly the kind of poise and polish Society adored. But something in the sharpness of her gaze, the subtle tilt of her chin, hinted at a nature less yielding than her manners suggested.

A shiver went up the back of Georgiana's spine.

As Lady Alderidge led Montrose away to make the introductions, Georgiana caught sight of Cecily, radiant in deep rose silk, laughing at something Nathaniel had whispered in her ear. They moved together with the easy grace of two people utterly comfortable in each other's company. Georgiana's heart warmed at the sight of them. If only Sophia could find the same kind of love.

But her attention was drawn back to Henry, who was now bowing over Miss Wood's hand with perfect courtesy while his eyes remained utterly cold.

"Think no more of it tonight, dear wife," James said into her ear. "Come and dance with me."

The music shifted, and soon the dance floor filled. James guided her into his arms, and together they moved through the steps of a gentle country set. Laughter rippled around them. Glasses clinked. Guests swirled around them in a kaleidoscope of silk and candlelight.

But Georgiana found herself distracted, her gaze drifting once more to Henry Montrose, who was now leading Lady Thornfield onto the dance floor with the same grim efficiency he might use to sign a legal contract.

Georgiana didn't want to worry but she did just the same.

THE LAST GUESTS had departed, the candles in the ballroom had been extinguished, and the laughter of the evening lingered like the soft scent of roses trailing through the corridors. Upstairs, in the quiet sanctuary of their bedchamber, James sat on the edge of the bed, unfastening his cufflinks while the fire cast a golden glow across the walls. They'd sent Digby and Molly off to bed earlier, content to undress each other without help from their valet or maid.

Georgiana stood at the window, still in her gown of midnight blue silk, her hands resting on the sill as she looked out into the darkness. The moonlight silvered the gardens below, and her reflection shimmered faintly in the glass. Her fingers traced absent patterns against the cool windowpane.

"You're quiet," he said gently. "Are you worried about Sophia, as I am?"

She turned to him. "I am, yes. But I have other things on my mind as well."

"Your mother's engagement?"

Not long after midnight, the rich American had asked for a meeting with James, where he asked for Lavinia's hand. Being

American, he had no qualms about Lavinia's lack of wealth or previous scandal. Georgiana couldn't help but think how freeing that would be. James had given his blessing. Mr. Whitaker and Lavinia would marry soon and then sail across the ocean for America. Her mother was beside herself with glee. So much so that she'd actually acknowledged James and Georgiana's contribution to this new life for which she would soon embark.

"No, I am delighted for Mother. I do hope she'll be happy and not trouble Mr. Whitaker with her exuberant personality or love of shopping."

"From what I hear, Mr. Whitaker has more than his share of wealth," James said. "I believe they will be very happy together."

"I have something else to tell you." Now that the moment was upon her, she suddenly felt apprehensive. What if he was not as overjoyed as she was about the baby?

James set his cufflinks aside, the small click of gold against mahogany loud in the hushed room. "What is it, love?"

She crossed to him slowly, her skirts whispering against the carpet, and brushed her fingers through his dark hair.

He leaned into her touch. "You were the loveliest woman in the room tonight." He caught her wrist to press a kiss to her palm. "Your skin looked particularly dewy and flushed. In fact, I've never seen you look more beautiful."

She smiled. "There may be a reason for that."

He studied her face. "Is it? Are you…".

Leave it to James to read her so well that he'd immediately guessed her secret.

She lowered herself onto the bed, the silk of her gown rustling as she turned to face him. Her free hand moved to her stomach. "It is true. I am with child. I did not want to say anything until I was certain." Her vision blurred with unshed tears. "Please tell me you're pleased."

"Georgie, don't be absurd." He cupped her face gently, his thumb stroking away a tear that had escaped. "How could I not be pleased? A child? What more could I ask for but to raise a family with you? The woman I love and adore? You'll be the best mother too. I'll do my best to be a decent father, but it will be you who will be the center of their world, just as you are mine."

She drew in a shuddering breath, her hand finding his and pressing it flat against her waist. "Thank goodness you feel that way. I never thought I would have a family and yet here we are. I am ecstatic to think of a child bringing even more joy into our home. James, you've made all my dreams come true."

"You're sure? You've seen a doctor?"

She nodded, happy tears spilling freely now. "I saw the physician while you were in London. He believes the baby will be here in early February."

"It feels very far away. I will be a wreck until then. Do you want a boy or a girl?"

"It doesn't matter to me, but it would be advantageous to have a son. Yet, we needn't worry, since young Edward will inherit his father's title."

"I suppose. Furthermore, imagining a little girl who looks just like her mother would be a dream come true. I shall be absolutely besotted with a little girl."

"Or a little boy," Georgiana said, smiling up at him. "You will be a fine father, no matter what. That I know without any doubts."

"My only aim in life is to make you happy. To think, there will now be a child. The blessings you have brought to me, Georgie, are too many to count. Or to describe in words."

"As are those you've brought to me, my love."

They held each other in the firelight, and Georgiana thought of the desperate widow who had arrived at Ashford Manor with nothing but her sister's future to bargain with, never dreaming she would find her own salvation within these walls. Now the house breathed with life again, its halls would soon echo with children's laughter, all proof that love, like hope, could resurrect even the most shattered of dreams.

The End

About the Author

Tess Thompson Romance… hometowns and heartstrings.

Tess Thompson is a USA Today Bestselling and award-winning author of clean and wholesome Contemporary and Historical Romance, with over 60 published titles. Her heartfelt stories feature family sagas, romance, a sprinkle of mystery, and all the second chances her characters deserve.

Tess is happily married to Cliff, affectionately known as "Best Husband Ever." Their love story is one for the books—they met on Tinder in their forties after both had endured heartache. Tess was a divorced mom of two girls, and Cliff was a widower raising two teenage boys. Now, their blended family includes two "Bonus Sons" and two daughters, all grown and forging their paths. Tess is incredibly proud of each one, even if she's still puzzled by her daughter's talent for Chemistry, which didn't come from her!

A small-town girl at heart, Tess grew up in a place much like the towns in her novels. After earning her degree from USC's Drama School, she dreamed of acting, but her passion for writing won out, leading to the career she cherishes today. Most days, you'll find her matchmaking fictional characters from her cozy office, often with one of her cats—Midnight, Mac, or Mable—curled up nearby.

Tess loves strong coffee, red wine, reading in bed, and spending lazy afternoons binge-watching TV shows, especially Masterpiece Theatre. She's a Zumba enthusiast, despite occasional knee protests, and has a soft spot for French fries over cookies any day. Cooking isn't her strong suit—her cakes often fall apart, even with a mix—and she's prone to a bit of messiness, especially when she's on a writing deadline. But she blames her forgetfulness on the constant swirl of stories in her head.

Grateful for her readers, Tess pours her heart into every story she writes. With Cliff's unwavering support, she's living her dream of writing full-time from their recently purchased dream house on a small lake—a place she still pinches herself over. Tess's books remind us that no matter how complicated life gets, love and second chances are always possible.